LIES

MAKE

PERFECT

Also by Ellie Banks

One Little Spark

ELLIE BANKS

LIES MAKE PERFECT

CANARY STREET PRESS

CANARY
STREET
PRESS™

Recycling programs
for this product may
not exist in your area.

ISBN-13: 978-1-335-00937-1

Lies Make Perfect

Canary Street Press
22 Adelaide St. West, 41st Floor
Toronto, Ontario M5H 4E3, Canada
CanaryStPress.com

Printed in U.S.A.

To mad women everywhere, who refuse to be silent. Believe yourselves.

It's nearly impossible to solve a crime when there's
no crime scene. No body to send to the coroner
to examine, to search for trace evidence, a cause of death.
No glass with lipstick on the rim, or an out-of-place
matchbook. No pieces of the puzzle to put together.
A crime scene is about the presence of clues.
A last known location is about absence.
The absence of any real evidence that
something happened at all.

Nothing but an empty place in the world
where a person used to be.

And a thousand unanswered questions.

—EXCERPT FROM *I KEPT THEM SAFE*, BY MARGO BOX

1

POPPY WAS CRYING.

Margo sat upright in bed, her breath frozen. Listening.

Listening for her daughter who wasn't here.

It was like this every night. When she got into bed. When she tried to take a shower. She could swear she heard a child crying.

She knew she didn't because she was alone.

She had been alone for six months.

The first time she'd heard it she'd looked everywhere. She'd torn her house apart like a child could be there and she might not know. She'd gone outside. She'd run through the streets.

It was silent. There was nothing.

It was inside her.

She went downstairs. She couldn't hear anything. Her living room was dark and empty, like the rest of the whole house. She let the silence settle over her, for just a moment. Then she started pacing. She paused and touched the spine on her book. *I Kept Them Safe* by Margo Box.

That book had changed her life. Writing it. Releasing it.

Earning money from the sales of it.

The living room felt darkly, oppressively empty.

It was a nice living room, though. Thanks to the book.

She wasn't sure if it mattered anymore that she had a nice living room.

For a moment she pretended she might go upstairs. Put on pajamas like a normal person. Go to bed. She wasn't working on a book. Her editor had been supportive of that. *Take all the time you need, Margo.*

But increasingly, she could feel an undertone: *We will be needing our six figure advance back if you don't hand a book in, so dammit, come up with something even if it's terrible.*

That wasn't her editor's fault. It was the company. Corporations were as silent and unfeeling as the universe, in her experience.

Without the excuse of being consumed by a book, sleepless nights weren't excusable. She couldn't blame a research hole or a late-night Adderall because she'd stopped doing both of those things. She just didn't care enough to do either anymore.

She wasn't going to go upstairs.

But she knew what she was going to do. She didn't know why she pretended she'd stay home tonight. She was as obsessive as she was routine-oriented.

And the new routine was walking the neighborhood until she was so cold she was tempted to lie down on the sidewalk and go to sleep and never wake up. Super healthy.

But then, her routines never had been.

She wasn't the kind of person who did moderation. She'd always thought it would be nice if she could. When she'd had Poppy she'd been torn in half by that. She'd wanted to give one hundred percent to her child, and one hundred percent to her writing. She'd found a way to do it, and it had involved not sleeping. Adderall for focus, and to keep her up, sleeping pills for the couple of hours she needed to go down.

It wasn't healthy. She knew that. She hadn't known how else

to do everything, all the time. To make it something she knew she could do, to make it so she knew she could give everything she needed to give.

She wasn't good at routines. But her daughter had needed one. So she had done Poppy's routine, and then she had done everything else.

She had been a perfect mother by day, and at night she had been free to be the perfect investigator, plunging into whatever the current obsession was with a cultlike devotion. Eschewing sleep and healthy eating habits for late nights poring over every message board, every internet rumor, and all the cold case files she could gain access to from different law enforcement agencies.

Except she hadn't been totally perfect. She'd lost Poppy at the park.

She blinked against the pressure in her eyes. Not tears. She'd cried so many tears she'd become a dried-up husk of herself. They didn't come as easily now.

Nothing did.

She needed passion to spark obsession. And right now, she was out of passion.

Her particular characteristics had always been a strange and difficult combination, but with them she'd accomplished so much. She'd never understood people who didn't. Who couldn't get things finished, who couldn't figure out how to pursue a goal. Who tried to limit hyperfocus, and chased lazy days and self-care and *balance*, rather than let themselves get a little bit burned by sparks of madness that produced brilliance.

Without passion, she was useless.

Without passion, her once widely read true crime blog that she'd started ten years ago, *Diaries of the Missing*, went silent.

Without passion, she had a hundred pages of a manuscript that was going nowhere, twenty boxes of case files stacked in the corner of her room that she hadn't even read, and if it weren't for her cleaner, she'd be buried under a pile of laundry.

You're lucky I'm here to take care of you.

Zach had said that a lot. With affection for probably ten years or so. Then increasingly without.

"Well, you aren't here, are you?"

She grabbed her jacket off the peg by the door and shrugged it on. She took her flashlight off the shelf above it, put the loop around her wrist and zipped her coat all the way up to her chin.

She went outside and took a breath of air. It was dark, and it was damp. Conifer, Oregon, was five miles from the ocean, but still, at night the mist rolled in, and the air tasted like salt. It had rained earlier, and the air was still heavy with the scent of wood and pine.

There was something familiar about it. Nostalgic even. But she pushed the nostalgia away. And all of the memories that might come with it. Because she simply wasn't in the mood for memories.

She was walking because she needed to do something.

Most of the houses on the street had their lights off. Her neighbor Julie went to bed early, because she worked an early shift as a nurse at the hospital.

Margo also knew that Julie had gotten a lot of money in her divorce five years ago, otherwise she wouldn't be able to afford a house on the street. Not on a nurse's income.

This was the kind of neighborhood that traded in exclusivity.

That wasn't why Margo had wanted to buy a house here. It had been a complicated mix of things. Nostalgia mixed with this feeling of triumph that she could do for her daughter what her parents had done for her. But mostly...

Wanting to be safe.

She stood and stared at the house across the street for longer than she needed to. Callie's mother's house. That should have been a cautionary tale, she supposed. You couldn't be safe if the monster was inside the gate.

She'd thought the monster was gone.

How could there be two?

She shoved her hands into her pockets, the flashlight dangling at her hip, beating against her side as she walked in quick strides. The neighborhood was well lit, but she kept the flashlight with her just in case.

She didn't like to go walking during the day, because then people wanted to talk to her. And she couldn't bear it. Not when she wasn't prepared to do the whole polite small talk thing. Easy chitchat while they smiled at each other and she could read the monologue scrolling through the other person's head: *Oh God, just don't mention the missing husband and child.*

She talked to Callie. Callie was her best friend, had been since middle school, and even when everyone else had stopped being friends with Callie, Margo had continued. It was hard for Margo to make friends. She'd had a tight friend group in high school, bonded by their love of books, alternative music and the general feeling they were square pegs in their small town. At first, her obsessive need to untangle what had happened had almost broken her and Callie apart. Margo knew her obsessiveness was hard for everyone who'd ever cared about her. But she'd done a good job putting a boundary around all of that so that she could preserve their friendship.

She'd tried. To be a good friend. A good wife. A good mother.

She'd failed. The cracks in her patched-together life had broken open.

She'd failed.

Her husband had taken her child.

She swallowed down the bile that was rising up inside of her.

She hated this. Because part of the routine was the thought loop that went with it. Julie's house. That was neutral. But then Callie's mother's house. *Not* neutral.

And then it got her thinking what good her supposed investigative reasoning had ever done for her.

Yes, it had made her a lot of money.

Yes, she had helped solve a decades-old mystery. She had brought a murderer to justice. She had brought peace to five families. As much peace as you can get under the circumstances. But she couldn't... She hadn't been able to solve the mystery that had haunted this street, this town for twenty years.

She couldn't solve the mystery that was haunting her.

She couldn't make her brain work. It was just this. Circles. Spinning her wheels.

Always. Over and over again.

When did you last see him?

I don't know. I realized he was late hours after I should have.

What was his mood?

I don't know.

Was there any indication that something was off?

No. And yes.

How did she explain that? She didn't know. She'd known things were off, but she hadn't been in the space to deal with it. There was never a good time to sit down and reckon with the dysfunction that had crept into their marriage.

She had known, but it'd been easier to pretend she hadn't. It'd been so easy to make small talk with him and ignore the distance between them. Ignore that it'd been easy to stay up half the night writing and let their sex life fade. Easy to smile and say *good morning, I love you*, and not ask questions. If she'd asked him if he was happy, he might have asked her if she was.

If she'd asked if there was something he wasn't telling her, he might've asked her the same thing.

She hadn't wanted to answer those questions. So she hadn't asked them of him.

That had worked for a while.

Until Zach had been the one to start asking questions.

Until she'd started to suspect he was having an affair. She'd been sure of it after she'd found the condoms. Or rather after she'd counted the condoms and discovered some missing.

She'd been in the middle of this new book, and she'd thought that maybe she could just let it go. Just for a while. Maybe it didn't matter all that much. Maybe it was only sex, as he came home to her at the end of the day. *She* hadn't been having sex with him as much as she should. It hadn't hurt when she didn't know.

She didn't have to let it hurt just because she did.

She'd told herself she couldn't throw stones.

Let he that is without sin…

She *hated* this loop, and she had to make it anyway. Every night.

Every damned night.

Memories of being a teenager, of being happy. Having friends. Her obsessiveness almost costing her those friends. Becoming a wife, feeling like things would be okay. Being a mother, being a bestselling author. Being a bad wife. Was she a bad mother? She wasn't sleeping. She couldn't remember everything. She'd taken her eyes off her…

Maybe it was all true. But he had no right to take their daughter.

He had no right to disappear.

He had no right to leave her in this endless, bottomless hell.

It's your fault.

That thought hit her along with the wind, wrapping her body in an insistent chill. And she kept on walking. To the edge of the community. To the gate. It was closed at this hour. But there was a code for the residents to get in and out. A code to keep them safe.

But he'd used it, and he'd left. He'd taken Poppy away from her.

Parental abduction.

It was *so common*. Not usually with people *like them*.

One of the police officers had actually said that to her. It was usually drug addicts. People who had lost custody of their children.

It slid under her skin like a knife's blade.

But she wasn't an addict. Not strictly.

Maybe that made it worse. She'd taken pills to try to do it all. Now she had nothing to do and she didn't take them. She'd chosen it. To try to be better. To try to be the best version of herself she could be. The writer and the mother. But in the end maybe it had made her worse and she hadn't seen it.

Her fault. What mother wouldn't feel like it had to be her fault, at least in part?

It's about the only way you're like other mothers.

She heard it in Zach's voice, even though she wasn't sure he'd ever said it. Was that true? She couldn't even tell anymore. Because she had a hard time remembering what kind of mother she was. Her memories of her relationship with Poppy were big, dark blotches. Swaths of failure. Of all the ways that she'd neglected her duties.

As a wife. As a mother. All of it.

She'd thought the Adderall/sleeping pills combo had been working. That she could rise on command and sleep on command and that was all she'd needed. Then she'd started making mistakes. She'd forgotten it was a short day at Poppy's kindergarten on Wednesday, and her child had ended up sitting in the office while she raced to the school twenty minutes late. She'd hit an intense part of the book and had forgotten dinner until Poppy had knocked and said she was hungry. Zach had been working late and Margo had lost track of time.

But then she'd lost her on the playground. She'd gotten an email from her editor and she'd opened it on her phone and just…forgotten where she was. She'd started to respond to it, and had lost track of minutes. Precious minutes.

When she'd looked up, Poppy was gone.

She'd stood up from the bench and had turned in circles. Looking, looking. She couldn't see her. She'd called Zach, panic in her voice as she'd run around.

You know better, Margo. God dammit this is your job. How many kids get taken from parks?

His words rang in her ears now.

She'd run, run until her lungs ached, into the woods at the edge of the park.

Poppy!

She'd screamed her name. And then Poppy had wandered back onto the path, one knee on her rainbow leggings dirty.

I was chasing a butterfly.

And she'd smiled at Margo like there wasn't a frightening thing in the whole world.

But Margo knew there was. There were so many frightening things in this world.

She simply hadn't expected her husband to be one of them.

She'd made mistakes. She thought of them every day.

Because six months of not having her husband or her child had taken away actual memories, and had left behind nothing more than guilt and blame.

And rage. So much rage.

But none of that could be cobbled together into anything useful.

So she just walked the neighborhood.

She arrived at the gate, and she stood there. She looked up at the top of the wrought iron. Then at the stacked stone wall that surrounded the entire community.

For all the good they did.

She hit the code, and the pedestrian gate opened. She walked through, taking her hands out of her pockets and gripping her flashlight, turning it on. She walked in front of the broad gate that opened and closed for cars, and down toward the Little Free Library that was perched just there.

Just outside the jurisdiction of the homeowner's association.

It had been a point of contention in the community. A Little Free Library was practically a *bargain bin*. It would give people permission to leave undesirable items at the edge of the community. It would attract people who didn't belong. The sort of person who needed to get something for free.

Margo, for her part, had wholly supported the library.

But then, for her part, she wholly hated the HOA.

Except Callie, who was a member of the board but didn't take any of this all that seriously. Margo knew that sometimes blew back in Callie's face. It didn't matter how many years had passed since her father, a respected teacher, had disappeared with his sixteen-year-old student—Callie was *his* daughter.

And every time she did something that put her on the outs with the majority, it was evidence that there was something wrong in her family. Something strange about *her*.

It was why Margo appreciated the way that Callie pushed up against it all sometimes.

They were two weird birds of a weird feather. That had bonded them closer than just about anything. But Callie had been raising her hand to volunteer for things since fourth grade. She'd been the one to take home the class hedgehog. To clean the whiteboards and to show the new kid around the school.

She carried that energy with her still.

She actually *wanted* to take charge of things in her kids' school, and plan playdates and birthday parties and myriad other things that Margo felt enervated by.

It was okay, though. Because Callie planned, and Margo showed up.

She had even done that for Margo's launch event of *I Kept Them Safe*.

Margo was not an author because she wanted attention. What she wanted was to be by herself in front of her computer.

And now you're by yourself. You must be very happy.

She heard that in Zach's voice.

She hated it.

She hated him.

"I'm not happy," she said, stopping in front of the quaint little blue house on a post just there on the side of the road.

In bright red lettering on the front it said: *Little Free Library*.

She opened up the glass door and looked at the contents. She laughed when she saw two copies of *I Kept Them Safe*. She never knew whether or not to be flattered by finding her books in places like this or not. On the one hand, it was nice to think that new readers were getting exposed to them. On the other hand, someone had discarded the book. It did not merit a position on a keeper shelf.

But she found some measure of comfort in the names that surrounded her. Nora Roberts and Debbie Macomber had also been discarded, and their careers were going just fine.

Not that Margo wrote the same kind of thing. They wrote the kind of books that you might hang on to, so that you could sit with the characters for just a little bit longer.

Margo wrote the kind of books that made you lose faith in humanity. She knew that.

She couldn't blame a person for reading one, and then needing it out of their house.

But she also felt like there were stories out there that needed to be told. She had always thought that. Especially after Sarah Hartley disappeared with Brian Archer, Callie's father. She had wondered and wondered what had happened. How they had all missed it.

If she'd been able to dig like she'd really wanted to, maybe...

God complex, much?

That was her own voice. She tried to stay on top of that kind of thinking. But she had solved a case law enforcement hadn't. She had seen things other people had missed.

She moved her hands along the spines of the books in the Little Free Library, and stopped when she came to another familiar one. *Devil in the Dark* by Jacob Spinner.

That book...

She remembered when it came out, so clearly. Their whole friendship group had been obsessed with it. A novelization of a string of unsolved murders that pointed out the grim truth that there was a monster hiding in a sleepy small town.

The scene had been set with a house on a well-manicured street, where no one locked their doors. All the neighbors trusted each other, knew each other. Kids stayed out until the streetlights came on, and walked the neighborhood freely.

When a young girl was murdered, it changed everything, and when the killer wasn't caught, and there were more and more victims, the fabric of the community unraveled. It was harrowing, and to a group of teenagers, the exact sort of real-world drama designed to hold them in suspense.

They'd all had theories in their group. They'd argued about it.

Sarah had been convinced it was the mayor. A man with power and influence pretending to do good while hiding his darkness. In hindsight, it made sense why she'd thought that.

Zach had thought it was a female cop, who'd zeroed in on a local boy in town, the son of a rich family who'd had a few brushes with the law, because it made for a good scapegoat. Margo had thought he'd just wanted it to be the unlikeliest person.

Callie had been adamant that it wasn't someone from town at all, but a trucker who drove through to make deliveries and had chosen to terrorize the town specifically to throw suspicion off it being someone transient.

Margo herself had simply been captivated by how Jacob had painted such a complete portrait with so few clues, how he'd looked critically at every angle and treated everyone like full, complete human beings, even if they might be a serial killer.

She'd wanted to be Jacob. She'd wanted to be able to write about real things in such a deep, evocative way.

It had been kind of a strange letdown when the case was actually solved. Ten years after the book came out, a detail in the story had suddenly clicked with a woman who'd lived in the town growing up, and had avoided reading the book all that time for that reason.

She'd managed to put a suspect in a location the police had never been able to place him.

They'd gotten a confession from him in under thirty minutes.

A whimper, not a bang.

The theories they'd created, the hours they'd spent discussing the book in high school, were somehow always more titillating than the truth.

Because it hadn't been a twist. Nothing as interesting as a villain masquerading as a hero, a sexually repressed cop or a manipulative trucker.

It'd been the rich boy, Cody Johnson, because who else would feel so entitled to women's bodies? He'd been able to cover his tracks as well as he had because his football coach had hidden a key piece of evidence—a bloody sock he'd found in the boy's locker room that'd fallen out of Cody's bag.

Because people were always happy to cover the mistakes of men they found more valuable than the women they hurt.

Boys will be boys.

Just like in her hometown, where the bad guy had been a teacher. A man with access to vulnerable teenage girls.

She'd often wondered who had known. Who had looked away.

When Brian and Sarah had disappeared, he hadn't even been wholly reviled around the school. He'd been a handsome enough man, and maybe he and Sarah had been *in love*. Maybe it was forbidden and exciting, even. Girls had giggled about it. Boys had elbowed each other and laughed about how Mr. Archer was getting more action than the band geeks.

Remembering that made her skin crawl.

At thirty-four, she recognized how very young they were when they were sixteen. She could now see clearly that there was no way it had been a relationship. It didn't matter that Sarah had left with Mr. Archer. It had been abuse.

She stood there for a long moment staring at the spine of that book. She was shocked by all the memories that were wrapped up in it.

That was the magical thing about books. Even if it was dark magic.

You brought yourself to them when you read. And everything that you were going through. This book had changed her. Because of when she'd read it. She was standing here, at the edge of this community because of that book.

She never would've written her own books if not for this one.

She pulled it out of the Little Free Library, the slow slide of the dust jacket against the other books loud in the silence of the darkness.

This was the original cover. For the original hardcover that had come out eighteen years ago. It looked exactly like the copy she'd had. Except she still had hers, tucked away on a bookshelf in her living room. Just above her own.

A little bit of hubris, maybe, to stick herself next to Jacob Spinner. But she was allowed to have hubris in her own house.

She opened the front of the book and saw that it was signed.

She closed the book, and held it up against her chest. It was like being young Margo again. She wanted to cry for young Margo. Who'd thought the worst thing she would ever have to live through was her friend vanishing with an older man. Who'd believed she would make a difference in the world, and who'd wanted to be like Jacob Spinner.

She was. She'd solved a cold case, like he had helped to do.

But there had been so much worse waiting for her than the disappearance of her friend.

So much worse.

She held the book tighter.

She'd actually found something out on her walk. Not anything that would make an impact on her life. Not anything that was going to help her progress with…anything.

But she didn't expect that anymore.

Every day for the past six months had been the same. She woke up, and Poppy and Zach were still gone. She didn't know where they were. When she tried to picture them, she only saw them surrounded by a void.

At first, she'd been worried about her husband.

He'd been having an affair. Things had been bad.

But she'd *loved* him.

It was that simple and that complicated.

She hadn't stopped loving him, even knowing that. She hadn't stopped loving him when he'd disappeared. Because what if something had happened to him? To them?

Two months ago, though, she had stopped loving him.

Two months ago she'd finally accepted what the police had been telling her from the beginning. Wholeheartedly, not in some strange, fuzzy way where she told herself that it must be some kind of mistake, or an accident. Like they'd had a miscommunication about the time of a parent-teacher conference.

She'd accepted it for real.

Her husband had kidnapped their child.

He had taken their daughter away from her, and he had done it with intent.

As much as she had ever loved Zachary Corbin, she hated him now.

She wasn't a bad mother. *She wasn't.*

She clung to her book even harder. And she walked along the edge of the wall, back through the pedestrian gate, back into the neighborhood. And she closed the gate behind her. Even knowing that it didn't matter.

Because for her, the monster had been inside the house.

2

WHEN MARGO WOKE up she had four missed calls from Callie, and her friend was knocking at the front door. At least she assumed it was Callie. Callie was the only person who regularly came to see her. Particularly without establishing contact first.

She heard crying.

Her heart slammed into her breastbone, her breathing going erratic for three, four, five breaths.

She would be tempted to believe she was locked in some kind of *Groundhog Day* situation. Except every day she was painfully aware of the passage of time, even as it all crawled by in distressing sameness.

She grabbed her phone and texted Callie, and the banging on the front door stopped, confirming her suspicion.

She didn't even pause when she went by Poppy's closed bedroom door. If she did, she couldn't move past it. She would end up standing there until time didn't mean anything. So she didn't look at it at all. Didn't stop.

She hadn't gone inside in six months.

She headed downstairs and opened the front door.

Callie Smith stood on her front porch. "Smith" was objectively a much worse name than her maiden name. Archer had been a good name. Margo also understood why Callie had given it up. She hadn't had any interest in maintaining the link to her father.

Callie was one of those women who seemed to understand how to harness her femininity innately. Like a superpower that she wielded effortlessly. And she had done so ever since they were thirteen years old. Her hair always did whatever she wanted it to, and over the years that had been many things, from some relatively unfortunate chunky highlights to the sleek shoulder-length bob she had now. When she moved her head, her hair moved with it in concert.

Margo's own hair was piled on top of her head in a haphazard facsimile of a bun.

Her pro styling tip was to grab a handful of her hair and pull it partway through an elastic band, wrapping it around twice. And whatever shape it made was where it stuck.

Callie had done Margo's hair and makeup for her author photos on the back of her books.

It was one reason Margo hadn't had a new one in eight years. It just all seemed like a lot of work. And she had looked very good that day, thanks to Callie.

She tried to imagine getting pictures taken now, and it nearly made her laugh.

And very few things made her laugh right now.

Her raccoon eyes and wayward hair would certainly add to the notion that true crime enthusiasts were cave-dwelling rats who rarely saw the light of day and didn't know how to properly interact with the world.

"I was afraid that you'd died," said Callie.

"No. I'm not dead."

"Good."

Callie did look legitimately worried. "That would be an awfully big coincidence, don't you think? Or do you think Zach is going to sneak back in and kill me?"

"No, Margo," Callie said, her gaze uncomfortably direct, "I'm afraid that *you're* going to kill you."

Margo let out a short breath, unsure quite what she was supposed to make of that. "You think I'm suicidal?"

"Not necessarily, though I wouldn't put it past you at this point. Could be accidental, though. Choking on a Hot Pocket, drowning in the bath. Who knows? I don't think you're taking care of yourself."

It's a good thing I'm here to take care of you...

Callie looked at her for so long, Margo felt like she was seeing under her skin. She wondered how much Callie knew. About the pills.

"I didn't even get my prescription refilled. I couldn't OD on sleeping pills if I wanted to," she said.

"I feel like you've thought about it."

"I don't need you to be my nanny, Callie. I can handle myself."

"If you ever needed a nanny, it's now."

"It's been six months."

"I doubt it's gotten better."

Callie knew her. That was the problem. Through elementary school playground games, to middle school boy drama, to the shattering of their high school friend group. Their own rending when Margo had gone too far pushing about things Callie might have seen at home that didn't seem important at the time. They'd gotten past that. Their friendship had survived them attending universities in different states, and Callie's gut-wrenching sophomore year breakup that saw her rebounding with a guy named DeVonte, who she'd gone on to marry and have kids with. Making DeVonte the victor, not the rebound.

She'd encouraged Margo to start the true crime blog.

You should do something with your obsession.

She'd said that while staring at the mountain of books Margo had about missing persons cold cases.

The way Sarah had vanished had always fascinated Margo and filled her with dread at the same time.

The way a person could just…disappear. It haunted her.

With a note. With evidence. A known person whom she was traveling with, a vehicle…

Sarah Hartley and Brian Archer were gone.

The dead body of a loved one was a horrifying reality, but what had always terrified Margo was the blank, bleak unknown.

Not knowing was hell. She knew it deeply, viscerally now.

But the idea of *knowing* was a level of terror she couldn't face.

She shook her head. "No. It doesn't." She swallowed hard. "Come in. I need to make coffee."

Callie was already striding through the entryway, and into the bright white kitchen. She had liked it because it always looked clean. Now it hurt her eyes.

Margo followed, rubbing a hand across her forehead.

"I'll make the coffee," said Callie.

"I told you, you don't need to take care of me."

"Well, Margo, it is after eleven in the morning, and you're just rolling out of bed. I think someone does need to take care of you."

"I've never been a morning person."

She had been for Poppy. She got her out of bed every morning and sang their special song.

Good morning, good morning, good morning, it's time to rise and shine!

She chose a cute outfit for her. She brushed her silky, baby-fine hair. Zach usually made them jelly toast, with hot chocolate for Poppy.

It was the only time she'd ever liked mornings.

Now she just wanted to sleep through them.

Losing Poppy had also stolen a thousand small joys she'd taken her in everyday life.

When she'd had Poppy she'd wanted to do *everything*. Be a mother, be awake in the morning. Be a writer, be awake at night.

She didn't want to be anything now.

Maybe Callie was right to be worried.

"Okay, maybe you weren't a morning person, but you used to get dressed every day too."

She watched as her friend bustled about the room, getting out the coffee canister, and taking the carafe out of the bottom of the coffee maker and walking it over to the sink. She touched the faucet, and water came out. Everybody had trouble with that. That it was a touch-activated faucet. Zach had thought it was cool. Margo thought it was stupid.

And she was stuck with it.

She didn't know why she was fixating on that. Sometimes it was easier to fixate on that kind of thing.

Callie was on her side. Margo wished she was completely sure it was the right side.

This morning her house felt empty. Without the cover of darkness, it was harder to feel so certain of who was good and who was bad.

"I lost her on the playground, you know," she said. "Seven months ago. One month before he left. One…"

Margo took a deep breath.

Callie didn't say anything. She was keeping her eyes attentively on the coffee-making.

"Zach was furious. I had a note that I needed to make. About the Detweiler case. This paragraph had just come to me. It was just right there, materialized. And it was everything I wanted to say. About that woman, and the unfairness of it. The way that her life was taken from her. And I had to do it, right then. I was sitting on the bench, and Poppy was on the play structure. I opened up the Notes app on my phone, and I typed it out. It took me probably a minute and a half. When I looked up she was gone. She was *gone*. And I didn't know where she was. And in that moment, it was like a canyon had opened up underneath me, and I thought it was going to swallow me whole. It was like I wasn't attached to the earth anymore. Because I didn't know where my daughter was. She was there, and then she was gone. I couldn't find her for three minutes. And in that three minutes I called Zach and I told him what had happened. He left work right away. A minute later I found her. She had gone down toward the creek by the edge of the park."

She stared at a spot on the wall, her heart starting to beat a little bit faster.

"He was so angry at me. It makes me think he did this on purpose. To make me live in that moment. For *six months*."

She hadn't told Callie that Zach was having an affair. She hadn't caught him in the act. There were no dirty texts or anything.

But there was the box of condoms.

They didn't use them, because she was on the pill. They had them for a backup. Just in case. In case she was on antibiotics or missed a dose. There had been eight condoms in that box for years. She had been looking for something in his nightstand drawer, and for some reason, she'd picked it up. And there were four inside. There were four missing.

And the four missing condoms had burned their way into her consciousness.

For three months before Zach had left, she'd been thinking about those condoms.

She had been over and over it. She knew that there had been eight. She did. There was probably an explanation. But that explanation was probably that he'd use them to have sex with someone else.

It was almost offensive that it hadn't been cleverly concealed. *I'm basically a detective, you fucker.*

Almost more offensive he didn't think she would look or care. Or maybe he'd even *wanted* her to.

Worse was that she hadn't been able to bring herself to ask about it. Or even yell at him about it. To throw the box at his head.

She had just buried it. She'd started working more. Longer. The pressure to do a follow-up to the last book was so immense. And he didn't understand that. She'd done something once in a lifetime with *I Kept Them Safe*. Her intervention had brought attention back to the case. Her intervention had helped them solve the crime. They had found those women. And they had found the person responsible for killing them.

How did you follow that up?

Before that book, the blog and her smaller books that explored the people left in the wake of unexplained disappearances had been enough.

But after she'd found those missing girls, it'd felt like *that* was the real mission.

Not simply talking about absence, but filling it.

Five years ago, she'd keyed in on the constellation of disappearances in the area of Lake Tahoe, with three girls having disappeared from resorts in Incline Valley and three more from the surrounding area, between 1998 and 2020. The idea they might be connected had been floated around law enforcement agencies, but it had never been followed up. There had been more disappearances that had come from further afield, never joined up by detectives.

Margo had been certain they were connected. There were too many similarities, too many similarities for her to ignore. The patterns were there, if you stepped back and looked.

The disappearances had been dismissed. The girls were partying. Holiday negligence. They'd probably gone willingly with strangers. Gotten into trouble while drunk. Simply wandered into the woods.

But their cars all went missing along with the girls. Margo couldn't believe that was a coincidence.

She'd pored over hundreds of documents, everything every agency who'd ever touched the disappearances had put a finger on. It had felt resonant to Sarah's disappearance, maybe because of the judgment that had been directed at the missing.

It was so familiar. It was so like Sarah.

Sarah, whose case she'd had to stop digging into because of Callie.

Because of *him*.

She'd pushed and pressed on, determined to figure out the connection.

The police believed if there was foul play the perpetrator was most likely a transient.

Assumptions could be good, Margo knew. When left with blank spaces to fill in, reverting to preestablished precedent made sense.

But she'd wondered if it had created blind spots, more empty voids that didn't need to be there.

She'd wondered if the dedication to preexisting narratives had made the mystery unsolvable.

And she'd wondered how the hell six women had gone missing, along with their cars.

It was the cars that had stuck with her.

How did you hide cars?

She wasn't sure she'd have figured that out if it wasn't for him.

After the success of *I Kept Them Safe*, her publisher had come to her with the next case they wanted her to write about. A high-profile missing children's case in Oregon. She'd liked that it was something near to her, and the picture of the smiling little boy had touched something in her. The stepmother had long been a suspect, but there had been no real evidence from the beginning. She'd wanted to tackle it. She'd wanted to fix it.

I Kept Them Safe had changed her goals. She didn't just want to ask questions. She wanted to give answers.

She'd allowed the pressure of that to consume her. To keep her awake at night. For eighteen months it had been her obsession. She took Adderall to stay awake. She didn't go to bed with Zach. When she finally let herself take her pills to sleep, it was almost always on her office couch, for two or three hours max. Then she was back up, medicated and ready to go.

Good morning, good morning, good morning!

She hadn't thought he'd leave. She'd thought she could keep putting it all off. Until the book was done.

She'd thought the money would buy her time.

It was such a terrible, shallow thing to think, but it was true. She'd been so convinced that the money she'd made from *I Kept Them Safe*, the subsequent documentary, and the movie that had come after, would keep him with her. In two years, they'd made so much. He hadn't had that kind of money, and he'd definitely enjoyed what it had given them. The ability to move from their small house closer to town, back into the neighborhood she'd grown up in.

It was funny to her now. She'd wanted to move back here because she'd felt like statistically it had to be safer. The big bad thing had happened years ago.

She was so good at ignoring the bad in her own life, and focusing on other people's tragedies.

And now she was living on her own and she didn't know what to do.

The signs had been there.

He had never been happy with her success, not really. He'd tried. But he'd resented it.

Sometimes answers just open old wounds.

He'd said that to her when she'd told him she had to keep pushing on her next case, to bring more people closure.

It had gotten to her. The idea that not only was she profiting off someone else's pain, but maybe she'd caused more rather than relieving it.

Especially now that her own daughter was missing.

She wanted answers, but what she really wanted was Poppy back.

"One time," said Callie, calmly pushing the button on the coffee maker, "I opened Jaden's bedroom door, and his window was open. And he was gone. I didn't know where. I had no idea he could open that window. I didn't know that he would do that. I knew that he wandered, and I knew that during the day I had to keep a close eye on him, but I thought that when he was in bed he was in bed. I called 911 at the same time someone across the street did. Because they'd found him. A four-year-old boy running around in a diaper, who couldn't talk and couldn't tell her which home he belonged to. I know that the police, that woman, they all thought I was a neglectful parent. I made a mistake. Nothing happened. He was fine. Thank God now he doesn't ever want to leave the house, because his iPad and his food are there. Everybody makes mistakes. Not everybody's husband leaves them and takes their child. You didn't do anything extraordinarily wrong."

"Thanks," said Margo.

She knew Callie was trying to be supportive, but she also didn't feel like she could compare her experiences with Poppy to Callie's experience with Jaden.

She knew how hard Callie worked to keep Jaden safe. He was autistic and it had taken him a long time to grasp cause and effect. When he was small, he'd done so many dangerous things. He'd wandered away from the house all the time.

For a while, they'd had special locks on the windows and doors.

Callie would laugh when she'd let someone in, then lock the very high lock with a key she kept hidden.

We're the Hotel California, you can check out any time you like, but you can never leave.

If we ever have a fire, we'll all die, she'd said to Margo once, laughing. She knew Callie hadn't actually found it funny.

Her situation with Poppy wasn't the same.

"I'm serious," said Callie. "Losing track of your kid at a playground happens. It's a thing that happens." She cleared her throat. "I know how you feel."

Margo knew now that Callie wasn't just talking about having experience with her child being out of her sight.

"I know you do."

"I know my dad was the villain in that story. But it's still so hard when somebody just disappears. And you can never have it out with them. I think maybe in that way it's probably more like Zach than with Poppy."

"Yeah," she said. "I just... I never thought he would do something like this. I knew things weren't great. I knew we needed to deal with it. But I thought there would be some big fight. I thought he'd tell me I was a bad wife, or a bad mom. I thought he'd tell me he was fucking someone else."

Just then the coffee gurgled and finished running into the pot. Callie slid it out from beneath the drip. "Was he?"

"I think so. I wasn't sleeping at night. Consequently I wasn't sleeping with him. He wasn't pushing that issue. And we had missing condoms from a box. If there's one thing I've learned investigating crimes, it's that the obvious answer is usually the correct answer. When it isn't...that's when you have cold cases. Even then a lot of times the answer is obvious. I just thought it was maybe...just sex, you know? Not like, a real affair."

"You think he left you to be with her?"

Callie poured coffee into a mug and handed it to Margo.

"I don't know," she said. "I'm trying not to think about that, because you know that means there's some other woman... Some other woman is raising my child. For six months, some other woman has been tucking her in. Dammit, I hadn't even been tucking her in every night. I was busy at night. I was working on my book." She took a drink of the coffee. Black. "I'm not going to kill myself."

Callie was staring at her.

"*I'm not.* She's out there somewhere. If I kill myself, then he's going to win. He wants me out of his life. He wants me out of their lives. Or maybe on some level he thought that I wasn't going to try to find them. But I am. And I will."

Except she had come up with nothing but dead ends. She had a private detective that she had worked with on a previous book looking for them, and there'd been nothing. She couldn't even find an interesting paper trail on her husband. He hadn't taken any huge sums of money out. There'd been small amounts, over time. Some things that suggested he'd definitely been building up to leave, but nothing that indicated where he was now.

Nothing had popped up in his name since. Which meant that he was using a different identity, but there was no indication of what that might be, or where he might've gone.

Zach was smart. It was one of the things that she'd liked about him.

"Not the best reason for not killing yourself."

"It's the reason I have."

Callie let out a relenting breath. "I'll take any reason. I just... I'm worried."

"You get it," Margo said, looking directly at her friend. "This isn't like grieving. It's not something that can just get better as time passes. The more time passes, the more she's been away from me. The longer it's been since I've seen her, held her. She's out there. She's..."

"I *do* get it. But I don't want you to self-destruct. Maybe you need to get a regular job."

"That is the stupidest thing you've ever said," said Margo.

Callie laughed, and poured herself a cup of coffee. "I appreciate that you're still opinionated. And kind of an asshole."

"I don't need a job."

"I mean, I realize that, Margo. You don't need to write another book probably either. But you were going to. My point is, maybe you need something to keep you busy. You could always volunteer for one of my—"

"I won't be doing that. I'm not interested in interacting with people any more than I need to."

"Right. But you might need to. Because this… This isn't healthy."

"My life isn't healthy."

Callie laughed. "I hear you. We don't have to talk about this. We can talk about other things."

Callie was very good at that. She was very good at asking Margo what shows she was watching. If she was working on her book. If there were any other adaptations happening with the previous book. It was strange that six months was this weird space where it was harder to not talk about it all the time. To not think about it all the time.

Right at first, there had been so much media attention. A *New York Times* bestselling true crime writer's family had disappeared. And she had taken every interview that had come her way, because she had thought that the more she could get Zach's and Poppy's pictures out into the world, the more of a chance she had of them being found.

But nothing had come of it. She was an expert at trawling online forums. And of course there was ugly shit on there. Implications that she had killed them. Or that Zach had killed himself and their daughter.

People loved it to be salacious. And grim.

And some of them got their knives out and smiled as they typed out anonymous bile in chat rooms and forums, couched in concern.

That poor child, I hope she's okay.

Innocents used as pawns by their parents.

Between every word she could see it: *I hope she's dead. Horribly. I want it to be as grisly as possible.*

And the worst thing was she couldn't be judgmental about the more normal people in the forums making accusations about her and Zach because she'd trawled those very same forms and had those very same thoughts.

She'd believed the worst. Countless times.

She wasn't sure what she believed now.

At first there had been a parade of neighbors. At first there had been media. At first, her dad had come back and forth between his house on Hawaii and here as often as he could.

At first, her brother and sister-in-law had rotated staying with her.

But at a certain point everybody had to get back to normal. And this was Margo's normal. This yawning void that felt as wrong now as it had the first day.

This unhealed wound that was beginning to fester.

Because they were out there. Somewhere. She couldn't picture them. Where they were, what they were doing.

If there was another woman.

It was the not knowing. That itch under her skin.

She couldn't pull up Google and know.

Not knowing was going to kill her.

"I'm not saying that you should move on," said Callie. "I'm not saying that you should try to get back to normal. I'm just saying you should do something other than prowling around the neighborhood at night and sleeping all day."

"How do you know I prowl around the neighborhood at night?"

"Because sometimes I don't sleep either. And I've seen you."

"How come you can't sleep?"

Callie sighed. "Same reasons as you. You kept me from drowning all those years ago. You were nice to me when other people weren't. You were there for me. Everyone else acted like they were going to get pedophile on themselves."

She laughed. Reluctantly. Because it was a terrible thing to say, but then all of these things were terrible.

"I wasn't always the best. I nearly ruined our friendship obsessing about it. Other people avoided you, I wanted to know more. Which is...very me."

"Yeah, it is. And it bothered me then, but it wouldn't now. I know who you are. I get where you're coming from. For some weird reason I had a hard time trusting people back then."

Margo laughed. "Wow. I wonder why." She cleared her throat. "It was never your fault. You didn't have anything to do with any of it."

"I know."

But the people in town had acted like Callie might have known something about her father and Sarah's plans. They'd treated her like she was stained by it and it had been wholly unfair.

Whether it was Sarah or Callie, the town had acted like teenage girls were responsible for the decisions of a grown man.

What Margo wondered was how much other people in town had known. If they'd seen disconcerting proof and pushed it away.

It was just now she understood the way that you could rationalize things. Push them down to be dealt with at another time.

His lies.

Her lies.

Hope was the thing with feathers.

Denial was a whole feather pillow. You could press it down over the top of your doubts, and just keep pressing. Until you suffocated them.

Though inevitably they rose up and fought back. Clamped an icy fist around your throat and squeezed. Until you were the one that couldn't breathe.

Dammit, if she were actually working on a book, she would put that in there.

"How come you aren't working on your book?" Callie asked, the words jarring alongside her own thoughts. "You were for a while."

Right after Zach and Poppy had gone, she'd kept writing. She'd kept writing and medicating like it was all the same and they were going to come back any day.

"Because for a while it didn't feel real. And now it does. I guess that's it. At first, I had hope. That it was a mistake. That he would change his mind and come back. And now I just have more days without them."

"It wouldn't hurt you to get obsessed with something else. Someone else's problems. You're good at that. I mean that in the best way."

"My obsessions are probably why this happened."

"No. Don't ever think that. Zach made his choices, and he didn't talk to you. If he was cheating on you...then he had plenty of time to sit down and have a conversation. If he had time to go stick his dick in another woman, he had time to talk to you. Half the time DeVonte and I don't even have a chance to *talk* about the day, let alone have time to fuck each other, much less *somebody else*. So just believe me, if he had time to go make a whole other relationship, he had time to deal with yours."

"What if I didn't let him? Because I was busy."

Because I didn't want to fix it. Because I wasn't being honest either.

"People make time for what they want to make time for. Okay? And you have been my friend this whole time. I saw you. Even when you were in the middle of the most intense part of the case, I saw you. The only time I didn't was when you were actually away. And you still texted. Don't let your anxiety about it recast the whole thing, okay?"

Margo nodded. But she could already feel herself taking that information and letting it simply filter through. She didn't let it stick.

Because it didn't matter. Guilt was at least something she could hang on to. It was something tangible. It was something more than a black hole.

And God knew she needed that.

"I have to go. I have a meeting at the school. Still fighting about Jaden's IEP."

"I'm sorry. Do you want me to write a letter?"

"If you would. I wouldn't say no to you using your powers for me. I need to tell them to pull their heads out of their asses, but eloquently."

"Sometimes direct works, but if it will help, I'll write something that expresses the sentiment with a little more coding involved."

"Yes. Please. If that would keep you busy, I would take that."

She would do something for Jaden. Because at least that was useful. It was better than sitting around feeling sorry for herself. She was tired of herself, and she could only be grateful that Callie wasn't.

Callie had become a mother before Margo, and it was Callie's children, the life she'd made, that had made Margo want kids.

Callie had so many reasons to not trust the world. To not want a husband. To not want to bring kids into this mess, but she had. Motherhood had taken all of this fierce love in her friend and made it expansive and beautiful. Margo had thought if she could love a child with the obsessiveness she felt for her stories it might…soften something in her.

It had.

"This is what I mean," said Callie. "You've never shut people out entirely. You were always there for me. You know how everyone else cut me off. Because of my dad. Because Sarah was gone. You actually listened. You've always understood that people were complicated. Yes, you're obsessive. Because you care so damned much. I'm really sorry that Zach has taken your whole sense of self from you."

She just couldn't think about all that right now.

"What's the specific issue?" Margo asked, eager to move on.

"They're not compliant with federal law. They're supposed to be putting him in more mainstream classes. But basically it's PE and music and nothing more. He could do math. On grade level, I know he can. But the district…"

"Okay. I've got it."

"Thank you."

"I'll email it to you in literally an hour."

"Thank you, Margo."

Callie hugged her, which she knew Margo hated, but Margo tolerated it for Callie, because she clearly needed to do it as a gesture of comfort, even though it wasn't comfort that Margo especially recognized.

That was the cost of friendship.

Margo walked home and went straight into her kitchen. She grabbed a Hot Pocket out of the freezer and stuck it in the microwave. Then she took it and a cup of coffee upstairs to her office. She pulled up a document and began to write, from Callie's point of view. Everything she knew about Callie's struggles and triumphs with Jaden. Everything about Jaden, and what a wonderful, brilliant child he was.

It felt good to write something. It felt good to remember that she could. Even if it was just a letter to a very disappointing school district.

She sent it off to Callie, and then paused. She'd set Jacob Spinner's book on the edge of her desk last night.

She felt something prickle at the back of her neck when she looked at it. A remembered excitement. Of what it had been like when she read that book.

It had been such a scathing indictment of law enforcement and their inability to work together. Of the way a community had rallied around a mediocre man to protect him, at the expense of the safety of young women.

How the desperate need to look for a villain outside of their midst had insulated one.

And how the reckoning had come too late for the victims. He had taken a story that would've been buried amidst countless tragic headlines and he had made it vividly real for millions of people. It was what she had wanted to do.

Especially after Sarah.

She'd always wondered if there had been signs. If she was the first girl Brian had molested. Manipulated. She'd thought that Sarah's story might be the first one she would tell. But she'd hit dead ends back then. Everyone had. Her parents had hired private investigators, exhaustive searching had been done, but there had never been a trace of Brian Archer or Sarah Hartley since they'd left, over eighteen years ago.

She'd had to focus on cases that weren't personal. She'd nearly ruined her relationship with Callie over her obsession, and then there was *him*.

So she'd stopped.

She'd chosen to pore over the lives of strangers, the echoes of their pain better at least than the echo of a crying child she couldn't reach.

She picked the book up and opened the front again, looking at Jacob Spinner's autograph. As she lifted it up off the table the pages relaxed, and there was a thunk on the surface of the desk. A white envelope that had been wedged inside the book slid out, the edge hitting the desk. She opened the book the rest of the way and the envelope slid down farther, revealing the first paragraph on page 102.

There are always signs. Everywhere you look, there are signs. But people see what they want to. They tell stories to try to make sense of the pieces of information they see all day long. Most insidiously, they tell themselves lies. To make the rough edges smoothed. To

turn wolves into sheep. To make their communities into safe
havens where nothing bad can ever happen.

The back of her neck stung, the hair there rising up.
She picked up the envelope and turned it around. There was
an address printed on the back.

```
Jacob Spinner
PO Box 795
Bainbridge Island, Washington
98110
```

There was no return address, no postage. No date. The envelope wasn't sealed, and she flipped it open and took out a lined
piece of paper, with frayed edges torn from a spiral-bound note-
book. It had been folded three times.
It reminded her of the notes that they'd passed in class.
Notes that Sarah had passed.
She unfolded the paper, slowly. There was a typed letter inside.

```
March 11th
Dear Mr. Spinner,
I read all your books. I love how brave your char-
acters are, and that they always try to do the
right thing even when they're scared. I'm like one
of your characters, but I'm not brave. And I'm not
like you. I know you wrote your new book about real
people, because you wanted to help them. I know
he's hurting her. But I don't know what to do. I
can't tell anyone.
    I thought I would tell you.
Sincerely,
Your Biggest Fan
```

3

THE BOOK COULD'VE come from anywhere. But the letter was dated two weeks before Sarah Hartley disappeared.

It could have come from another town. It could be about anyone.

It really could be about anything. Anyone.

Maybe it was about Sarah, maybe it wasn't.

But she had to know.

She had to follow the letter, because it'd come to her.

She hadn't touched the box for years. Her Sarah files. She'd kept them, because she'd never been able to bear the thought of discarding them.

She'd had to leave them, because of Callie.

And she'd stopped for good after that day. When *he'd* grabbed her arm and left bruises on it. When the pain in his eyes had left her cut so deep she didn't think she'd ever heal from it. Not really.

She went into the closet in her study, and looked at the box in the back that was labeled *Case #1*.

She hadn't put Sarah's name on it. That had felt too invasive.

It felt like she was breaking a vow by touching that box. To Callie. To herself.

But she touched the top of the box, running her hand over the top of it slowly. Then she lifted it down from the shelf and carried it to her desk.

She didn't have any police files on Sarah, nothing official. But she knew how to order those now.

As she sifted through the box, her heart contracted. She'd thought of it as a box of case files back when she'd been seventeen and wanting to save her friend.

But it was a box of memories.

Inside were pictures. Pictures of Sarah, of the friend group hanging out together. Their yearbook, which she'd included because there might've been pictures of Sarah and Mr. Archer in there.

She had notes. She took one out and opened it, immediately feeling deflated when she saw that the handwriting on the note did not match the note inside the book.

mall after school?
Sarah

yes
Callie

no. Boring.
Zach

Yes!
Amber

Yes
Margo

That was how they'd always passed notes. Kind of a round-robin, circulating to everyone in the group, then back to Sarah.

Sarah was the instigator to Callie's planner. Less practical than Callie, and with a softer personality. She'd been one of those girls everyone liked. She was bubbly and sweet and caring. And no one would've ever guessed that there'd been something dark happening in her life. That anything had been wrong.

That drove Margo insane. The idea that blind spots were so easy to develop and maintain. Had Sarah been happy? Had Sarah been as easygoing and content as it had appeared? Or had they all been making up stories?

Like when they'd sat around dissecting Jacob Spinner's book. Putting their own prejudices, ideas and motives over the top of the truth.

She opened up a Word document.

I'm the kind of woman who reads about serial killers to relax. I'm kidding, I never relax. I sit at my computer hunched over the keys, scrolling until my hand cramps up and my eyes are dry. I don't believe in the innate goodness of humanity, not after what I've seen. Not after what I know.

But I still bought into the lie. That if I bought myself a perfect house, on the perfect street, that if I married the perfect man and got my daughter into the very perfect preschool, I could make my life safe. From all the bad buys at the gate.

I knew better. I've known better since my tenth grade English teacher kidnapped my friend, and left a note telling the town they'd run away together.

I knew better, and I still let myself believe that nothing bad could get me. But my perfect husband took my perfect daughter away and now I'm left with nothing but the truth. That nowhere is safe, not when there are secrets.

It isn't a need for relaxation that makes me want to uncover the truth about Sarah Hartley. It's the feeling that somehow, if I can tear down the secrets in this world, expose the hidden things, if I can tear down every wall and steal every shadowed space, maybe I'll find my own truth.

Sarah's life was perfect.

She had it all.

How much of that is true? And how much of that is us, needing to make simple something complicated. Needing to make edits to the story. Taking a red pen to the truth and fashioning it into a narrative that's easier to swallow.

If someone difficult dies, how quickly they become everyone's friend. The nicest guy. And when a grown man runs away with one of his underage students, everyone holds up their hands and says: he was the perfect father. The perfect husband. The perfect teacher.

No one saw the signs. No one saw the warnings.

I tell myself that, when I think of my own marriage.

But how much of that is true? Were there truly no signs?

Or it possible that in order to find the truth we have to look beneath the surface?

She stared at that for a long while. It was a ramble. It might not be the right choice, to bring in her own personal situation. She might need to edit all the mentions of it out. But right now it was tangled around everything. Every breath, every thought, and every sentence she wrote.

But at least this was a part of herself she recognized. This thing that had woken up, all bright-eyed tenacity and wanting to know.

Wanting to know something she might actually be able to find an answer to.

Sitting in the silence of her house, trying not to go insane, hadn't helped.

This might not help. She wasn't sure anything would help. But this note…

Maybe it was a sign that she needed to go back to the beginning.

Where had Brian Archer taken Sarah Hartley? Had there been signs that it was coming?

Was it possible that there were pockets of truth hidden everywhere within this community? Just like there had been truth hidden in her own house that she hadn't taken the time to look at.

One thing was certain: she wasn't going to be starting this without talking to Callie. She had to do that before she talked to her publisher. She had to do that before she talked to anybody.

There was a story here. She didn't have to solve it for that to be true.

But she ached to fix it.

She always had.

She'd built a fence around it to protect the people she loved from herself.

And here she was, six months into the middle of her own personal tragedy. Her own missing person.

She wasn't any closer to answering the questions.

She was going around and around in circles, trying to untangle the knots that might be impossible to get at.

But something else…

Getting involved in something else…

It at least made her feel like herself. For a brief moment. Like maybe the Margo Box she'd once known hadn't been taken along with Poppy.

Or with Zach.

You don't love him anymore.

She wished that were true all the way. That there wasn't this one last piece inside of her that thought of him and felt twenty-three. That thought of him and saw him holding their tiny daughter in his arms, beaming with pride.

That was the thought where the love died. Because he'd taken that baby away from her.

How could he? Zach.

She could still see him at twenty-three, ready to start his own financial consultancy business in his hometown after working for just one year in Seattle.

He was crazy, she'd told him that.

But then she'd gone out with him and he'd kissed her. And she'd gone home with him.

"I'm not crazy," he whispered into her hair, and she could hear his smile. "I'm just very ambitious."

She'd practically moved in with him the next day.

They'd lived together for five years before they'd gotten married. And a couple years later Poppy had come along. And changed everything. Changed her fundamentally. She'd loved everything more. She'd wanted everything more.

She'd been so happy. Deliriously happy.

But the demands of being a mother and a writer had changed things between her and Zach. It had been subtle at first. So much so that she hadn't fully realized how long it had been going on until she'd paused to look back.

They'd been little things. Easy to write off as new-parent problems.

She'd already been writing books at that point, and they'd definitely contributed to their income, though Zach had been the main breadwinner.

Until *I Kept Them Safe.*

The research for that had been all-consuming. It had taken more time than any of her previous books. She'd gone over deadline as she'd found new case files to go through. In the end, she'd been spending twelve hours a day reading files, triangulating the failures of law enforcement.

And worrying away at the one thing she'd felt they'd missed.

When it led to the discovery of all the missing girls, when it led to the arrest of a serial killer, the potential of her book, and her life, changed.

The whole experience had been a crossroads. But she'd decided to take the road back to Zach.

She'd thought it might make things better between her and Zach. He could work less if he wanted. They were more comfortable. Didn't have any financial stress.

She'd hoped he might be proud.

He'd always been proud of her writing. Her small advances had been a welcome contribution. When she'd sold the concept for *I Kept Them Safe*, it had always been intended to be a hardcover. A bigger deal, owed to the fact that she was hooking into a true crime/serial killer zeitgeist.

When it had gone off like it had, she'd been sure it would be the key to them finding their way to each other. Her obsessiveness had been worth it. The fraying of their sex life, the distance. She'd decided that she'd recommit to them.

It had made things worse.

She'd had to travel to do interviews. She'd gone to New York to do the morning show circuit. She'd gone to LA.

It hadn't been in her comfort zone. She preferred to be left to her own devices. And she definitely didn't like putting makeup on every day.

She hadn't had her Poppy mornings.

She'd been…not herself.

But all the publicity had fueled the book sales enormously.

It had been such a whirlwind of excitement and it had brought her into a life that was bigger than the one she'd been living before.

How proud he'd been…

She sat there for a long moment. She knew that she was going to have to call *him* too.

It had been a while now.

She looked at the clock and saw that it was past time for school to get out. She called Callie.

"Are you home?"

"Yeah."

"Can I come over?"

"Sure."

Callie sounded a little bit weirded out, and that was fair, because it wasn't like Margo had been needlessly social the past six months. It was one thing for Callie to come visit her, but it was another for Margo to return the favor within the same twenty-four-hour time frame.

Still, she grabbed her coat and zipped it up, heading out the front door.

Callie's mother, Gail Archer, was directly across the street, standing on the porch, sipping something from a mug. "Hi, Margo," she said.

"Hi, Mrs. Archer," she said.

Gail Archer had been her fourth grade teacher. It was almost impossible for her to figure out what to call her now, as an adult. You would think that she'd have that figured out. But there were so many things she had not figured out, and that seemed like the least important of them.

Gail didn't ask, *How are you?*

She was probably one of the very few people that Margo would mind having asked that.

Because she couldn't imagine what it had been like for Gail to walk through this community after her husband had run off with one of his students. How every time someone asked her that it must've been laden with barbs.

With suspicion.

With questions of whether or not you'd known something. Or if you were even responsible.

That thought made her feel as if someone had grabbed hold of her heart and twisted it hard to the left.

Because Margo understood exactly how that was.

"I got up this morning," said Margo. "And I'm going to see Callie."

Gail nodded. "Good."

She didn't tell Margo to cheer up, or to keep the faith or anything like that. Because she knew.

She knew what that was like.

Margo waved and turned, heading three houses down to Callie's place.

The large white house had a row of purple flowers out front, and those flowers had a big trail that cut through them. Jaden, Margo assumed.

If Jaden had a route he wanted to take, it wasn't going to be changed simply because there were flowers there.

She liked that about him.

She walked up the path and to the front door, and before she could knock, Callie opened it. "Come in. But Jaden and Hayley are fighting."

"That sounds about right," said Margo.

Truth be told, she had stayed away from her friend's house over the past few months because of the kids.

Margo loved Jaden and Hayley. But watching her friend mother them… She'd been afraid of that. Afraid that it might shatter her.

She was brittle as it was.

Hayley came into the room with her arms pinned down at her sides, and her eyes downcast. She was nine, and wholly overdramatic. She was followed by her older brother, who at eleven was getting tall, and looking more like a man than a boy.

Six months.

It's been six months since she'd seen Poppy. Poppy was only four, so the changes might not be that extreme when she saw her again. But she would've changed. Learned new things. And Margo had missed it.

"Please apologize," Jaden said to Hayley.

Hayley turned around, her curly hair swinging behind her. "No! You're the one that's being annoying!"

"I'm not annoying. Don't say that."

"Stop following me!" Hayley growled and marched from the room, and Callie stood and put her hand on Jaden's shoulder.

"She set a boundary. And you need to respect it."

Jaden frowned. "Boundaries?"

"Yes, Jaden. Sometimes when you've upset somebody they need time."

"I apologized," he said. "At 3:27."

"I know you did," said Callie. "I'm proud of you. But you need to give Hayley a minute, okay?"

Jaden lifted one shoulder. "Okay."

"Why don't you go play on your iPad?"

He nodded. "Hmmm."

Then he turned around and walked out of the room, and she could sense her friend's anxiety that he might actually just go follow his sister and start all over again.

"Some days I swear they can go all day at each other."

"That's why it was nice having an only child."

The words left her mouth before she could really think them through. The past tense statement. When had she accepted that?

She wanted to stuff the words back in. And to her credit, Callie didn't follow them up. Like she sensed that Margo regretted saying them.

"I feel sorry for Jaden. He can't let go of things, and then it just sends her over the edge. I don't really blame her either."

"Siblings are hard. Nobody can infuriate me like Christopher."

"Well, he was infuriating. Hot though."

"No," said Margo. "Your feelings for my older brother are gross."

"Relax. It's not like I ever dated him."

Which was actually a fair point, because Callie had dated a number of older boys when they had been in high school, but she had left Christopher alone.

It had been kind of a surprise when she got married and started having kids right out of college. Though Margo had long suspected that the pregnancy had coincided with the decision to get married. But Callie had claimed it hadn't. That they had actually wanted to be pregnant that quickly.

"What's up?" Callie asked.

"I found something," she said.

"What do you mean you found something? About Zach and Poppy?"

Margo shook her head. "No."

Her forehead creased. "Um. What then?"

"I went down to the Little Free Library last night. There was a copy of my favorite book by Jacob Spinner in there."

"Oh. You mean *our* favorite Jacob Spinner book."

"Right. I pulled it out and looked at it. It was signed, so I decided to take it. Today when I was flipping through it, a letter fell out." She took the letter out of her pocket and handed it over to Callie.

Callie opened it, and unfolded it, frowning as she read. "What do you think it means?"

"It made me…think of Sarah."

"Why?"

"Sarah used to pass notes like that in class. It's not her handwriting, but something about the note, and the book, the timing of it made me think of Sarah."

"That's a pretty big stretch."

"It is. I admit it. It's a huge stretch. But trust me, that is actually how you piece a story together. Sometimes you have to swing and miss wildly. And… Maybe this means nothing. But the point is that I would like to look into it. I think I want my next book to be about Sarah. And what happened."

"Margo, we made a deal a long time ago about this," Callie said, looking at a fixed point on the table.

"I know. But I'm different. We're different. I'm not in high school anymore, and I know how to do this without making you miserable."

"Margo," she said, slower this time. "You're an amazing person. An amazing friend. You also don't know a boundary if there isn't a very, very hard one in place, and that was why we…" She looked at Margo long and hard. "You didn't really stop for me, did you?"

"I did," Margo said.

"It wasn't *only* about me, though."

She looked down. "No. It wasn't." She cleared her throat. "I'm not the same person I was when I was in high school. First of all, it isn't just being nosy. I have a platform, I have experience."

Callie sighed. "Yes. Okay. But let's be honest about…the *you* of it all. You think that you're going to solve this after eighteen years?"

It made her sound…well, either egotistical or insane. Maybe both.

It was also not…*not* true.

"On some level, I guess. But I think I have to believe that in order to ever get started on something like this."

"I don't know. Margo, I really don't know if I can stand to have this resurrected."

"I get it. But I'm drowning, Callie. And this is the first thing that's made me feel like myself. That's made me feel like a human being in a long time. But I won't do it if it bothers you."

"That's not fair. Not when you put it like that."

"I'm sorry… I really didn't… I'm sorry."

Callie put her hands over her face. "No. I'm sorry. I'm sorry because I'm just not equipped to deal with this. Because as a family we had to just not talk about it. It was so great to meet DeVonte, and to have him be from a different high school. A different college. He didn't know. And he knows, but he doesn't *know*, you know?"

She nodded. "Yeah."

"He never met Sarah," Callie said quietly.

"People were unfair to you. To your mother."

"You don't have to tell me that."

"I want to fix that. I want to show the whole story. The way that the town reacted, and why it was wrong. There was so much blame to go around, and only one person is to blame."

"But that person is my dad."

"I know that."

And Margo had never understood the complication of that more. Because it was her husband who had taken her daughter away from her. And he was still her husband.

Because sometimes she missed him lying in bed beside her, even though she hated him now. Because sometimes she missed him as much as she missed Poppy. And there were moments when she couldn't breathe. Because the loss of both of them made her want to drop to her knees and never get back up.

She was far too acquainted with how complicated something like this could be.

"If anyone is going to tell the story, and actually listen, and actually understand, it's going to be me. Not just because I was here. Because I get it. I know what it's like to have somebody be there one day and gone the next. I know what it's like to hate someone as much as you love them."

"Do you hate Zach?"

Margo nodded slowly. "Yeah. Sometimes I dream about killing him. And sometimes I dream about kissing him again."

That was about the most fucked-up thing that lived inside of her.

She'd said it out loud, which she thought was probably a good thing.

"He was my husband for a long time," she continued. "I can't just…not feel that way." She took a deep breath. "I'm really not the same person I was the first time I tried this, Callie. I'm not even the same person who wrote the last book. Everything is broken. I just want to fix something."

Callie was silent for a long moment.

"Are you going to promise this to your publisher…today?"

"No. I can wait a couple weeks. And you can see everything that I've pulled together. We can work together. Because this is actually a story about a community. Where we were all supposed to be safe. When nothing bad happened. And I want to know, was your dad actually hiding this, expertly and perfectly, the whole time, or were there signs, but other people ignored him? Let it go? And were there others? No, there's really no way that he comes out of this looking good, but I feel like there are ways that we can thoroughly explore how blame shifting disrupted your life. Because if Sarah had to carry some of the blame for this, then so did you, so did your mother."

"Yes. That is true."

"And you were friends with Sarah."

She nodded slowly. "Yeah."

"I'll be careful with this."

"You're going to be honest though, aren't you? Because that's what you do. I read your book. Don't forget that. That one girl's family… Natalie. Her parents didn't call because they were angry at her. Because they thought that she was off partying and having sex. So they didn't call the police. They thought she was just experiencing a consequence for her actions. They didn't realize she'd been abducted by a serial killer."

"Yeah. I'm going to be honest. Like I was about them. It wouldn't have saved her. But it did feel particularly cold knowing that their daughter was dead and they were worried about whether or not she smoked marijuana."

"I can't imagine that. You know, that is the one thing, when your family breaks apart the way that mine did, you know how important it is."

Callie instantly looked filled with regret.

"I'm sorry, that was…"

"It's okay," Margo said. "You're right. I've never understood more than I do now. Just how important my family was. Now that they're gone."

She stayed at Callie's for a little while longer, then went outside. She had a book that she could throw herself into completely. No one else and nothing else needed her attention.

She would give anything to have that change.

She also knew that if she was going to proceed with this, she needed to call *him*.

She could go to his house. But it was possible he was out of town. So it would be better just to pick up the phone. She went to her recent calls, and scrolled down all the way to the bottom.

It had been forty-five days since she last made contact with Dane.

A brief text asking if she was okay. Mostly, like Callie, she assumed he'd been checking for signs of life.

They hadn't talked at all for months before Zach had left. Because she'd needed distance. Because she'd made her decision.

If she was going to do this, though, she had to talk to him. *Him.*

She was about to open up his contact in her phone when she heard her name.

She looked up, and saw Julie. Her neighbor.

"Hi, Margo," she said.

Her little white dog pulled on the leash she was holding, and tried to make a break for Margo.

"Tinkerbell," said Julie, scolding.

"Hi, Julie," said Margo.

"How are you? Can I bring you a casserole or something later?"

"I…" She didn't know how to say no to casserole. And she wanted to. Because casserole was disgusting. And people insisted on bringing it to her. If someone was already sad, what was the point of piling a casserole on top of it? Margo would never know. "Yes. Thank you."

She didn't have to eat it in front of her. It was nice of Julie to offer. Because actually, that was one of the difficult things. The way that people had dropped off after time.

"Wednesday?"

"Yeah. Thank you."

This was why she didn't leave her house, though. Not that any of the interactions had been bad. It was just they were all about Poppy and Zach.

Well. Everything is about them. Every day of your life was about them when they were here, so of course it's going to be when they're gone too.

She tried to hold back the wave of pain that rolled over her. She didn't have time to feel it. Not right now. She looked back down at her phone, and hit Dane's name as soon as she walked in to her house. It rang. And rang all the way until she got his voicemail.

This is Dane with Sonar Recovery, leave a message and I'll get back to you as soon as I can.

"Hi, Dane. It's Margo. I was wondering…if you'd give me a call. I wanted to talk to you about something. It's about Sarah."

She hung up. She wished she had never said that. It made it sound like she might know something more than she did. And she regretted that.

She didn't want to give him any kind of false hope. She hadn't wanted him to think it was about Zach or Poppy either.

She went into the kitchen and rummaged around in the freezer until she found a frozen potpie. Okay, maybe a casserole wouldn't be bad. Maybe she needed something other than frozen meals.

She heated it up in the microwave, and took it on a plate over to the couch, where she sat with her feet curled up under her and watched a mindless TV show. But the whole time, she was thinking about Sarah. She almost missed the phone call. Because it was on silent. The faint buzz from it vibrating against the couch brought her attention back to the present. Her heart thumped against the front of her breastbone. It was Dane.

She answered it. "Hello?"

"What's this about, Margo?"

"Right. Sorry. I don't know anything. I don't know anything new. But I was thinking about Sarah. And…"

"Dammit. How are you?"

His voice sounded raw. Exhausted. He must be working a job. She recognized that sound.

"I don't know."

"Functional?"

He was the only one who knew how little she'd been sleeping when they'd found the girls. He'd caught her with Adderall in her hand, her whole pill kit clutched in the other, one day when she'd gone back to her SUV, and he'd gripped her wrist. Not hard like he'd done once. Not bruising. But he'd been angry.

"I have to see this through. I can't do it all if—"

"You aren't doing it all if you need drugs to do it."

"They aren't drugs. I have a prescription."

"I see your light on, at all hours."

"If you see it, you're awake too."

"I know what my demons are. What are yours?"

"All the missing girls. Just the same as you."

She cleared her throat.

"More or less. I just wanted to talk to you about Sarah. I'm considering looking into her case. Writing about it."

"If you want to do that, that's up to you."

"You don't have a problem with it?"

"It wouldn't matter if I did."

"It actually would." Of course he wouldn't know. That she'd stopped pushing all those years ago in no small part because of him. He'd been lost in his own hell. But what she'd done…it had been for him.

"It shouldn't. If you think there's something to write about, write about it."

She couldn't read that. Couldn't read his tone.

"I'd like to see you," she said.

Those words felt heavy. Felt like an admission of something deeper. No matter how much she wished they didn't.

"I'm out of town. Looking into a cold case in Ohio. I just got out of the water."

"Shit. You're not… You didn't find a body?"

"No. Nothing. I wish that we would've found a body. Otherwise…it's going to feel like a waste."

"How many more places you have left to check?"

"We're going up to a reservoir tomorrow. Kid might've driven by."

Her heart jolted again. "A kid?"

"He was seventeen. When he disappeared twenty years ago. Thanks to the Incline Valley murders we've got a lot more funding and a lot more interest. It's hard to sort through all of it. But when people call about missing loved ones…"

"Yeah. That's good. I mean, it's amazing how many people you've been able to help."

"I need to go. I'm freezing."

"Thanks for calling me back."

"I'll always call you back."

He hung up, and she rested the phone against her cheek. Leaning against it.

She missed him. But there was a very specific reason they hadn't seen each other much since they'd worked on the case together.

His appeal had always been broad. He was tall, muscular. In the years since high school he'd added tattoos and a beard that only made him seem all the more compelling. Dangerous. He had been for a while. Then he joined the military, and she knew he'd seen things there that had left him changed.

As if his sister disappearing hadn't already done that.

Dane Hartley.

Her phone buzzed again, and she jumped. But this time it was a text.

i'll be back in two days. Let's meet up.

Sure.

Well, he hadn't said no, even though she could sense he wasn't happy. She also felt like he probably didn't think he could say no, given her specific state at the moment.

Working with him had been…intense.

Especially when he'd found the cars buried beneath the surface of the water. The cars that could be connected back to the man who'd killed those girls. Not a local, not a transient. A very rich man who'd owned a vacation home that overlooked the lake.

That overlooked the watery graveyard that he'd used to get rid of all the evidence.

She tried to steel herself, tried to imagine meeting up with him again. And for some reason, it brought back a memory, something he'd told her when they were getting ready to dive in Lake Tahoe.

Very few people are actually missing. The truth is, more often than not, they're gone before anybody ever realizes they're missing. Dead before anyone looks.

Margo closed her eyes, and tried not to dissolve.

4

SHE DIDN'T SLEEP much over the next two days. She had finally found something to focus on. And once she'd zeroed in on it, she became obsessed.

She had pulled out everything that she'd ever kept relating to Sarah, and had started to piece things together.

She had kept the door to her office firmly closed when Julie had come over with the casserole, and again when Callie came over.

"How's it going?"

"It's going. I don't have much to share yet. It's mostly just going over things everybody already knows."

"What did Dane say?"

She didn't want to get into it, and she couldn't quite say why.

"He was out of town. I'm going to talk to him tomorrow."

"Oh."

"Yeah."

Callie cleared her throat. "I have a question, and I feel like it's maybe not appropriate timing for it, but I…"

"What?" The question was sharp, daring Callie to proceed.

"Did something happen between you and Dane?"

Her brain supplied every piece of evidence for why Callie might ask that. That Dane had come to the house the night Poppy had disappeared. That Margo kept her interactions with him compartmentalized. That she saw him, but clearly didn't talk about him.

But all of those things could be attributed to the fact he was Sarah's brother.

Dane had been one of the people who'd hated Brian Archer's entire family on principle. Dane had hated everything on principle back then. Margo could remember the alarming unraveling he'd undergone back then.

She could remember calling Sarah and hoping he would answer the phone, just so she could hear his voice for a second. She could remember walking into Sarah's house right when Dane was coming down the stairs, her heart slamming itself against her breastbone like she'd just experienced a jump scare.

But it hadn't been fear creating that reaction.

Then after Sarah was gone she hadn't had a reason to call. Hadn't had a reason to visit.

The worst thing ever to be upset about in that moment, but she had been.

Because Dane had been...something to her.

"No," she said. "I never know how much you want to hear about him."

It was true. And it was a lie. All at the same time.

She was getting very good at those.

"Right. I don't have an issue with Dane. He's not the same person he was then. I'm not either."

Margo remembered trying to see him once, when she'd come back to town for a visit while she was in college. She hadn't seen him in a couple of years, and the last time she had it had been difficult. She'd asked him questions about Sarah, her moods, any signs he might have seen.

You aren't a detective.

I just want to help.

He'd brushed her off, told her she was just one of Sarah's annoying friends and she wasn't going to uncover anything the police hadn't.

But she'd really felt compelled to see him.

She'd heard that Dane was convinced he'd seen Sarah at a trailhead just out of town. The police hadn't listened. But Margo had wanted to know. What he'd seen. When. She'd promised Callie she wouldn't dig, but Callie didn't have to know about this. Anyway, her support for Dane, her feelings for Dane, were different.

He'd lived in an apartment by the ocean, small and grimy and smelling like the sea and too much damp. When she'd arrived, it was barely noon, and he'd been drunk.

"I want answers to…"

"Give it a rest, Margo."

"Dane, I just feel like I could fix this. I feel like…"

He reached out and grabbed her arm, the touch of his hand on her bare skin electrifying for the moment, until he tightened his grip and propelled her toward the door. She resisted, pushing back against him until he released his hold and she fell backward against the wall.

She'd never told anyone where the bruise on her arm had come from.

He wasn't that same person now. The one who'd been lost in despair and on a fast track to drinking himself to death. Hurting himself or someone else because all the anger inside him was like a living thing.

He'd enlisted shortly after that. She'd been almost certain he'd hoped he'd get deployed somewhere he might die.

He hadn't died.

He had come back different.

"Okay, well now I know."

"You used to like him so much."

Margo bit the inside of her cheek. "You used to claim you'd lie down in the street to let Justin Timberlake run you over because even being crushed by his car would be an erotic experience. We all change."

The corner of Callie's mouth twitched. "Sure. But I don't live in the same town as Justin Timberlake."

And for years she'd lived in the same town as Dane and hadn't associated with him. She'd made her choice.

Zach hadn't known she'd spent her teenage years nursing a huge crush on Dane, and he certainly hadn't known about the tense encounter at Dane's apartment. In hindsight, she wondered if that was weird. That they'd never laughed or joked about people they'd once had crushes on in their small town, before they'd found their way to each other.

She'd never felt like her feelings for Dane were something she could make light of though.

When she'd ended up with Dane for that two weeks during their search in the Tahoe area, Zach had been...strange. She could tell he hadn't been entirely comfortable with it.

She'd thought maybe she was projecting.

After the book had released, she'd ended up giving interviews with Dane in New York, in LA.

The sense of tension with Zach had gotten louder. The silent accusation she could see in his eyes. But she hadn't known if she was just seeing her own guilt reflected back at her.

But she'd chosen Zach. Their marriage. Their life.

The silence had erupted eight months before he and Poppy had disappeared. Before she'd ever found those condoms.

She'd told him good-night, and headed toward her office as he headed to their room. Zach had stopped.

It's not the book, is it? It's him.

The guilt, regret and rage that had twisted up in her had left her immobilized. She'd just stared at him. Except of course, she didn't have to ask who *he* was. Which made her outrage feel a bit unearned.

You were away with him for two weeks, he'd pressed.

Yes. I was. We were working on a case, and it's been over a year and a half—

Did you fuck him?

"Zach had some concerns about Dane too."

They'd stitched the wound back up after that. She'd denied that she'd slept with him. Zach had believed her.

Then Margo had found the condoms.

She'd blamed herself.

She hadn't said anything.

She hadn't said anything to Callie until now either. But she was raw. And she didn't see the point in holding anything back now.

Callie closed her eyes. "I'm sorry." She opened them again. "I channeled high school again and I wasn't thinking that in terms of accusing you of having an affair, which I know you wouldn't do."

She was glad Callie was confident in Margo's fidelity. Margo wasn't.

She hadn't fucked Dane.

She'd wanted to, though.

In the end, was that better? It was, she supposed. But it was a line crossed all the same. One thing she'd discovered over the years of investigating different crimes was that the internal gerrymandering of morality was a lot more dangerous than people realized. Once you moved the boundaries, the lines you could consider crossing, inside yourself, you were laying the groundwork for the actions you could take later.

In her experience, every cold case was littered with multiple failures. People who were protecting themselves at the expense of justice.

They may not have committed a crime, they may not have

known for sure who had, but all the little things added up to complicity.

Sometimes what you didn't do, what you didn't say, could be just as harmful.

"Zach thought there was something between Dane and I. I don't blame you for thinking the same, I guess."

"Right. Well. It wasn't my business anyway."

There was a glimmer in her friend's eyes then. And Margo was so very familiar with that look. She'd seen it in countless law enforcement officers' eyes. The eyes of family members trying so hard to convince themselves they believed a loved one's alibi.

Doubt.

Callie doubted her, whatever she said.

Margo would love to be offended.

She'd never touched him. He'd never touched her.

They'd never talked about the fact that they wanted to. It had been coded in the intensity in their every interaction. In that long-ago remembered touch that had left her bruised and haunted him like a ghost.

She knew they'd stood on the edge of that invisible line that would have shattered her marriage. She hadn't walked over it, though.

After they'd found the girls. Watched a mother drop to her knees on the edge of the lake and scream in anguish when they'd confirmed that her daughter's car had been found beneath the surface of the water, a license plate serving as proof.

It had been a shot of whiskey, layered with fire, joy, deep, deep sadness. It had been the break Margo'd needed, that law enforcement had needed. They'd found answers. But they'd found death.

They'd been high on that afterward, the wrenching, discordant emotion that no one else would be able to understand them.

They'd stood in front of her hotel room door. He'd been

physically exhausted, his hair was still wet from the dive. She'd wanted to hold him.

She'd wanted that back then, when his sister had disappeared.

She'd wanted it when he'd been angry and drunk and on the verge of self-destruction.

It would have been reasonable to invite him in to have a drink. To discuss what had happened that day.

He'd looked at her, and she could see it all in his eyes. What would happen if she did. An invitation to go over the line.

She had made vows to Zach. She'd loved Zach.

But she'd loved Dane first, even if he'd never known it.

She could remember her mother telling her that she didn't believe in ever being alone with a man she wasn't married to. Not for dinner, not to socialize. She definitely wouldn't invite a man into her motel room to share a drink.

Margo hadn't. She'd kept that door firmly closed.

She'd wondered what would have happened if she'd made a different choice ever since.

But she'd done the right thing.

But the truth of what she *felt* remained. Whether she'd touched him or not.

She'd wanted it, and she'd done the hard thing. She'd walked away from it. Maybe that made Zach's infidelity worse. Was she hurt by it, or just mad her husband had gotten the sex he wanted when she'd denied herself?

"We've been through enough that you can always ask me difficult questions," Margo said.

Callie looked at her for a long time. "You're very good at being there for other people. But you're a little locked box. You're always there for me, but you make it hard to be there for you."

Well. She didn't like her own feelings. She liked writing about other people's lives. Other people's secrets. She liked talking to her friends about other people's problems. She liked hearing about theirs.

"I don't know what to ask for," Margo said.

It was honest.

Callie wrapped an arm around her shoulder. "Yeah, that doesn't surprise me. I'll just keep trying."

"You can ask me," Margo said. "It doesn't irritate me. I think sometimes I don't know how to share voluntarily."

"Good to know. I'll keep harassing you then."

"Thanks."

She meant it.

The next day, when Dane texted her that he was ready to meet up, she gladly took his suggestion that they head out to the local tavern, Sea Dog, which was overly nautical for a tavern that sat five miles inland.

It was dark and crowded, the green vinyl and fake wood-paneled walls making it a cave. It wasn't the kind of place she typically frequented, which made it all the better.

It was a small town, so not only did a lot of people know her because she'd grown up here, the notoriety she'd gained in the past eighteen months, then again six months ago when Poppy and Zach had vanished, had compromised the small amount of anonymity she'd had.

So she gave thanks for the darkness, and the fact she looked about five years younger without makeup and with her hair in a ponytail. No one would recognize her.

Or at least, not quickly.

As soon as she walked in, she zeroed in on Dane. He was sitting with his back to the door, his shoulders so broad he looked overlarge in the chair. He had one arm resting on the table, and her eyes went to the vivid red dragon that was inked all the way down from where his shirtsleeve ended, to the back of his hand. He had a glass of whiskey in front of him, and he was already partway through it.

"Hi, Dane," she said, moving around to the other side of the table and going to sit across from them.

"Margo."

"I…"

"Drink?" he asked.

"A Coke."

"You're not a big drinker, are you?"

She shook her head. "No. I like to be able to think."

She liked a substance, but she needed it to be useful. Alcohol made her foggy.

"Still? That's really something." He stood for a moment and went to the bar, and she watched as he exchanged words with the woman behind the counter. She was fascinated by the way he talked to other people.

He'd softened so much when he'd talked to the families who'd been present when they'd found the girls. A completely unrecognizable version of Dane Hartley.

Right now, this woman was flirting with him. Looking at him up from beneath her lashes, smiling in that coy, sweet way every time she said something. Then she'd look up again, checking for his reaction.

Dane didn't notice. He was a brick wall. He didn't give her a reaction at all.

That, Margo could see, only made that poor woman want to reach him more.

Relatable.

"Here you go," he said, returning to the table with a large glass in his hand. He set it in front of her.

"Thanks," she said.

She wrapped her hand around it, grimacing because it was already wet with condensation. She moved her hand away and wiped the water drops on her pants.

It reminded her of being in Tahoe with him. In a small place like this, tucked out of the way. They'd been there for two weeks trawling the lakes in the area. All based around a hunch that she'd been unable to ignore.

She'd explored so many theories. She'd had maps posted all over her office, with strings connecting different points, each color part of a different theory.

Where he'd come from—she'd always known it was a man. How he'd gotten to them. What he'd done with them.

If they went from these origin points, where did it make sense for them to end up?

What was the pattern?

She'd been over and over it.

And one night, late, she'd been up in a medication-fueled fury, and her break had been to indulge in trying to trace where Dane Hartley was at.

She was friends with his sister Kerrigan online, and she was off living her best life in Boston, a young single professional with constant girls'-night-out posts and endless selfies. She was still in her twenties. It was forgivable.

Through that connection she'd started hunting around for info on the very-not-online Dane. Very little hard evidence turned up on social media. Instead it was, oddly, a news article. Sonar Recovery was a nonprofit, entirely donation-funded team that searched for missing persons in lakes and rivers.

Almost entirely comprised of vets, the team used sophisticated sonar to search for people who'd disappeared without a trace.

They'd made twenty-seven recoveries in two years.

"My sister went missing sixteen years ago. I know the pain these people are going through," says Hartley, a veteran who served two tours in Afghanistan with the US Army. *"This is a way of providing people with closure they wouldn't otherwise get."*

She'd read the article over and over and then she'd gotten up to look at her map.

Those women had disappeared.

Cars and all.

How? Why?

It'd made her wonder.

Burying someone underground in a vehicle would require equipment. It would draw attention.

Burying someone in water...

She'd messaged Kerrigan immediately to get Dane's contact info. They hadn't spoken since she'd run into him in town at the grocery store when she'd been pregnant with Poppy and he'd been getting beer and bread.

She could still remember the brands he'd had in his cart.

She hadn't felt uncomfortable asking for the info, because she'd had a reason. It'd been for work. But she hadn't been able to deny the weird thrill that went through her when Kerrigan gave her his number, and she'd sent the text.

I need your help with something. I think your organization could be exactly what I need.

She'd realized then he wouldn't have her number. He wouldn't know.

This is Margo.

Dots had appeared at the bottom, like he was thinking about what to type.

Then finally: What are you working on?

She'd switched from sending messages on her phone to sending them on her computer because she'd had a lot to say.

It's a book about six missing persons cases in the area of Lake Tahoe. I'm working on the idea that they're linked, and that it's potentially the work of a serial killer. All six disappeared within a 50-mile radius of each other, three from Incline Valley. Their cars also vanished.

Interesting.

Yeah. I think so too.

He looked up at her and his hard gaze brought her back to the present. "What's going on?"

No *How are you doing?* Which was actually fine. She wasn't doing well. Obviously.

If Dane wanted direct, she could give that to him.

"I found a copy of *Devil in the Dark* in the Little Free Library by my neighborhood."

"I think the last time I saw that book it was in the grocery store with an emblem that said 'five million in print,' so that doesn't seem unusual."

"It was a first edition. The one we all had back then."

"Okay."

"I found a note inside."

She told him the whole story. The Little Free Library. The note.

"I don't know if it's related to Sarah," she said. "I feel like it's possible, though. The time frame would be right."

"You're assuming only one girl was being raped in this town."

The words were hard and stark. "I'm not. Believe me, Dane, I don't make assumptions that give too much credit to human nature being benevolent. Most of all, it made me think of her. Most of all, I have a feeling. I would think someone who is in your line of work should understand the importance of following a hunch," she said.

"I don't do hunches." He took a drink, then set the glass back on the table. "I do sonar."

"But to get on the water you have to follow a hunch first.

You have to be willing to connect vague dots. To think of any possibility. Any reason a person might have been on the road near where you're going to search."

"Yeah. Fair point."

"I just…"

"What's the purpose of dredging it up? She disappeared with the guy. Brian Archer doesn't want to be found. I think maybe Sarah doesn't want to be found. At first, I imagined that she was being held prisoner by him. But after all this time? I don't know. I guess she chose to be with him."

"She was sixteen."

"Not saying it wasn't fucked up. I'm saying that I can't think of any reason she wouldn't have come home now other than the fact that she chose it. Okay?"

"It was still a kidnapping at the time. A sixteen-year-old who leaves with her teacher even by choice was coerced. Manipulated. Even if she felt she made the choice, the whole situation was wrong, and we know that now. We know things we didn't because things change, because we've changed. We had a predator living in Conifer, teaching at the high school. I want to dig into that, and I want to know…how everyone missed it."

Dane shook his head. "Because people are selfish. Because they see what they want to. They turn away from the difficult things. I've done fifteen recoveries in the past three years. Very few of those recoveries were accidents. The vast majority were suicides. And when you start digging and talking to people, signs were all over the place. I'm not saying anyone could have stopped it, but I am saying that people usually do show you what's happening. We just don't stop to look."

"Then I want to know what we missed."

He shook his head. "Why? What's the point of dredging all this up?"

She was right back in that day all those years ago. When he'd broken. When he'd lashed out. She had never understood him more. Maybe because she'd seen him break, she found herself shattering beneath that familiar gaze.

"Because I don't know what happened to my child," she said, all of her restraint suddenly gone. The rage and desperation clawing at her chest made it difficult for her to breathe. "I can't figure it out. I hired someone to help me, and he can't figure it out. I have exhausted every resource that I know to use. And it just keeps bringing me back to Sarah. Because that happened here too. And nobody ever answered the question. And maybe on some level I think if I can't ever answer that question, then I'm never going to be able to find Zach and Poppy. He took her from me. *He took her from me.*"

His hand moved slowly across the table, and for a second she thought he might put it over hers.

Their eyes met. She wondered if he remembered the last time he'd grabbed her wrist. When he'd been so angry.

He pulled his hand back. "I'm sorry."

A wave of sadness threatened to pull her under. Whether it was because he hadn't touched her or because of his apology, she wasn't sure.

"Cold cases are a long shot," she said. "But the thing about cold cases is sometimes you end up digging into the police work and you find connections that weren't made, and balls that got dropped. Sometimes distance and time are what it takes to put the pieces together. To see clearly where things got missed. Or mishandled."

"What I don't understand is why you're asking me what I think."

"Because I want your… Your permission. To write about Sarah."

"Has anybody asked your permission to write things about your husband and child?"

She curled her fingers tight into fists, and realized the tabletop was vaguely sticky. "No. Of course not. You can't stop speculation. And you can't stop people from posting their opinions. On the internet or in publications."

"I can't stop you from writing about my sister."

"It's more than that. It's more than just writing about something. It's investigating. And anyway, those people are my friends. And I thought maybe we were…"

It was like shutters closed behind his eyes. "No. Margo, it's not like that."

That hurt.

And maybe he was right.

Maybe they weren't friends. She'd wished they could be that at least. When she was fourteen she'd have given her left arm to have him look her direction.

It was why she'd gone to his apartment when she was twenty-one, filled with so much empathy and concern she thought she might implode from the sheer force of it.

She'd felt drawn to him.

Compelled to be near him.

But maybe that couldn't be friendship.

"Right. Fine. But even if it isn't that way for you, can you respect that *I* care what you think?"

"You are the most single-minded, tenacious person that I have ever met. And I don't understand the performance of coming in here and asking my permission. Because we both know you're going to do what you want. You did what you wanted the whole time you were digging into things with the Incline Valley Killer. You ruffled a lot of feathers. Law enforcement, some family members. Your own husband. The phone calls between you two made it clear he didn't want you traveling around unearthing things about a serial killer. And you did it anyway, because you thought it was important."

"It was important."

"I didn't say it wasn't. My point is, you're going to do this thing that you think serves the greater good no matter what I or anyone else tells you. Your problem is that you want what you want, and you want other people to agree with you. But if you're going to be this big of a pain in the ass, Margo, you need to own it. You have to deal with the fact that people are going to be pissed off at you."

She sucked in a sharp breath, and felt irritation and pain well up inside of her. "But I don't want to hurt you. I don't want you to be hurt. I don't want to dredge up things that you don't want to deal with."

"You're lying. You don't care about that. You want me to thank you. You want me to fucking *thank you*, because now you're a famous writer, and you're going to bring the same kind of attention to my sister's case that you brought to the Incline Valley Killer. You're not doing this just to look into it. You think you're going to solve it."

She hated that he saw through her so clearly. That what he said was both extremely flattering and very unflattering all at once.

"It doesn't matter that I'm a famous writer," she said. "That's not why I'm doing this." She put her hand back on her Coke glass, but she was shaking too hard to pick it up. "I'm a woman whose daughter is missing. That's what I am right now. I'm a woman whose marriage fell apart in the most improbable, insane way that I could never have seen coming. And this is the first thing that has made any sense to me since that happened. I cannot fix my own life. But I need to do something. Because I'm driving myself insane."

She leaned back in her chair. "Do you need me to admit that this is selfish? Is that what would make you happy? Do you need me to say out loud that I'm doing this in part for me? Because I do want to do it for me. But not just in the way that you think. I have a box. Of all these things that I hoped were clues back when she went missing."

"She ran away," he said.

"She's still missing," said Margo. "And I know that it still hurts."

Had *she* hurt him? She doubted that was possible. Not because she didn't think he had feelings, but because she didn't think an unspoken attraction during an intense time would be something that would rattle him like this.

"Did you end up finding the boy?" she asked.

She decided then to switch the conversation to his work. Because that could explain his mood as well.

He nodded. "Yeah. Doesn't get easier. With a case like that, though, the family knows it's a recovery effort. Twenty years and you do know. I mean, in those sorts of circumstances. Especially when someone was in a bad place mentally."

Suicides. He'd said it was mostly that.

"He did it on purpose," she said.

"Yeah. His girlfriend had broken up with him, he was in a fight with his parents, he left a note indicating that he planned to harm himself. It was just then he disappeared without a trace. But we finally did sonar near a quarry where I guess the kids used to go drink. As far as we can tell he deliberately drove his car off the edge of the embankment there. And it was deep. Straight down. But you know, you don't need that much water to hide a car."

Those poor parents. Twenty years. Twenty years of not knowing where their child was. They'd aged, and he was forever seventeen.

She looked down at her hands again, and suddenly she felt dizzy. It felt like the table was tilting to the side.

He reached out and wrapped his hand around her wrist.

Finally.

His hold was strong, but it was gentle.

There was no anger in his touch.

"You okay?" he asked.

She shook her head. "No."

She met his gaze, and she realized something. He wasn't angry at her. He was uncomfortable. He didn't want to be sitting there with her. This whole thing was about his discomfort.

"You think they're dead, don't you?" Her mouth went dry, icy dread skating down her spine.

He tilted his glass of whiskey to the side, the amber liquid pooling there. Then he looked up at her. "I'm not an optimist. I look for bodies. That's what I do."

"Is that why you don't want to see me? Because you're afraid you're going to, what…shout that at me? That my kid is dead?"

Even saying it like that, flippantly and with guarded disbelief, flooded her mouth with the metallic tang of panic. Made her stomach turn over on itself.

"No. But there's a reason that when we do searches like the ones we do, it's with families who ask for it to be done. They have to be ready. They have to be ready for the answer."

"You think I'm not ready. You think that I'm unrealistic."

"No. Not necessarily. Parental abduction is different than somebody just disappearing. I'm not an optimist. I don't know that you necessarily need to be around me."

He didn't want to be around her. That was the real truth.

Do you think they're dead?

She hadn't specified when she'd asked that who she'd meant.

Zach and Poppy.

Sarah and Brian.

"Maybe that's really the question I'm trying to ask about Sarah," she said softly. "If I go looking, and I find out the truth, are you ready for the answer?"

"You think you're going to find it. You think you're going to find my sister, when she and Brian Archer have spent eighteen years avoiding everyone who's ever known them. When no law enforcement agency could find them. And you know they put out an APB for an adult traveling across state lines with a minor. There was an AMBER Alert. They considered it a kidnapping. You know, when people in town didn't consider her a slut for tempting him away from his family."

"I *do* think I can find her. Because I really do believe that the way she was partly held responsible for that prevented law enforcement from engaging in a serious search for her. I believe that there is more to find out about Brian Archer. And if we can get that information, we are going to be able to start building a bigger picture."

"You're infuriating, do you know that?"

"Why?"

He looked resigned then. Tired. "It's not you, I guess. It's me. I like watching you do this too much to tell you no."

"Does that count as your blessing?"

"It's as close to one as I'm giving."

And yet again she was thankful they were on neutral ground. Because the air between them never felt neutral. And it was hard enough contending with that.

"That's good enough for me." She didn't order a drink. She left him sitting there with his alcohol.

She wasn't sure if that had been a good conversation or not, but she had made a decision. She felt certain about something. She'd made a decision. And right now, in her life, that felt like something.

Right now, she felt something like passion stirring inside of her.

Right now, it felt like a reason to breathe.

5

SHE'D WOKEN AT 11:00 a.m. thinking she'd heard crying, and by 11:15 she'd stepped outside her front door and was on her way down to the police station.

Zach had taken their black SUV when he'd left. So she had their little red electric car and that was all. Not that she needed an SUV when she didn't have a child. She drove through the gate, and out onto the two-lane highway, down the winding road that ran along the Columbia River, and headed into town.

Most of the main part of the community was settled on a bay, the harsh call of seagulls serving as a soundtrack after she parked in the small lot behind the little blue police station on the end of the street.

There were different ways to do things. In other towns, she might have emailed first. But here, with the small-town department, she thought she would go in person.

She walked in the front, and was a little surprised to see Amber Harding from high school sitting in the reception seat.

Her instant reaction to Amber was a violent, soul-deep *hell no*. It was hard for her to remember Amber had been a friend once. Part of their group, even. But not after Brian took Sarah.

Amber had been so cold to Callie. So convinced she must have known something.

When they'd read *Devil in the Dark*, Amber had sided with the cop. And with some of the invasive policing tactics. She was law and order all the way. It wasn't super shocking to see her working in the small-town department.

She genuinely couldn't remember ever liking her. Not now.

"Hi."

"Oh, hi, Margo."

It was interesting to watch as Amber's expression shifted to one of…pity.

"I'm not here about me," said Margo.

She hoped that the clear and concise sentence would throw up a verbal wall between them on that topic. She wasn't in the mood to discuss Poppy.

She was here about Sarah.

"Right. Of course. How can I help you?"

"I'd like to speak to Officer Daniels."

"Right," said Amber. "Why?"

Lord. Why were there high school dynamics happening to her now? It was that little snare of being in her hometown. It was good when people knew her, mostly. It validated her questions and made people trust her. She could just walk into the police station and ask to speak to an officer, and he would know who she was.

But also, there was this.

"Does it matter?" she asked, forgetting to be polite. "Is he in or not?"

Amber looked to the side. At nothing. Just not at Margo. "He's here."

She didn't move to do anything.

"Should I just head back to his office?" Margo asked.

"I'll call him."

Amber picked up the phone and typed in an extension. "Dave. There somebody here to see you."

She heard footsteps a moment later, and looked up to see Dave Daniels heading toward her. She had an instantaneous flashback to the night he'd come to the house to talk to her about Poppy and Zach. That had been a strange experience. Because she had also remembered a younger him. Remembered talking to him about Sarah. What she knew, if she had suspected anything. If Sarah had confided in her at all.

His hair was white now. It had been light brown then.

"Margo. Come on back."

She gave Amber one more glance, and then walked down the hallway to a small, faded office. The floor was a lighter blue than it had once been, she was sure. The windows were just slightly foggy, hard water buildup from a sprinkler, likely.

A small-town police department with limited funding.

"What brings you in? We haven't heard anything about…"

"That isn't why I'm here." She didn't need to talk about Poppy and Zach.

"Then what brings you in?"

"I remembered that you were the lead on Sarah Hartley's case."

He blinked, taking a moment to adjust to a comment that must seem wholly out of nowhere to him. "Yes. I was."

"My understanding is that it's considered a cold case now."

"Yes," he said. "There hasn't been any new information on that case since the day she was kidnapped. Never another sighting. Not of her or of Brian Archer." He lifted a shoulder. "None confirmed, I should say. You know how it is."

"Let's say I don't know how it is."

"Sightings of missing persons are common, particularly by loved ones. But we've never had any reason to believe that any of the supposed sightings of Sarah or Brian were legitimate."

"But people reported seeing them."

"Sure, someone reported seeing Brian Archer at the bait and tackle shop a year after. Sarah Hartley's brother swore he saw her six years later walking down a trail by the highway. But when he stopped to go and look, he couldn't find her. He wanted me to send out a unit to follow that up."

"Did you follow it up?"

"I sent a guy. But you have to admit that sounds far-fetched." She could remember Dane then. Drunk and messed up. Beside himself. She couldn't imagine his report had been taken seriously.

It did sound unlikely, of course. But the problem with missing persons, rapes, kidnaps, murders...they were already outside the rules. Humans lived together in a society because they agreed to follow the same rules. Because they agreed not to hurt each other, not to commit certain violations. And when a person took the shape of society and bent it to conform to what they wanted instead...

There was no way to say what was normal and what wasn't. There was no way to say what was too outside the box.

"But this is all part of the investigation? Officially?"

"Every dead end."

"I'd like to have access to the case files," she said.

"You're welcome to them. I don't know that you'll find anything interesting. Nothing substantial has ever been found. No major developments. A few people who suddenly acted like they'd always known something was funny about Brian. Or who said Sarah was a Lolita."

Margo felt her expression scrunch involuntarily. *"God."*

"Everyone's a great detective after the fact. Very observant when they already know the truth."

Did they know the truth though?

That question settled in her breast uncomfortably.

"The case files..."

"Physical," he said. "If you want to come back to the evidence room with me you're welcome to. Our cold case corner is small. It's Sarah."

She nodded slowly and started putting pieces together in her mind. An underfunded small-town police department that didn't have experience with investigating abductions. Nothing but dead ends beyond the borders of the town, so even the inclusion of other agencies hadn't brought about more evidence. If people thought they'd had sightings, they were more likely to be locals with an emotional connection to the crime, so most likely yet again to circle back to the local department.

These are the people looking into what happened to Poppy too.

That echoed inside her. The truth of it. Eighteen years and nothing. They'd found nothing. They'd found the one sighting far-fetched.

In eighteen years Poppy would be twenty-three. No longer a little girl. No longer hers. She would miss everything.

No. She couldn't think about that now. She couldn't sink into that now.

She followed Officer Daniels down the hall and toward a back room, which was locked up. He took the keys out of his pocket and opened the door. The evidence room was like many she'd been in. Dimly lit and filled with shelves and boxes upon boxes.

He took her to the back of the room, to a corner with a stack of four boxes.

"These two are Sarah Hartley."

"The others?"

"Things like 'Bigfoot stole my hiking boots.'"

She laughed. "You're kidding."

"No. We keep those reports too."

"I thought filing a false report was illegal?"

He smiled. "I'm not convinced those people always think they're filing a false report."

She wondered how a man who'd worked in law enforcement as long as he had had avoided becoming cynical. She wondered if it was a benefit of living here. Except she lived here too, and she didn't believe in the essential good of man.

Of course, her obsession was peeling back the layers to get to the *why*. And maybe when all you had to know was *how*, it didn't get quite as dark.

I kept them safe.

The book was called that because it was what that madman had said when he'd been interrogated about the crimes. Six women, abducted, assaulted and restrained in their cars, which were then put into the lake. So that they could drown.

The world was going to corrupt them. I kept them safe.

There had been no sleep for her that night.

The way a person could twist the story, the truth so profoundly that they could commit murder and call themselves a hero...

Maybe that was the divide between herself and Daniels. He believed in good guys and bad guys. Cops and robbers.

She believed they could all be bad guys, if they told themselves the right story.

That anyone could stand outside a hotel room door and think of all the reasons that sleeping with another man wasn't really a sin, when your husband and child were waiting at home.

That maybe taking your daughter away from your wife was okay if you...

Were in love with someone else?

If she...

Loved her job more than she loved her?

The story you told yourself could reshape your own limits. Easily.

"You can take the boxes. I know where to find you if I need them."

"Thank you."

"Just sign them out."

He indicated a clipboard that was affixed to the wall, with a form on it.

Date. Item. Out. In.

She picked up the pen and pressed it to the paper.

"Southpaw," he said.

He'd said that to her before, when she'd had to sign a statement after being questioned.

"Yes," she said, trying to smile.

2/18 Sarah Hartley Files MB

Then she went over to the boxes, those brown cardboard file boxes that she'd found were pretty standard across departments, and slid them off the shelves, holding them close to her chest as she followed Daniels out of the evidence room.

"See you around, Margo," he said, separating from her at the door to his office, while she went past, heading back toward the front doors.

"See you," she said, continuing on down the hall.

When she passed the reception desk, she didn't need to lift the boxes slightly and grin at Amber. But she did.

Because everything might be bad right now, and Amber might pity her now, but Margo let herself head back to high school and enjoy her petty triumph.

Then she pushed the front door open with her shoulder and headed back out to her car. She held the boxes against the side of the car with her hip and opened up the trunk, shoving them inside and getting back in behind the wheel.

She thought about going to get coffee, but decided she didn't want to deal with any more small-town dynamics today. At least beyond the ones she couldn't avoid.

She drove back through town. It was so easy to superimpose images of the group of them, walking down the street after school. Going to the diner for a milkshake, going to the candy store for fudge. The boys hopping over the pylons by the shore. Zach tripping and falling. Laughing.

She captured that image and held it still, then turned it over slowly. It was strange to think that she had married that boy. The man she'd spent the past eleven years with had slowly turned into something unrecognizable to that memory.

But the man she'd spent the past eleven years with still didn't seem like someone who would kidnap his own child. Who would disappear without a word. Without a trace.

She tried to focus her memory on Sarah.

Mall today?

Can't. Busy.

She had gotten "too busy" to hang out in the few months before she'd been taken. Margo was going to start making an effort to think of it that way. It was easy to think "missing" or "ran away." But she'd been taken away by a grown man, and even if he'd gotten her to think she wanted to leave, he'd *taken* her.

It was important to her to cement that. Firmly.

It was the story she was telling.

When she was back in front of the gate she entered the code. She drove up the street and when she neared her own house, tension crept up her shoulders.

Guilt.

Since Zach left it had become like a sacred garment, one she had to wear at all times. There was no putting it on or taking it off. It just was. So this new layer of it slithering up her spine to set her muscles on edge was notable.

Debbie Hartley.

Sarah's mother. Dane's mother.

She should talk to her.

Maybe it was more than guilt. It might be intuition.

She pulled her car into her garage and got out, opening up the charger port and plugging it in before going around to the back and standing in front of the trunk where the files were.

Then she got back into the car and drove back out of the neighborhood.

This was what it had been like when she was looking for the Incline Valley Killer. She'd been driven sometimes by gut feelings that had surpassed logic. That was the nicest way to look at it.

Sometimes she wondered if it was just obsession that surpassed social acceptability. That made her numb to what should embarrass or shame her.

She was good most of the time. But there were times...

Times when she followed a rabbit trail of information down the dark of the internet, so that the bath she ran her daughter sat cold, and she forgot to ever put her in it at all. So that when she didn't realize the sun had gone down and the mountains around them had gone dark and she hadn't made plans for dinner, that when she got out of bed at midnight and left her husband sleeping and took an Adderall so she could keep on going, it was because she had a hunch.

Not just squinting in the dark, certain she saw something that wasn't there at all.

She'd solved the case. So it should have been worth it.

It hit her sometimes, in the dark of a sleepless night, that maybe it had just been the single-mindedness of turning over every rock in a field until she'd found something. That it was a testament to what a person could accomplish when they embraced the utterly unhealthy drive to cut out everything except one singular mission.

So maybe it was obsession that carried her down the highway now, moving farther away from town to the next town over. Or maybe it was guilt.

Or a hunch.

Maybe it was all three.

Astoria was right on the ocean, five miles from Conifer. Sarah's mother had moved there, into a much smaller house right on the water, nearly a year ago. She remembered the move clearly because it had felt so significant.

Sarah's parents had divorced two years after she disappeared, and Joe Hartley had moved away shortly after. But Debbie had stayed. For a long time. Sarah's childhood bedroom had been a tribute to her for years, unchanged, unmoved. The day she'd moved, the day she'd put so many possessions out in the yard for sale or to give away while she prepared to downsize, had felt like a shift.

She knew her daughter wasn't going to walk through the front door again. And she'd accepted it.

Margo remembered walking by the yard sale with Zach and Poppy. Poppy had been on her scooter a few feet ahead of them, and when Dane had come out from the garage, carrying a heavy box and setting it in the lawn, she'd felt Zach's mood change.

Did you fuck him?

That echoed between them like a gunshot.

They hadn't stopped. She'd waved, and so had Dane. But they hadn't stopped walking.

Maybe Debbie wouldn't be home. It had been a pretty big leap for Margo to think she could just drive to the next town and knock on the door.

She pulled up to the dark gray house, and noted how sleek and minimal it all was. It was so different from the sprawling white house at the end of the street in the gated community.

She walked up the front steps and stood, poised in front of the door, then rang the doorbell.

It took a few minutes for Debbie to answer. She looked confused, then shocked. Then sad.

"Margo. Hi."

"Hi, Mrs. Hartley. I'm sorry to just…come over like this but I…"

She looked alarmed then and Margo felt that creeping guilt again. She was being given entrance into the house because

Debbie thought she was vulnerable and felt bad for her. She'd heard the stories, of course, because everyone had.

Maybe she'd even talked to Dane.

"Come in," she said. "Please. I'll get you something."

"I'm not having a breakdown," Margo said as soon as she was inside, because she felt like leading with honesty might be for the best before Debbie wrapped her in a blanket and gave her a cup of tea.

That only made her look at Margo with greater alarm.

"I'm not here to talk about myself," she said, trying again. *I'm not having a breakdown.*

She doubted her own thoughts. She had just driven here with no warning. No plan.

Maybe she was having a breakdown.

Maybe this was all her trying to keep from drowning in her own impenetrable mystery.

Maybe it didn't matter.

"Come in and sit down," Debbie said.

"I should have called," Margo said. "But I wanted to talk to you about Sarah."

She felt a little bad for springing that on her except she knew. She knew that Debbie thought about her daughter all the time.

Even if she'd traded a house with a perfectly preserved bedroom for a girl who never came home, on the street she'd raised her children, for a modern town house overlooking the bay.

Margo knew, because she thought about Poppy the same way and knew no matter what she always would.

Debbie nodded. "I'll get you some tea."

She was getting tea anyway.

Debbie led her through the bright white entryway and into a small kitchen with a square table that had only two chairs.

In contrast to the Hartleys' house in Conifer, this was bare. Margo could remember how cheerfully cluttered the other house had been. Always shoes in the entryway and jackets on the floor under the pegboard by the door. School schedules and Post-it notes all over the fridge.

The sort of house that showed that the people in it lived lives that centered on family. Where everyone was, what everyone was doing.

This house, bright and clean and empty, no visible schedules, was for a woman who didn't have to worry about what anyone else was doing. A woman who minded her own life, her own schedule.

Margo was very aware she was collecting all these details and mentally composing paragraphs about them already.

Every exterior marker of the woman she was has been erased, and I can't blame her. Her whole life used to be about every move her family made. When her husband had his bowling league. When Sarah had speech and debate and when her son had football practice. She knew where everyone was, all the time. But now her daughter is gone. If you can't know where she is, ever, it would be easier to just let go of it all.

"We haven't actually spoken," Margo said. "But I'm sure you're aware that Dane's work during the research of my last book was essential to me. To solving the case."

She nodded slowly. "Yes."

"I was very grateful and…" Her throat went tight. "I guess that's all, about that."

"It's important to him." His work, she probably meant. Or maybe helping Margo, but she doubted it.

"I appreciate it. I appreciate the way he's taken his own tragedy and decided to help other people." She did her best to meet Debbie's gaze. "I'm trying to figure out what to do."

"There's nothing right that you can do," Debbie said. "And nothing wrong either. That's what happens when the world is so broken. You can't put it back together. You can either sit there over the shards, or walk over them, over and over again while you bleed. Or you can walk away. But it's all broken anyway."

Margo was the person who tried to piece it all back together. Even the parts that had been ground to dust.

So far though, she hadn't managed to put any of her own pieces back together.

"I have to do something," she said, looking at her hands. "I want to write about Sarah."

She looked up at Debbie when she said that. She decided not to tell her about the letter. If Dane did, that was fine. Somehow though, she knew that he wouldn't.

"For a book?" Debbie asked.

"Yes."

"Why? They've never found anything."

"I know. But I want to try."

She looked exhausted. "I'm out of hope. I don't want any more."

"I'm not offering hope." Margo felt an answering weariness in her soul. "I'm clinging onto what little I have for myself. But I can offer Sarah a story. A better one than they told when she was taken."

Debbie looked to the left. At the fridge. Stainless steel, with no calendar, no notes, no photos. "She was taken."

"Yes, she was. The story of a teacher and a sixteen-year-old girl isn't a star-crossed romance."

"You solved the last case you looked into."

She nodded. "And I haven't solved the others. It isn't why I started writing about cold cases. It isn't why I started getting into true crime. Every victim has a story, and it's one that's bigger than the moment they were made a victim. Every person touched by a tragedy has a story. I just want to hear yours."

"I've given testimony over and over."

She nodded. "I know. I know that and I also know... I also know she's with you every day. That these memories, and this story and this truth, are with you every day whether I'm here or not. I understand."

"I'm sorry that you do."

Margo nodded slowly. "Me too."

"I think about her all the time."

"Of course you do. Six months. Eighteen years. What does it matter when it's your...your child? It's just endless."

Eighteen years.

She cleared her throat. "I have that in a box in my car. I have Sarah's case files. I'm going to get them out tonight and read over them. Those are cold, dry. Bare sentences. I want everything that goes in between. The things *they* didn't think were important. That's what I want. Because what the mother knows is important. I get that. I know it."

This was painful. Far closer to the bone than she'd expected.

A look at her own potential future.

Eighteen years.

She pushed that thought aside.

"I wanted to know...how did you continue to live on the same street as Gail Archer? You didn't move until last year, and for all that time...you drove past her house. So many people villainized the Hartley family, and you stayed in close proximity to them."

Debbie stared at the wall behind Margo. It took her a minute to begin speaking.

"At the time...at the time I was angry at Sarah. Right at first. I couldn't believe she'd run away. I couldn't believe she hadn't told me. If something was wrong, why wouldn't she tell me? I'd always made it so clear that I wouldn't judge her. That if she needed help I would give it to her. So I thought... I thought she had run off with this man. I was sure we'd find them in a week. I was sure... And I felt sorry for Gail. I felt ashamed. Like we'd done something to her."

Margo kept her expression neutral. "But later?"

"She never came home. That's not right. That makes no sense, it never has. And as time went on... I thought he probably did something bad to her. I thought… I don't know. Either my daughter was killed by a sexual predator, or she decided to never come home. She hated us so much she never came back." She shook her head. "That's what I realized when I finally moved out of the house. I stayed there in case she came back. Like someday she would walk in as if nothing happened. But then it hit me. She's either dead or he made her hate us. She's an adult woman now. It's possible she had children. That I have grandchildren, and not once over the past eighteen years did she…" She blinked, long and hard. "I'm angry at my own daughter. I'm angry at the man who took her. I'm angry, all the time." She wiped at her cheek. "I'm sure that isn't what you want to hear."

"It's exactly what I want to hear," Margo said. "Because it's the truth."

6

DANE WAS IN her driveway.

She pushed the garage door opener and passed him so that she could plug her car in.

When she got out of her car he was standing against his truck with his arms crossed, and there was something about him being here that made her feel like a child who'd been caught doing something she shouldn't.

If anyone saw him here…

Did you fuck him?

"Come in," she said.

There was a quick flash of memory. To the moment in front of her hotel room door when those words had hovered at the base of her throat, begging to climb up, to be let out.

She'd denied them then.

She said them now out of desperation, but not the desperation she'd felt then.

He stepped into the garage and she closed the door, then popped her trunk. "You can help me carry these boxes inside," she said. "They're Sarah's case files."

She wasn't sure if she should have said that, but if he was going to be here, knowing what she was doing, then she felt like he had to know there would be case files.

He said nothing, but picked both boxes up out of the trunk and headed toward the door that connected the house and the garage. She moved ahead of him quickly and unlocked the door.

She stopped and looked at the house like he might, but only for a moment. It was shabby, even though her cleaner had been there at the beginning of the week. She'd left every dish she'd used piled in the sink and the only reason the house wasn't *messy* was she was the only person living there.

"You can put them there," she said, gesturing to the kitchen table. She never ate at the table.

He set the boxes down on the table, and turned his focus to her. "You went to see my mom."

Of course that was why he was here. His mother must have called him when she left.

"Yes, I went to talk to her."

"My mom is trying to leave this behind her."

"But she hasn't," Margo said, touching the top of the box. "Because you don't leave your kids behind."

He gripped the back of one of the dining chairs, his knuckles white. "In the future, if you want to see my mom, talk to me first."

"She seemed fine with my being there, and she could have asked me to leave if she wasn't."

"You said you wanted my blessing to do this. So I'm giving you a stipulation and if you were sincere at all about asking me, you'll honor that."

The room seemed to shrink around them, the air compressing over her skin, making it feel tight.

"I told her how much you helped me," she said, not sure if it was an appeal to his ego or just the truth.

She'd only told his mother about the way he'd helped with

the Incline Valley Killer. Not about the way he'd been there for her personally.

She should have known appealing to Dane's ego was impossible.

He'd left it somewhere at the bottom of a bottle years ago. He was *better* now. Not healed, but better. He had a mission that seemed to serve as a competent bandage.

She understood that better than she would like to.

"I was about to open the case files. You're welcome to be here if you want."

"I didn't come for a social call. Or to be part of your research project."

"I don't think you know what you want," she said. She ignored the way the words reverberated around them. The way they carried more than one meaning.

"Neither do you."

That was a lie.

As far as Dane was concerned, she'd known what she'd wanted since she was fourteen. It was just that life had layered on complications that made the answer less straightforward than she would like it to be.

What had been a long shot when she was his sister's annoying friend had become impossible after the years had splintered their connection, wounded him, changed him.

She knew what she *wanted*.

What she hadn't known was if she wanted it at the expense of being Zach's wife. Of being part of a nuclear family that was still together. At the expense of what she considered to be her own moral code.

She hadn't gotten married just to ignore the vows that had come along with it.

"I know that I want to go through the case files."

That wasn't what he'd meant. She knew it. But it was all she could handle.

"This is it?"

"As surprising as it is, this is a fair amount. Though, I already got warned that it isn't very substantial. A lot of reports of sightings that aren't substantiated in any regard. And I assume a lot of testimony from people who live in town."

"Probably not anything I don't already know."

"Maybe. There probably isn't anything I don't already know either. That is why I went to talk to your mom. Because sometimes facts aren't enough. Sometimes you find things in between facts."

"I don't get that."

"Yes, you do. Because you find people. That's what you do. So you listen when their parents tell you about everything that happened leading up to their disappearance. You listen to the way their friends describe their mental state. And because you aren't their friend, because you aren't their family, you are able to put things together that they can't. That their brains won't let them put together. Sarah was my friend. I'm not neutral here. But it's been eighteen years, and I'm evaluating the situation from a different place. With different experiences in my life. I think I can trust the way that I'll think about this information more than I could back then. First of all, because I'm not sixteen."

"Right."

"Second of all, because I've actually done this now. I know, I'm trying to think of me solving the case of the Incline Valley Killer as a fluke. Something never to be repeated again. But I can't help but think… I've done it now. I've taken information that police and other law enforcement agencies went over. Over and over. Individual private investigators couldn't do it."

"And you can't find Poppy."

"No," she said, firmly pushing past what she thought might be meant to puncture her confidence. "I'm too close to it. I can't figure that out. Not right now."

"All right. Let's dig into these."

He went over to the table, and she realized that there were no lights on in the house. They'd just been standing there in the dimness of the late afternoon. She flicked the light on and then took the lid off the first box, taking the first stack of papers out of the top. Initial statements.

The reports were typed up, interviews that had been done with teachers. With Sarah's family. With her friends. With Brian Archer's family and friends.

Interesting, because of course she'd been aware of Callie's perspective on all of this. She had some concept of the Archers, because she'd been there for dinner sometimes, she'd spent time there. She was friends with their daughter, and that meant that they weren't entirely unknown to her. But the concept of Brian Archer as a whole human being and not a teacher, not the father of one of her friends, not a boogeyman, was jarring in the moment.

They had interviewed his friends, because of course they had. If you're having an affair with a sixteen-year-old, perhaps you would hint at that to people that you were close to.

Men did that sort of thing. Engaged in bravado. Bragged about their conquests. And maybe Brian Archer wouldn't have confessed that she was underage, a student, but perhaps he would have given an indication that he was having an affair.

She started with the statements from his friends.

No indication of anything out of the ordinary.

He had been a bit distant.

Had been around less.

I asked him if he had some woman on the side, because he was in a better mood lately. He laughed. But he didn't deny it.

The perspectives of his drinking buddies were inconsistent. It made her wonder if they'd been similarly inconsistent as Sarah's friends.

They had discussed some things about it, in the beginning.

But then fractures had started to form when some people in the group had felt like Callie shouldn't be considered a friend anymore because of what her father had done.

Callie of course gave a statement as both a friend of Sarah and as Brian Archer's daughter.

I didn't know anything was going on. Sarah didn't seem any different. My dad didn't seem any different. If I would've known, I would've called the police. But she seemed fine. Everything was normal. My dad took us to get ice cream yesterday.

She stared at that sentence. She wondered if Brian Archer had been taking his kids out to say goodbye to them.

She didn't humanize Brian when she thought of him. There were strange divisions in her heart and mind when it came to him. He had abandoned her friend. He had hurt her other friend. But he had been a husband and father, and he'd left his children.

Right now that felt like such a raw thing.

He'd left his children.

She looked up at Dane.

He was staring at a paper in front of him. "Our statements," he said. "I don't know why I was hoping to see something I didn't know. I thought I'd read it and maybe…maybe I'd find that I'd said something useful." He made a gruff sound in the back of his throat. "I had no idea that anything was going on with Sarah. I didn't notice a mood change. She wasn't acting like somebody who was upset or hurt. Or somebody who was about to say goodbye. But when I think back, I realize how wrapped up I was in my own shit. An upcoming football game. Whether or not some girl liked me back. How we were going to get booze for the bonfire party we wanted to have later in the week. My sister could have told me outright that she was being abused and I'm not sure that I would've listened. I can't even remember the last thing Sarah said to me. Or the last thing I said to her. It might have been: 'Why did you eat all the cereal, idiot?'" He shook his head. "A statement from an eighteen-year-old boy who only cares about finishing out senior year? It's useless."

"What about your mom?" She thought of the calendars. The schedules that had been everywhere in the Hartley household. Debbie Hartley had known about every move the children in the family made.

"She would've said something to us."

"Maybe." She thought about the woman she'd talked to today. Defeated. Exhausted. Accepting of the fact that answers wouldn't fix anything. And yet deep down wanting them all the same.

He pushed his hand over the top of the papers, sliding them to the side, and paused at one. "Sarah was busy. She had picked up a couple more extracurricular activities recently that kept her at the high school. I didn't think anything of it. She was an overachiever." His lip curled. "Fuck that bastard."

Margo nodded. Because she agreed. Because of course it had been easy to cover all of this with a story about picking up more extracurricular activities. She would have even been able to get proof from a teacher.

Because a teacher was violating her.

Had Sarah believed that it was a relationship? Had he manipulated her into thinking that it was love?

She cast her mind back, tried to remember how Brian Archer had looked to her when he had been a neutral figure in her life. Just her friend Callie's father and her English teacher.

Back then, her take on forty-six-year-old men was generally that they were old, and in no way attractive. But she'd known that wouldn't necessarily be true for *everyone* her age.

She was trying to get a bigger picture of all of this. Get into the heads of the people who'd witnessed it, even if the headspace was fucked up.

She didn't want to get into Brian Archer's head.

She didn't care what he thought. Whatever he believed

would be boring. No different than so many other middle-aged men who were staring down their mortality as the women who'd once praised them for simply *existing* got older and wiser and demanded more, and highlighted deficiencies that had always been there.

Men wanted to go back to a simpler time when it had been possible to garner dewy-eyed wonder in exchange for the bare minimum.

A high school teacher who had never reached the heights that he had once dreamed of, bored in his marriage, blaming his wife, probably, for the fact that his life had slid into a tide of mediocrity, because *surely* he had been meant for excellence.

There was never any insight. Never any self-awareness.

Never the possibility that perhaps their lives were mediocre because they themselves were mediocre.

No. It was everyone around them. Their jobs, the women they had married, the demands of their children. The women who refused to get on their knees and suck them off when they demanded it.

Those were the people responsible for their unhappiness. For their dissatisfaction.

And the men were never different from each other. Only their actions varied.

A serial killer who raped strangers and drowned them and convinced himself that he was somehow their savior was no different from a man like Brian Archer.

Because their motivations all came from the same place.

She didn't care about *them*.

Right then, she saw a picture of Zach's face in her mind.

I don't care about you.

She stood for a moment, staring at her dining room wall.

I don't care about you.

She let out a hard breath and forced herself back to the case in front of her.

It mattered what Sarah had thought, though, because it might give answers to where they were today.

People don't just go missing.

No one had seen any signs that Brian had been planning on leaving his life. No one had seen any signs Sarah had been planning on it, but it was clear that they had been. Sarah had left a note.

It had been written on her computer the day before they had vanished. The fingerprints on the note itself had been Sarah's.

She had left it in the kitchen. On the fridge where her mother had kept the family schedule.

Margo stood up and looked in the box again, and found the note tucked away in the section just behind the witness statements.

She sat there staring at the note, and she sensed Dane get up and reach into the box again. "Jesus." His face had contorted into an expression of clear disgust.

"What is that?"

His throat worked. "Brian Archer's browser history. A porn habit I didn't need to know about."

"Is it…"

"Student-teacher. And BDSM shit," said Dane. "He got off on power. Obviously. Considering how he applied his interests…"

"That's disgusting."

"Nothing about leaving, though. No searches for hotels, no…"

"Is there anything in there about school computers?"

Dane skimmed the paperwork. "No."

"What about Sarah's computer?"

"You can look at that," he said.

Meaning he didn't want to.

She reached across the table and collected the papers in front of him.

She riffled through the section that had contained the information about Brian's computer. "I don't see much in here about Sarah's computer. There are notes about the computer along with the letter that she left. Confirming its origin. But nothing about her complete browser history."

"That seems like a pretty big oversight."

"Yeah. It does. She could have done the searches for where they were going. But also, he could have done it on a work computer. And there is no way that whatever he was using at the school is still operational. He could've done it in the library. The school library or the public library."

"Do you think he was that smart? He had student-teacher porn right there on his personal computer. I'm not sure that he was doing a great job hiding who he was."

"Well. They ran away together. He exposed that part of himself by doing that. But maybe he had the presence of mind to try to hide where they might go."

"Possible. The whole next box is potential sightings," said Dane. "I had no idea there were this many."

"Officer Daniels brought up that time you thought you saw her."

Their eyes clashed. "I didn't."

"But you *thought* you did."

"I thought it all the time. But yeah. A few years after, I really did think that I saw her. Enough that I reported it."

"That was why I went to see you. I heard—"

"We don't need to dredge that up."

"I'm not upset about it."

"I am. I hurt you."

She'd been so wrapped up in her own anguish for him, she hadn't realized he'd noticed how hard he'd held her.

"It was just a bruise."

"Never, I have never in my life touched a woman like that. Not before then, not after then. I'm not that guy. I'm really not."

She reached out and put her hand over his. The way that he had done with hers in the bar. "I know that. If I didn't, I wouldn't be sitting here with you."

"I think you might have a blind spot when it comes to me."

The irony of that was how exposed it made her feel.

"I don't think so. I'm pretty cynical about human nature. It's a side effect of my job."

He didn't say anything, but she could feel what he was thinking. She continued. "Yes. I obviously had a blind spot where my husband was concerned. Believe me, blind spots that existed before are pretty well taken care of now. I understand what you were going through… You would've done that to *anybody*. It wasn't about being the kind of man who likes to lord his strength and power over a woman. It wasn't about hurting me. Or scaring me. *You* were scared. And you were out of control."

"Yeah. That's when I realized I needed to do something. Something other than drinking myself into an early grave. It's when I joined the military. I figured if I was going to put myself into an early grave I might as well do it…" His lips curved upward. "Honorably?"

"I get it. Because some days since Zach and Poppy left I feel like there's no point. But you know what, I would rather be doing something. If I'm not going to sleep, if I'm going to… If I'm going to be obsessive. But I want to do it with a purpose, rather than just indulging my own despair. I'd rather accomplish something."

"A mission is helpful."

"I hope to God that it is."

She looked up at him. He was staring at her, in a deep, studying way that she could feel sinking down beneath the surface of her skin. She would have given anything for him to look at her like that years ago.

She hated that she liked it. Even now.

What was wrong with her? What was wrong with her that

she could still feel pleasure blooming inside of her *even now*. When her daughter was missing.

She was angry at physical needs a lot. The need to eat. The need to sleep. At least those things kept a person alive.

Sex was unnecessary. That she could feel the pull to him when everything was just so dark. So grim.

Maybe that was why.

She'd read about people who had sex after near-death experiences. That it was life-affirming.

Maybe it was just something else she wished she could use to block out reality. To block out her feelings.

A long look was hardly an invitation.

But feelings laced between words had become their preferred method of communication. Maybe that was why it was difficult to talk to him on the phone. Or over text. Maybe that was why before this week they hadn't spoken for forty-five days.

Maybe that was why she had so happily put distance between them after the Incline Valley Killer case had broken.

Well, not entirely.

They'd been put on the same floor in that hotel in Times Square, when they'd gone on *Good Morning America* to interview about the book and the way it had ignited a new investigation after a decade of having no new leads.

They'd arrived on separate flights. Separate airports, at separate times. They'd still managed to end up in the hotel lobby around the same time, checking in one after the other.

And then they'd gotten on the same elevator.

"What floor?"

"Twenty-nine."

"Me too," she said, forcing a smile.

They'd been silent the whole ride up. And she'd felt it growing between them. Maybe they would just talk. Because he'd understood. The intensity of that whole experience. Because he'd understood what it had been like to be there.

Because she'd been back at home with Zach, who hadn't understood at all, and who had been angry that the experience had changed her.

Who'd been suspicious of everything she'd done, and who'd taken the distance between them that had grown on its own those past few years and had seemed determined to force the chasm wider.

Dane had *understood*.

They could just talk. About the case. Share memories. Share a drink.

And maybe they would sit in the chairs in the room, and not on the bed. Maybe they would never touch each other. Maybe they would keep enough space between them. Wouldn't succumb to gravity.

But she'd known she couldn't take the risk. The elevator had reached its floor, and the doors had taken too long to open. It'd reminded her too much of another time. Another place. Why did she have to make this choice again?

It had been so hard the first time.

When the elevator reached their floor, and the sign on the wall indicated that his room was to the right, and hers was to the left, she'd said a prayer of thanks that they would be going in opposite directions.

She'd said good-night. Gone back to her room alone and ordered room service. Stared down at the relentless neon below. Flashing advertisements rolling through the color wheel, making her feel dizzy.

The next morning they'd arrived on set separately. They'd done the interview together. She'd been about to ask him to breakfast. Because surely *that* would be okay. But then Zach had called, and she had taken it immediately. And by the time she was finished with the call, Dane was gone. She'd decided to take it as a sign.

Other than brief exchanges to clarify details over text, and two other interviews, they hadn't seen each other over that next year.

But he'd come to the house the night Zach hadn't come home. She'd called him. She hadn't known what else to do.

He'd never been inside of her house before, but he'd come right in like he had every right to be there. Like he'd known the layout of the place. But of course he'd grown up in a house on the same street, another house that was supposed to be safe at another time.

"It's probably nothing," Margo said.

"It's probably nothing," he repeated. She could see that he didn't believe it. That even then, he had been certain that Zach not coming home, that Poppy not being in her room, was intentional.

"He took her out to dinner."

So that she could get some work done. It had been a nice thing that he was doing for her. And he had made sure that she knew that.

At nine o'clock she had been sure she'd heard Poppy crying. She'd gotten up from her desk and realized that Poppy and Zach weren't home. There was no one here.

What kind of mother waited that long to get worried?

She'd been so caught up in writing. In her research. She hadn't even realized how much time had passed. And anyway, she was out with her father. Shouldn't she have been able to trust that?

But that was when she'd realized that some of Poppy's things were gone.

She'd relayed that information painstakingly to Officer Daniels.

"Her backpack is gone."

"Could she have just left it in the car?"

"I suppose so. But also, her blanket. Her stuffed rabbit. His name is Sherbet. I bet that isn't relevant. I went through all of her clothes. She's missing three pairs of shoes. Red, white and black."

She'd cataloged the other things that were missing. Almost to prove to herself that she had been paying attention. That she had known what was happening. She had just lost track of time that night.

Her husband's wallet was gone, which was normal because he had gone out to eat. But his passport was missing too. She'd checked the safe in their closet. He always kept cash there. He was a financial advisor. She'd asked him once if that meant he should be the antitheses of the old man with his money buried in a coffee can. He'd laughed. *"Hell no, Margo. My problem is I see too many weird things happen to people's money. It's always good to have assets on hand."*

There had been ten thousand dollars in there.

It was also gone.

And that was when it had become clear.

Zach hadn't taken Poppy out to dinner.

He had taken *her*.

The first thing they did was try to track his cell phone.

They'd found it in the garbage can on the street in front of their house.

She hadn't called anyone else that night. Not Callie. Not her dad. Not her brother. And Dane had stayed with her.

She had wanted to cross the space between them on the couch and fold herself into his arms. But she'd never done that before. It'd seemed like the wrong moment.

So they'd sat there, with him on one end of the couch, and her on the other. Sleepless. Motionless.

The police had put out an AMBER Alert.

She could dimly remember, sometime around five in the morning, Officer Daniels came back to the house. *"If he got rid of the cell phone, the odds are he had a plan to get rid of the car."*

"Right." She could think of a hundred ways you could do that. But the best would definitely be to take it to a chop shop, where they would remove all identifying markers, and take the vehicle off your hands. Probably supply you with another vehicle that would be difficult to track or trace.

That was the problem with having a brain that ran toward conspiracy. That obsessed about crime. She could think of so many ways her husband could do this and get away with it.

He had taken his passport, but the odds were he wouldn't use it. He'd been saving money. And it hadn't even occurred to her that that was strange. Cash.

What were the chances he didn't already have another identity? Another bank account?

How had she missed this?

How had she missed it?

She was suspicious. Paranoid, sometimes. Her mind lingered on the most disturbing aspects of humanity as a lifestyle choice. You couldn't do that and not emerge with a suspicious nature. Not suspect a gaze that lingered overlong from a stranger on a public street. Not trust the unsettled feeling in your gut that you got when you made eye contact with a man in a diner who just gave you a bad vibe. The one place she hadn't felt that way was in her home.

She'd known they had problems.

She'd known that he was probably having an affair.

She still hadn't seen *this* coming. She was that woman. The one who'd been certain she knew that her husband was a good man, whatever his flaws. That there were limits. But people's limits moved.

She'd been sure that they'd had time. Sure that they would have a conversation. Maybe it would end in divorce. But she'd been putting that off. What kind of woman didn't leave her husband when he had an affair?

Maybe one that felt guilty.

One that felt like it was probably her own fault for being neglectful. One that felt like she probably had a hand in it, since she was too emotionally entangled with another man.

Even though she'd never touched him.

Margo's high ground was a technicality. And she knew it.

It was why she hadn't pushed it. It was why she hadn't been ready to have the conversation.

Zach had never intended to have a conversation. He had always intended to rip the rug out from underneath her. To take everything from her.

To consign her to spending the past six months in a dark, bottomless hell, where she had no idea what her life had become. And Dane had been there. That whole first night.

And here he was again, at her kitchen table.

Because she'd decided to make his sister her mission.

Because she'd found the letter, yes.

But maybe also because he'd been distant. And she didn't want him to be.

Perversely.

She stood up from her chair, and he did the same.

"I don't think I've ever really thanked you," she said. "For being there for me. The night when…"

"I told you. I'm always going to be there when you call."

"Why?"

"I don't know," he said. "Maybe for the same reason you wouldn't leave me the hell alone all those years ago, even when I told you to. Even when I should have scared you away. And I'm glad you didn't, by the way. Because I would be dead now if you had."

The thought filled her with hollow, unimaginable grief.

"You wouldn't be. You would have found your mission."

He shook his head. "I wouldn't have. You're the only person, Margo. Just that one visit… No one else was speaking to me then. Not Kerrigan or my mom or dad. You were the only one who came. They couldn't deal with me. My dad had already left, and he just wanted to get some distance from the suffocating grief. From the way my mom refused to move anything in Sarah's room. He couldn't handle it. I don't really blame him. But I did at the time. My mom had Kerrigan to focus on, and so she did. She wanted to make sure that her life was still good, normal. She couldn't do that with her drunken son careening around the property, could she? You were the only one that still thought you could reach me. So yeah. I'm here. No matter what."

"Even when I make you angry?"

"You always piss me off," he said, taking a step closer to her. "You were my sister's annoying little friend. Always."

For some reason, it warmed her. "I've always been annoying?"

"Every goddamned day."

So there, Zach. You knew exactly what you were getting into. You did it anyway. It's not my fault you were unhappy.

For one moment, she let that burn in her chest.

It's not my fault.

You knew.

Her eyes met Dane's. And she felt a swift, sharp tug low in her stomach. Zach had known about this too. It was what had made him so jealous.

That she had a special connection with Dane and had for years. So maybe that wasn't her fault either.

Maybe…

Forsaking all others.

She had never done that. Dane had always occupied a particular place in her heart, and she had never done a damn thing to kick him out of it.

She didn't want to. It was that simple and that complicated.

She wanted this. This moment. The two of them alone. Him looking at her like she might have the answers that he wanted. She wanted to have the answers.

What's wrong with you?

So many things.

She couldn't blame a bad childhood. Unsupportive parents. Yes, everybody had problems that originated in their childhood. She was no exception. She had definitely learned to internalize that her reactions to things were often too big. That she was irritating when she grabbed hold of something and wouldn't let it go. That she worried her every impulse down to a nub before she moved on to the next thing. That her obsessions were unwieldy, inconvenient things for those around her. Her mother had often wondered why she couldn't just play baseball. Why she wanted to spend hours at the library researching something strange. Or why she wanted her mother to drive her out to an old cemetery so that she could get some arcane piece of information for a school project that she was working on.

She had been indulged. At least in part. Even if it had been with an eye roll.

She missed her mother terribly. Though for the past six months she had, at some point nearly every day, thought that it was probably a good thing her mother hadn't lived to see this. She wouldn't have been able to survive her grandchild being kidnapped.

She hadn't survived long enough to meet her grandchild. But still, Margo knew her mother. A woman who'd had definitive ideas, and who'd definitely thought her only daughter was odd. But who had also been willing to challenge her own ideas to make sure that Margo felt loved. Felt supported.

Even with all of that, her mother had made mistakes. Had reinforced some of the things that Margo feel wrong sometimes.

The crush Margo'd had on Dane hadn't just been a crush. She'd been fourteen and it had instantly turned into a wild, uncontrolled sort of love. The kind that made your heart hurt. That made you feel like your whole world was turned on its head when the other person walked by. It made going to her friend's house an adventure every single time, because if Dane was there, then she was submitting to having a full body experience.

She had embarrassed herself with overly confident opinions expressed without any hesitation. She had betrayed her emotions to those around her because she hadn't known how to hide them.

And over time, she had learned to deflect, so she didn't get hurt. Over time, she had become the person that Callie had recently accused her of being. Closed off, one who preferred to dig into other people's issues because her own were simply too big. Too unwieldy.

This feeling right now was too big.

She was a woman whose daughter was missing.

She was a woman whose husband had kidnapped their only child.

She was a *woman*.

Right in front of Dane, it seemed stripped down to that.

The way that he looked at her. The way it made her feel.

Not a single vow she'd ever spoken to Zach mattered now.

But she was no less a mess.

Right then it all overwhelmed her. Because she could see it. What it would be like if she crossed the space between them, if she wrapped her hand around the back of his neck and stretched up on her toes. If she kissed him—finally—because it was what she had always wanted to do. Something she couldn't do when she was fourteen. Something she hadn't been able to do when she was twenty-one and trying to bring him up from the depths of his despair. Something she hadn't been able to do as a married woman standing in front of a motel room door.

But she could do it now.

The woman she was might be broken, but she could kiss Dane Hartley if she wanted to.

It was too big. Too overwhelming. She couldn't breathe past it, that realization.

Instead, she took a step back.

And she did what Callie had told her she did best of all.

She sidestepped. She looked the other way. She looked past her problems. At someone else's pain.

Rather than trying to dig into her own. And suddenly, something crystallized.

"Dane. Have you ever done sonar on this stretch of the Columbia?"

7

HE STOOD THERE for a moment, then another. And it was like watching a caged animal. One that had expected the door to be opened to his enclosure, only to find it still locked.

He didn't relax. All the tension that held him there only seemed to compound.

"Have I ever done sonar on this part of the Columbia?"

"Yes," she said.

He scrubbed his hand over his face. "You're something else."

"It's a valid question."

"No. I haven't."

"You said it yourself, many times. You said it when we were there in Tahoe. Most people aren't actually missing."

"Are you talking about Sarah and Brian?"

"Yes."

"It isn't that I haven't considered the possibility that something happened to them. Both of them. But honestly, they could be anywhere. They left a note, and nothing indicated that they were planning on harming themselves. Nothing indicated that this was some kind of Romeo and Juliet situation. The police never even came close to closing in on them."

"What if they had an accident?" she asked.

"It's possible. And yes, we could sonar the spots on the Columbia we think they might have passed. But it's a needle in a haystack. But who knows where they went? Who knows... It may be all haystack, no needle."

"Maybe. Understandably. But what's the harm in checking? Even if it's just you. Can you get permission to use the equipment?"

"I'm sure that I can."

He didn't make it sound like he necessarily wanted to. Or maybe he was just upset about the pivot. Because it had been a pivot. Because it had been either turning hard into the reason that he was here or kissing him.

Unless...

Unless that was why he was here.

The same way it had been why she was there all those years ago. When he had grabbed her wrist. When he had bruised her, and her heart had broken a little bit.

It had been about Sarah.

But it had been about him.

About her feelings for him.

"So why won't you?" she asked.

"I don't even have a starting place. There's no last known sighting of the car."

"The route out of town. Vulnerable places, no guardrail. The bridge."

"That's like trying to stab somebody in the dark when you don't even know if they're in the room."

He made sense. But sense could be the enemy of gut feelings.

"I don't disagree. It's just a feeling. It's a feeling that I have."

Was it? Or was she lying, because she had needed to do something to cover up the feelings she was having looking at him? Maybe she was just a coward. Or maybe she was a one-trick pony, and this was the trick she had. Asking him to dive to try to confirm a hunch.

Of course, with the Incline Valley Killer she'd had more than a hunch. This was something that had just come to her out of thin air. Or more like ash from a fire, swirling around her. Pieces she couldn't put in order, but that she knew were there. And she wasn't entirely certain she hadn't set the fire herself.

Wasn't entirely certain that this was just a self-serving redirect.

She had never been less certain of herself than she was now. That was the problem with her husband up and leaving her. Her husband destroying their lives like this.

"I understand that your life has been completely overturned. But you are asking me…"

"Do you think they're dead?" she asked, meeting his gaze.

"Probably," he said. "Probably. I think it would be an awfully big coincidence for this to be how, though. Do I think it's possible he killed her and then himself? Yes. It was never a relationship. It was always power and control, and years down the road what would have happened when she grew up? When she realized she didn't need to stay with him."

She could imagine that clearly. But she felt like they should turn this stone over too. "This is your skill set. And like you said, a mission helps."

"I made other people my mission a long time ago. For a reason."

"Dane…"

He reached out and wrapped his hand around her wrist, and pulled her close to him. Her heart was beating wildly. His hold was different now. He had figured out how to use his strength without causing hurt.

He was older now.

Time had changed him.

He was still burning with all the things he always had been. He was still intense. He was still compelling. But the rough edges had been sanded away. Or perhaps it was just that he'd learned how to walk through the world without making other people bleed.

His hold now didn't make her afraid.

If she was honest, it never had.

He had always been terrifying in an entirely different way. She knew that he could hurt her. Not physically. But deeply.

He brought her in close, and she pressed her palm flat against his chest. She could feel his heartbeat raging there. Beneath that solid wall of muscle.

"I'll do this. *For you*. Do you understand me? It's for you."

"Why?"

His eyes went sharp. So much so she felt they might cut her. His breath was raw and ragged. Matching her own.

"You know why."

He dipped his head, and his mouth took hers. That was the best way to describe it. There was nothing gentle about it, nothing tentative. There was something about it that felt like a first kiss. Not in her experience. There was no question being asked. Just like there were no answers. There was only sensation. And it completely overtook her. Threatened to carry her under.

He was hot, and he was strong. And he gave no quarter in this, just like he gave no quarter in any other area of his life. It was a storm. And it was more than she had imagined it could be. Brutal. Devastating. And when they parted, he was breathing hard. And she could see that he meant to walk away. That he meant to leave her standing there, with her heart beating like a bruised, bloodied thing against her breastbone.

"Dane…"

"You're still married, Margo."

He might as well have slapped her.

It was somehow the most devastating thing he could have said. And he was deflecting.

"That isn't why. You don't care that I'm married."

His jaw hardened. "You're right. I don't. *You* do."

He meant *before*. She'd cared before. He wasn't wrong about that. How dare he make her feel bad about that? Like she'd done the wrong thing. It had been right. And it had cost her.

He was just...

You asked him to use sonar to look for his sister's body.

God.

She pushed her anger down, her hurt. Her desire. Not because it wasn't important, but because she couldn't handle it. It hurt. And there was no more room for hurt inside her.

Of all the things happening, this didn't need to be one of them.

She kept her gaze focused on him. Tried to regulate her breathing.

Maybe he would leave. But he didn't. He just stood there, being Dane. Being impossible. Always impossible.

She couldn't do anything about this. About him.

It wasn't her mission.

She let out a slow, shaking breath. "When would we be able to run the sonar?"

His eyes were level, never leaving hers. As if he was just as determined as she was to look, unflinching, at this mess between them. "I'll have to make a call. I'll let you know."

He was still here, but he was already gone. Everything was all sharp edges with him, and she wished it wasn't. She wished *she* wasn't like this.

That was so simplistic.

She wished she wasn't living in this hell. She wished her daughter was here. She wished her husband was the man she'd thought he was when they'd gotten married. She wished she had been the wife she'd imagined she'd be. She wished she hadn't imprinted on this broken man all those years ago. She wished *she* wasn't broken.

He had kissed her. After all these years.

She had thought everything was already so fucked it couldn't possibly get harder, worse, more confusing.

How nice to know that even hollowed out, she was still human enough to feel ruined by a kiss.

He turned and walked out of the dining room, his footsteps heavy.

"Good night," she said.

He didn't respond. He just walked out her front door and closed it heavily behind him.

10:30 AM Sunday. Meet at my place.

Ok.

That had been the only exchange between her and Dane after the kiss.

Her brain felt like it was too full. She should be used to that. It was how she'd always been, but everything felt harder now. She'd always been the type to go in a hundred percent. On everything.

Grief. Loss. Love. Hope.

Hope.

That was the problem. No matter how bleak or realistic she wanted to be about anything she always had hope.

She called it tenacity, a lot of people did. Stubbornness. Obsessiveness.

Maybe it was just hope.

It was definitely the kindest thought she'd ever had about it.

She had dinner at her brother's house, and she tried to be engaged. She and Christopher had always been close, even though they disagreed on just about everything from politics to what made good TV. He had been gentle with her to the point of parody since Zach and Poppy had disappeared.

It made her want to shake him and demand that he go back to being her annoying older brother.

Her nephews were too little to know what was going on. It made it easier. They didn't ask about Poppy or Zach. They just accepted that for now, only Aunt Margo came over.

Right at first Christopher had been at her house all the time, or inviting her for dinner every night. But he and his wife had jobs and lives, and they had to live those lives.

She still went for dinner at least twice a month. She steeled herself to see the little boys. To open herself up to the joy of their sticky hands and chubby cheeks instead of only feeling grief.

Or worse, anger. Because they were here, and Poppy was gone.

Christopher resolutely didn't ask how she was. He didn't ask about the investigation. He knew her well enough to know if there was any new, relevant news she'd let him know.

He made a space for her to try to pretend things were okay.

She couldn't. But it was nice that he tried. She wished he'd be meaner to her, though. She wished he'd be normal.

Maybe none of them would be again.

Maybe that was the real reason she'd grabbed on to this investigation into Sarah.

Normalcy or hope. Maybe it didn't matter.

As soon as she got home from Christopher's she was back at her computer, back in front of all those files, making notes about things that she had discovered, and trying to figure out what might be relevant.

That was the problem. You had to assume everything was relevant at first.

You had to eliminate things.

Again, that scratch to get something in her mind, she couldn't quite say what. It also pushed her mind right back into thinking about Dane, because it was what she'd been thinking about the last time she had that thought.

Her obsessive thoughts could get so circular. And they were so strong that they ended up all linked together. An unbreakable chain. So through all of this, she had been replaying yesterday with Dane. The kiss.

His rough, hot hold. The way that it had been the fulfillment of so many fantasies, but at the worst possible time.

Maybe not the worst time.

There had surely been worse times.

No. This was hell.

She went to sleep at 4:00 a.m., knowing that she had to meet him in just a few hours.

Knowing she didn't have the luxury of sleeping in as late as she had been.

It didn't matter anyway, because she ended up rolling out of bed at six thirty. She was too hopped up on adrenaline to sleep.

Because when it came right down to it, stabbing in the dark was an upgrade compared to the listlessness of the last few months.

At least it was something.

At least it was something.

DANE'S HOUSE WAS down a long dirt driveway, nestled back in the woods. It was all unfinished timber and rough wooden shingles. There was a wide covered front porch that didn't have any furniture on it. It seemed like a waste to her. To live out here in nature, and to never sit there and enjoy it. It also didn't really surprise her.

She had been up here once before when she was working with the sonar crew. She had been too distracted to scan for personal details then. Or maybe she had been trying to force herself to not collect personal details about him.

It had seemed like the better part of valor. Of course, in the end, her valor hadn't much mattered.

Two days ago they'd kissed anyway.

Her inability to hide her feelings for Dane had contributed to the cracks in her marriage's foundation. She'd resisted. She'd thought that had mattered. Zach…had done this anyway. He'd left anyway. He'd taken Poppy anyway. And she'd ended up kissing Dane. What good had it ever done to resist?

She could have torn it all apart in a big way back then. Maybe they'd have divorced like normal people.

If when he'd turned to look at her and said: *Did you fuck him?*

What if she'd been able to round back on him and say: *Yes, I did.*

Maybe it would have been different.

Dane had a big trailer hooked up to the back of his truck, and she imagined that the boat was in there. She'd seen them before. Red rubber boats that were suited to getting around in water of all different depths. They had a larger boat too, but the small boats were the ones they sent out the most often.

And they got the job done. They were laden with sonar equipment.

She had ridden in the boats when they had found the girls.

She already knew what it looked like, to be going along the water, and to spot a car. Sometimes a definitive shape. Sometimes not. Depending on the angle you picked it up at. Depending on the depth. Depending on how much silt was around the vehicle. On how long it had been there.

The team explained to her that cars that had been under for a long time looked different than a car that had only been under there for six months to a year.

They reflected light differently. Took on different shapes.

Clinging to details was comforting. Because it allowed her to turn away from the feelings.

She parked her car, and got out. As soon as she closed the driver's-side door, his front door opened, then closed behind him. Obviously she wasn't being invited into the house.

"You ready?"

"Yes," she said.

"I have a route mapped out. We're going to get in the water about five miles from here. There's a decent-sized stretch of road where there is no guardrail. There's a lot of foliage, though, and if a car had gone in, in most places there would be signs.

Broken trees, bushes. For the most part, they're going to stop a vehicle from going in. But there are a few places where it's possible. And then I want to trawl out by the boat ramp, and underneath McKitrick Bridge."

"Okay," she said. She started building a mental map in her head.

"It's going to take all day. You sure you want to come?"

"Yes. I want to come. I want to write about it."

"If you really want to."

"Do I strike you as somebody who's uncertain about what they want?"

"Selectively."

"Is this about us?" she asked.

Because someone ought to bring it up.

"Yes. It has no right to be. Because I don't know what I want either."

"Great."

She went around and got in through the passenger-side door of his truck. And he got in on the driver's side.

"That isn't true," he said, starting the truck engine and putting the truck in reverse. "I do know what I want. I just don't know what I'm prepared to do about it."

"Also unhelpful," she said.

"Are you in a place where you want to start a relationship?"

"I…"

"With a man who's never been in a serious relationship? With a man who's not even sure he can do it?"

"No. But that doesn't…"

"Yeah, it does. Because we're working together right now, so we need to try and…" He trailed off when he realized what he'd said.

"I didn't know we were officially working together," she said.

"You're looking into my sister's disappearance. And finding people is what I do now. So yeah. We're working together."

And he was right about all of it, there were logistical issues. She couldn't add another thing to her life anyway.

To her empty, sad life.

She swallowed hard. "He thought we were having an affair, you know."

"Zach?"

"He was so jealous after I got back from Tahoe. And it's why I had to answer the phone so quickly when we were in New York. Because I didn't want him to accuse me of... I had already told him that nothing had happened."

"He didn't believe you."

"No. I don't think he did."

"What a dick."

She laughed in spite of herself, as they headed down the road to go put a boat in the water to try to sonar for Dane's sister's body. Because it was all so absurd, it was all so dark. "I mean, that's an understatement."

"I guess so."

"It's complicated, though. I think he might've left in part because of that. Because he thought that you and I were..."

"You told him that we weren't."

"I told him we weren't *sleeping together*, yes."

She couldn't tell Zach there was nothing between Dane and herself. And neither of them had to say that, because it echoed as loudly between them as if it had been shouted.

"You said...you said I cared that I was married," she said. "And you're right, I did. I loved Zach when I married him. You weren't part of my life anymore. I chose him. I had to keep choosing him. I made vows to him and had a child with him. So yes. It mattered. I chose him even when he wasn't what I wanted most. Because I wanted to give Poppy her house and her parents and it wasn't worth sacrificing that to have sex with you in Tahoe. Or in New York. No matter how much I wanted to." She shook her head. "You're all mad at me about it, but you just said yourself you don't know what you can give me. How can you judge me for not burning my life down over this attraction?"

He let out a slow breath. "I don't judge you. I admire you. That doesn't mean I didn't wish you'd made a different choice."

"Then I really would have given him a reason..."

"Do his reasons really matter? What he did was insane. Unhinged bullshit. Even if you and I had been fucking in your marriage bed while he watched, he didn't have the right to do that to you." He rubbed the back of his neck. "Honest to God, Margo. There is no version of this story where you deserve this."

She held that one close, because she wanted to believe it. She did believe it. It was just that it was difficult to get that to sink beneath the surface of her skin. It was difficult to make it seem real. Because it was so easy to go back to all the things she had done wrong.

But have a court case about it. Get a divorce.

Running away with a child? Taking that child from her mother?

Zach was the kind of nightmare bad guy she would chase. The kind that she would write about.

She didn't know why she became her own personal online forum comment section whenever she turned the facts over.

The mother must've had something to do with it.

She must've done something.

Why else would a loving, good father feel like he had to flee with his child?

She wished she could click *hide comments* on all those asides that scrolled through her head all the time.

Instead, she focused on the view out the window. On the shafts of sunlight shining through the pine trees that lined the winding road.

Dane was right. There was so much thick foliage that ran along the river it was difficult to see where a car could go in.

But there was a break. Then another one.

"We'll start at the boat ramp. Work our way back."

Like he was reading her mind.

"Good idea."

When they arrived at the boat ramp, he backed the trailer up to the edge of the water, and opened up the back. He pulled out the red inflatable boat, and dragged it down toward the water.

And then began the process of setting up the sonar equipment.

She knew a little bit about the process from having worked with the team previously. Knew about the live sonar on one screen, and the other screen that would show them a broad view of where the boat sat in the river, and both the width and the depth of the waterway.

The reading was amber colored, and showed vague, apparitional shapes.

She could easily remember what it had looked like when they had found the first car.

The most alarming thing had been how much it'd looked like a car. After squinting at all the shapes and thinking it might be like a sonogram, where you had to pretend that you saw the foot so that the technician didn't think you were a bad mother in advance. She had thought it would be like grasping at ghostly straws.

But no. When they had come upon the car, it had been clear. They'd been able to see the slope of the roof, the nose, spots where the windows ought to be, and the shape of tires.

It had been chilling.

But even more so when Dane had gone down into the water after they'd flagged it, and had come back up with the license plate, and confirmation that there was a body in the driver's seat.

They'd had to use the license plate to help identify the girl behind the wheel.

To figure out exactly which parents they had to report back to.

But before the dive was finished, every single parent of a missing daughter that had vanished at Lake Tahoe between 1990 and 2003 had been given devastating news.

She couldn't forget that, as they got into the boat and launched it out onto the water.

The river was moving slow, wide and placid.

The water was opaque. A resolute steel gray that reflected the sky back at them.

And knowing what they were looking for today made it all take on a slightly chilling cast. She swallowed hard, crossing her arms against her body as if it could keep out the chill. But the chill wasn't coming from the air.

She kept her eyes glued to the sonar screen, as indistinct shapes flickered onto the screen. But none that seemed to pull Dane's focus more than any other.

Normal things. River debris.

"What's that?" she said, indicating a big, indistinct shape on the screen.

"Probably something like a tarp. Nothing that I'd worry about."

She nodded. "Right. You're looking for…something a bit fuzzy."

That was the best word she could think of to describe it. She remembered the way the cars had looked, the ones that had been down there for more than twenty years.

"Yes. Actually, sometimes the older cars are a little clearer than a newer one. It has to do with the way the waves bounce off it. When there's more algae and silt it's a little easier to spot."

She nodded. "Okay."

He was stoic, and serious. She could see that he had gone into the mode he went into during work.

Watching him do this, that was when she had realized just how deep she was with him.

She'd always found him compelling. It would be tempting to tell herself it was because he was so different from Zach. But she'd found him compelling when he'd been a seventeen-year-old football star who hadn't had a single rough edge.

But he'd had this, single-minded, focused, the way that she was, it was like a clear, ringing bell inside of her.

She recognized this. Recognized him. And it made her want to reach out and touch him. Made her feel like he might be the only other person on earth that really understood her.

And that, she had told herself then, was a trap. The kind of thing you convinced yourself of so you didn't have to work on the problems in your marriage.

There was a certain point where anything felt easier than untangling the mess that you were in.

Better to tie a new knot than worry at one that was hopelessly stuck.

So it had seemed attractive, she told herself, to convince herself that Dane was the only man who could understand her. That sex with him would fix something in her because she had lost her connection with Zach somewhere along the way. And sometimes she couldn't escape the cold, distinct feeling that she was having sex with a stranger when he turned over and reached for her in bed.

What a lot of mental gymnastics to try to justify a visceral attraction to a man with tattoos.

Because frankly, that was probably what it was.

And yes, there was a history there.

He was also dangerous, with the rough edge that her husband who worked in finance didn't have.

And she had spent the better part of the past few years trying to make cerebral something that was very likely just basic and physical.

People did absolutely insane things in the name of sexual desire.

Brian Archer was a prime example. A man who was willing to uproot his entire existence. A man who was willing to compromise his reputation to satisfy his own twisted form of gratification.

It was another one of those things that she knew people were often tempted to find ways to pretend they were excluded from.

It was what she was doing now. It was what she'd been doing.

Pretending that there was some deeper reason for wanting Dane. Sitting there in the boat now, thinking about that attraction, looking at him and feeling her stomach flip like she was a teenager, she had to concede that it was nothing more or less than that same sort of impulse.

Maybe Zach had been looking for the same excuses. The same reasons.

Looking for a clean break. A clear-cut reason so that he could run off and start a new life with the woman he'd decided he liked having sex with better than he liked having it with her.

Helen of Troy had a face that launched a thousand ships, but everyone knew Paris and Menelaus weren't in a fight over who got to stare at her for the rest of their lives.

It was about sex.

Because it always was.

She looked up at him, but he was busy watching the sonar reading as the boat moved along the banks. They came to the first spot he'd identified as a possible place a car could've gone off the road.

"I'm going to cross back and forth here. Make sure to cover all of the space."

"Do cars drift?" she asked.

"No. The pressure and weight of the water keeps them right

where they are. But they can still be pretty damned far from the shore. Depending. If the car was going at a high rate of speed then it's difficult to say where it would land. And I would have to know how to reconstruct the entire accident to get an accurate guess. But we don't have an accident scene. Which is why we're going to be thorough."

It was a very wide river, but still a river. Traversing the different sections where it was possible a car had gone took time, but not too much of it.

They'd covered two sections along the highway, and then came to the large bridge that ran across the river. It was all steel gray with round cement pylons providing support, rimmed in green algae where the water lapped against them.

"We'll go along the bridge. I have a hard time believing that a car could accidentally go up over the side, but it's definitely possible. Especially if it was slick, or the car rolled. It's not the highest guardrail. There was an incident not unlike that up the river a few years ago."

"Well, that's going to give me nightmares."

"All the shit you look at and *that's* going to give you nightmares?"

"Yes. I drive over this bridge every time I go to town."

He slowed the boat's pace and made his way up to the bridge.

"Oh shit," he said.

"What?"

"That looks…"

He looked over at the sonar screen that offered an overhead view of the boat, and a wide field of the water. He pointed to the far right of the screen. "That looks like a car."

It didn't look as much like one as what they'd seen on sonar in Tahoe.

It was a strange, indistinct shape to her eye, where in Tahoe they had been so chillingly obviously vehicles.

"You think so?"

"I can't be sure. I'm going to want to see if I can get a magnet to hook onto it. And if it does, I'm going to have to go down."

His expression was like stone.

"Dane, that doesn't mean that it's hers."

"No. I know that. Most cars that are abandoned in the water are ditched stolen vehicles, or insurance fraud. Fact of the matter is, the vast majority of cars we find were put there on purpose. And they don't have people in them."

But she could sense the change in his posture.

She wanted to ask if he had a hunch. A feeling.

She did but she wasn't experienced with this. Her only experience had been dredging up cars with murder victims in them. She had never seen this sort of find turn out to be nothing.

He maneuvered the boat over the top of the object and dropped anchor.

"I think it's a car," he said.

"Why doesn't it…look like one?"

"Too much reflection. If I had to guess, it's because it's a newer vehicle."

"Oh."

"I don't know that for sure. That's just…" He didn't really need to explain this. He'd done this so many times, of course he knew.

He reached behind them and pulled out a large magnet on a chain. She had also seen this done before. It was how they verified that the object they were above was metal. And how they would ultimately flag it so that it was easy for the divers to find it.

He took the magnet and started to lower it down.

She stared through the water, until the magnet disappeared.

"What's the depth here?"

"Over a hundred feet. So, no mystery why you can't see anything. Though sometimes cars can be completely invisible in ten feet of water. It just depends. On the color of the vehicle, on the way the sun is shining. On how much buildup is on it. It's crazy. We did a job one time in a pond and one of our guys could stand on…" He stopped. Then he jerked the chain he was holding, and it held fast. "Metal."

"It's a car," she said, her heart beating faster.

"Yes. It is. At least, I'm going to say I'm 90 percent sure. Could be a boat."

"Right."

"But usually isn't."

"Okay."

"I'm going to get suited up."

She looked out at the trees and listened as he shed his clothes, put the wet suit on. Once he was suited up, he spoke. "All right. It should be quick. We're right over the top of it, and I can follow the chain down."

"Okay."

"Hopefully I won't need your help to get back up in the boat."

She suddenly felt frozen with the horror of it all.

Was he actually going to dive down and…

"Maybe you should have someone else do this."

"I don't need anyone else to do it," he said.

Her guilt over the enormity of what she'd asked him to do was hitting too late. "Dane, I shouldn't have asked you to do this."

"Margo, do I look like a man who can be talked into something he doesn't want to do?" He did not. "If on the very off chance it is her, I'll be glad that I was the one that found her."

"But you'd have to see…"

"I wouldn't recommend that, it's true. For most anyone. When we have family waiting at the shore I always advise they leave when it we have to bring bodies to the surface. I believe—strongly—that it shouldn't be anyone's last memory of their loved one. But I've seen this, a lot of times. I know what to expect." His voice went rough. "If someone gets to bring her home today, then I'll be glad it was me."

She nodded slowly. "I…"

"Don't go feeling sorry about it now," he said. "It's too late. We're right here, and we found something. And listen, odds are, it's some car a group of kids stole and were joyriding in, and they shoved it into the water to get rid of the evidence. Odds are, it's nothing. But don't go apologizing to me now. You convinced me to come out here. You're on a mission, Margo. You want to end this. So, if it's possible, then let's end it."

And on that note, he sat on the edge of the red boat and went backward into the water.

She gripped the edge of the rubber raft and leaned over the side. There was no sign anyone was down there.

It was still. Smooth. And for some reason, she felt a strange foreboding rising up inside of her.

Her fingers were freezing. But the air was cold. The edge of the boat was wet.

It wasn't why she was cold.

Dane broke the surface of the water, then wrenched his mask off. He was breathing heavily. His eyes were wild.

"Dane…"

"I need to call backup. We need to flag it."

"Dane," she said. "Is it them?"

"We need to get back to shore. I'm going to flag it," he said, his voice going hard.

"Dane," she said, a thread of panic beginning to unravel in her stomach. "Is it them?"

"We just need to get to shore…"

"Dane," she said, her entire body starting to shake, but her brain hadn't caught up with the visceral, physical reaction she'd had. "What's happening?"

"I'll talk to you more when we get out of here."

He hauled himself up into the boat, and she didn't know where he got the strength from.

And he started to work to get a flag together. She had seen him do this before, plant flags on cars.

She felt dizzy. Like her head was spinning.

"What's in the water?"

"Margo, we need to get to shore."

"What is it?" That came out in a scream.

"I can't talk to you about it out here," he said. "We need to get to shore to…"

Her brain was blank and suddenly, she saw an image in her mind.

Zach.

She moved to the edge of the boat without thinking, and started to go over the side. She had to see.

She had to see.

She felt strong arms come up around her. "What the fuck are you doing?" he roared.

"What's down there?" she asked.

"Stay in the fucking boat. Do not jump into the water. For God's sake."

"Is it his car?"

"I'm taking you to shore, and we'll talk there."

She didn't need to talk. She knew.

God help her, she knew.

She looked at Dane, at the haunted, hollowed-out look in his eyes.

He hadn't found Sarah and Brian.

She met his gaze, and refused to look away. "It's his car, isn't it?"

9

HYSTERIA WAS OVERTAKING her. She felt herself separating from her body. A complete break. With everything she knew, with everything she could see and feel.

She knew that you couldn't just jump out of the boat and into the water, and yet knowing that the car might be down there made it impossible not to. If her child was down there, she had to be there too.

No. That was impossible. Poppy couldn't be underwater. Because if Poppy was underwater then Poppy was dead. And she couldn't be. Margo couldn't handle it. It was supposed to be a mystery and she was supposed to be able to solve it. She was supposed to be able to fix it.

If Poppy was dead then everything was broken. There was nothing that could be fixed. Nothing would ever be fixed again.

Dane was still hanging on to her.

She was cold. His body was hot. But wet at the same time, and she couldn't make it make sense.

"I'm going to let go of you," he said, his voice fierce. "It is going to take me ten minutes to get us back up to the river and out of the water. You need to let me do that."

"No."

"You need to let me do that."

"You need to tell me…"

"I will tell you when we are on land. I will explain everything to you. But you need to stay in the boat. In the goddamn boat, Margo. Okay?"

She slid down to the floor of the boat, and put a hand on her stomach, and he went back up to the front. He picked up his cell phone. "I need the crew out here. As quickly as possible. Yes. We're going to need a crane. Yes. Yes. We need law enforcement. Okay."

The ten minutes could have been ten days. It could've been a few seconds. She felt like she wasn't living in reality anymore. She felt like she wasn't connected to anything. She couldn't process anything. They got out, and got onto land, and she just sat in the boat.

He lifted her up, picked her up like she was a child and carried her onto land. "Can you stand up?"

"Yes," she said, but then he put her down on the ground and she felt her knees buckle, so he held tightly to her arms.

"I found a black SUV, upside down."

"No," she said, a whimper.

Black SUVs were common. She repeated that as many times as she could before he spoke again.

"I can confirm that there is a body inside. An adult male, buckled, in the driver's seat."

"What about the back?"

"Margo…"

She grabbed hold of his arms and squeezed him as tightly as she could. She wanted to hurt him. She wanted to bruise him. "What about the back?"

"The windshield is out. Driver's side is down, passenger side is down. The back is full of debris, I can't see anything. I'm going to have to get into it…"

"Is it Zach?"

"I can't say that for certain. Not given the way that… I can't say for certain."

"Do you think it's Zach?"

He looked at her, completely grim. "I do."

The sound that exited her body wasn't human. It didn't come from her throat, it didn't come from her stomach. It came from her soul. She heard it before she was aware of making it. She bent down at the waist, and threw up, dropping down to her knees, ignoring the small rocks that bit through her jeans and into her knees.

"Do I need to call an ambulance?"

No. There was no point calling an ambulance. They were dead. *They were dead.* You couldn't call an ambulance for someone who was dead.

She hadn't realized she'd said that out loud.

"No, for you. I think you're in shock."

"How… I don't understand."

"I know. I don't understand either. That's not what I expected. I didn't expect to find anything."

She tried to scrabble back up. "Why don't you let me…"

"You don't need to see it. You don't need to see anything."

"I'm going be here when you pull the car out."

He shook his head. "No."

"How come you got to go down and rescue your sister, but I can't be here to see if my child…"

He grabbed hold of her, his grip firm, keeping her from falling. "Absolutely not. It's my sister, and it's been eighteen years. I have experience with this kind of thing. But nobody, *fucking nobody* should ever see their child like that. Do you understand me?"

"You didn't see her. Poppy…"

"No," he said. "I couldn't see anything in the back of the car."

"You aren't lying to me."

"I'm not fucking lying to you. I wouldn't lie about that."

"You're not trying to make me feel better."

"I was just looking at what I think is your husband's body. I'm not trying to make you feel better. Nothing is going to make you feel better. I'm being a hundred percent honest with you. And so you need to trust me when I tell you I am being honest with you about whether or not you should be here, and I think you need to go. You need to call Callie, and you need to have her come sit with you."

"No," she said.

"Great. Okay. I'm going to call Callie, and she's going to come down here and sit with you."

He took her phone and found Callie's number.

"Callie, this is Dane Hartley. I'm with Margo. We just did a dive, and I think we found Zach's car."

She couldn't hear anything on the other end of the line. Couldn't hear her friend saying anything.

"I need you to come down here. She won't leave. No. She's being stubborn. But somebody needs to sit with her, and I've got to get down and help with this."

She looked up at his face, at his eyes.

He looked… He looked terrified. She'd never seen that look on his face before.

No. She had.

When he had grabbed her wrist and bruised her, he'd looked like that then.

Like he was plagued by demons and didn't know how to exorcise them. Like they might win. Right now, she felt like the darkness was going to win. Suddenly she realized how cold her lips were. That she felt like she was on the edge of consciousness.

And that was how she found herself wrapped in his arms

again, sitting down on the ground, on the boat ramp, the cement cold, biting against her bones.

She leaned her head back against his chest, and she tried to keep breathing. But it was hard.

Callie arrived when the police did.

And shortly after that, Dane's crew got there.

Everyone was familiar to her. The police, the sonar rescue crew.

But this situation was not.

Callie moved to sit beside her, and took her hand. "Maybe we should get up out of the way. We can sit in my car."

"I don't want to," she said.

"Honey, we need to get out of the way."

She lifted her up onto her feet, and propelled her toward her SUV.

A black SUV. Just like theirs.

The one that Dane had found at the bottom of the river.

"No," she said.

"Okay. Then we'll stand here, but we're going to give them space."

"We need to go down to the bridge. I need to see."

Callie shook her head. "Dane said it would be best if you didn't."

"He doesn't know anything. He doesn't know what I need."

It wasn't fair. Because he did know about this. And he knew her too. But she was so angry. She was so angry, and she decided that she was going to lash out at something, because she felt like a monster was growing inside of her, taking shape, taking over.

"He said that you tried to jump in the water?"

"When did he tell you that?"

"I talked to him over there." She didn't remember that. She didn't remember Callie actually arriving. She'd just suddenly been in front of her. "You're kind of out of it. We can't go stand on the bridge. It's not safe." She grabbed her arm. "Come here."

She dragged her over to where Dane was standing, talking with the police.

"It's a crime scene, so of course we're going to treat it as carefully as we can. But we know how to…" He cut himself off, and looked over at them.

"Dane, I want you to promise me that you will call Margo with details as soon as you have them. Don't wait. Not even five seconds. Okay? She needs to know exactly what you see when you see it."

"Okay," he said.

She wasn't sure why her friend was saying that.

"There. So you can stay over here with me. And we can sit where it's warm. It's going to take time."

"But I need…"

"You're going to know everything right when he does. There's no benefit to looking. You need to trust me," said Callie. "You need to trust me, because you know… Because I know what it's like to lose sight of my child. To be worried that I might've lost him. And if this were my son, then I would need you to tell me this. I want you to picture Poppy always smiling and laughing and happy. And I do not want you to ever imagine her as a body, okay? And that's what he's trying to save you from."

"He didn't see her body," she said.

"No. But you have to accept that he might. You don't know what phone call you're waiting for. I don't want you standing up on that bridge because you're hoping against hope, okay? I want you to be where you're safe. I'm afraid." She wrapped her hands around Margo's arm. "Because I know you. Because you're the fiercest warrior that I know. And you will jump right off that bridge. But we can't have you doing that. Okay?"

That was when she let Callie help her into the car. She sat holding her phone in her lap, and stared at the screen. She didn't know who to call. Should she call anyone? She didn't know anything.

And all she could think was that she had been willing to put Dane into this moment, and here she was.

Maybe it had been intuition all along. Knowing that sonar of the river needed to be done.

It had been her intuition. And now she was sitting here.

She'd written paragraphs about this.

About the sounds mothers made when they found out their children were dead.

About the utter bleakness of the loss.

How it was the death of part of a parent's soul. She'd taken those moments of pain and examined them, pulled them apart so she could describe them, do them justice. But on some level, give a voyeuristic view of grief to the observer who picked up her book.

And she couldn't even make sense of what was happening to her now.

She had no words for this. Time passed at random, great chunks roaring into darkness, while sometimes seconds crawled. Images were too sharp, and then gone.

It was like retribution for the clarity she'd had in the face of others' pain.

"Please take me to the bridge."

"Margo, I need to…"

"I'm not going to jump off. I'm not. It's going to take hours for them to pull the car up. I just want to be there when Dane comes out of the water, okay?"

"He thought…"

"He doesn't get to make this decision for me. Nobody does. Nobody but me. That is my family down there."

"Okay," said Callie, starting the engine of her car.

Because Callie was her champion in every way and Margo

had never loved her more. Even while everything in her was breaking apart.

She pulled down to the highway, and started to drive toward the bridge.

There was a road that led past the bridge, down to the shore, and Callie took that.

There were people standing on the shore, the police department, and now some gawkers. God damn them. And then she had to wonder how many times people had felt like she was a gawker. When she had been writing and researching about other people's pain. Putting it together like it was a puzzle. This didn't feel like a puzzle. It felt like a bomb. This felt like the destruction of her entire life.

And people were just watching.

And then she saw Dane, coming up out of the water in his scuba gear. And he had something lavender in his left hand. Waterlogged and filthy.

It was Poppy's backpack.

"Oh no," she said. "No no no no."

She unbuckled, and stumbled out of the car, a scream lodged in her throat. But it couldn't escape.

She felt like she was entirely bound. The horror that was consuming her now was so oppressive it made it so she couldn't move right. Couldn't think right. Couldn't make the sounds that she needed to make. The only thing that would bring relief. That would ease some of the pressure in her chest.

She went toward him, and just stood there. Staring at him.

"Margo…"

"Did you find her?"

He shook his head. "No."

"What did you see? What was in the back?"

"Is this hers?" he asked.

"Yes," she said.

She didn't have to open it to know.

She would find two pairs of shoes in there. The ones she hadn't been wearing. The white, and the red. She would find the missing rainbow tights. And Sherbet.

"Tell me," she demanded, the words shattered.

"I looked in the backseat. I didn't find her. I can only confirm one set of human remains."

"She wasn't in the car?"

"No."

It wasn't relief she felt. It was a fire. Burning savagely through her veins. A conviction she had to let consume her. "She's alive. She *has* to be alive."

His gaze was steady, never leaving hers. "The windshield was out. Two windows were down." He'd told her this already and she was impatient he was repeating himself. "The child safety seat wasn't buckled."

"He would never have had her in the car without it being buckled. And if she was under the water it's not like she could… unbuckle herself. If Zach was up there buckled in, there's no way that a five-year-old could…"

"He might not have had her secured in the car."

"He *would* have. It's completely unsafe to have a kid in the car and not have her in the car seat."

She could hear the words. She could hear how insane they were.

"He might have done this intentionally."

"But he… He just, he would've buckled her in. He was so angry at me. He was angry at me when I took my eyes off her on the playground." She wasn't making sense. She didn't think she'd told Dane about that. He didn't ask her to clarify. He was looking at her the way she'd seen police officers look at grief-stricken mothers before, who denied their child's death even as they stood next to a body bag. A kind of pity that had barbs in it.

"Margo, you know that people do this. You know that."

"That's not what it is. It's not what happened. She isn't in the car, she could be alive."

"The windows were open, she also could've gotten swept out with the current."

"No one found a body."

"I know."

"So she could be alive."

"She could be. But Margo… I don't think this is a good sign."

He was using her name so much. Like he was trying to keep her grounded. Like he was trying to temper her… Her expectations? What expectations could there even be when this kind of thing happened?

"Is it Zach for sure?"

"Yes," he said.

She nodded, feeling dizzy. Her husband was dead.

She'd been so consumed with knowing about Poppy that she'd skipped over that.

He was dead.

She had been angry at him. Outraged. But he was dead.

Had he killed their daughter?

She felt dizzy. She felt like she needed to sit down. What if Poppy had never been in the car? What if he'd done something with her? And then in despair he'd killed himself. Driven his car over the side of the bridge… What if…

Dane was right. People did this. They did this to punish their spouses.

"This is where we're going to let the police handle the investigation," he said. "I figure out where. But figuring out why is their job." He pointed to the police officers standing there on the edge of the water.

Figuring out why was *her* job. Digging into the truth. Digging into the reality of everything. To the truth. But this was what her life was. This was where her marriage had been. And she had no idea.

She'd thought it was cheating. An affair. A lack of trust. But that was… That was the kind of thing that happened to a lot of people. This was not the kind of thing that happened to a lot of people. This was like fiction. Like horror. Not life.

She reached out and took the backpack, held it against her chest. And then she found she couldn't let go.

Her body wasn't in the car. Poppy wasn't in the car. And that meant there was hope.

She could hold on to hope.

She could remember those parents. The ones that had stood on the edge of Lake Tahoe, praying that their daughters wouldn't be found. The ones that had believed for the past twenty, thirty, thirty-five years that their children weren't dead.

And she understood it now. Because it felt wrong to believe that they were gone.

It felt like they might need you.

Like they were somewhere, crying in the dark and you could hear it echoing through space.

And Margo couldn't believe, not for one second, that Poppy was already gone. Because what if she was here? What if she needed her?

She was clinging to the backpack now, holding it hard against her chest.

Zach was dead.

Zach was dead and that was something she knew. It was something she could grab on to. Wrap her brain around for certain.

Zach was dead.

Zach was dead.

It was the most bizarre, crushing grief laced with a rage that stole her breath. Because how dare he? How dare he make this mess and die? How dare he get out of ever having to explain himself?

He had done it. He had gotten out of the last, most complicated conversation they could have ever had in their marriage. It was such a fucking male thing to do. To mess everything up like this, and then die so he didn't even have to answer for any of it.

So he never had to have a conversation about it.

He was never going to have to admit that he'd had an affair. He was never going to have to explain himself.

He was never going have to tell her why he had taken their daughter away from her.

What she had done to be so insufficient for him that he would do this. Why the success that she'd found, and the money that he had enjoyed, money she had made, hadn't been enough.

Why the way she had *loved* him hadn't been enough.

Yes, she had feelings for Dane. But it was a testament to how much she'd cared about their family that she hadn't acted on them. Because she and Zach might not have been happy, but Poppy was. Because Zach had been... He'd been a good dad.

And it was Dane who was there for her now, while Zach was fucking dead.

All of that raged inside of her. Burned bright.

"They're going to pull the car up soon," said Dane, moving near her. "Believe me when I tell you, you don't want to see it."

"I don't care," she said.

"You feel that way now. You're in shock, and you're numb. You're angry. I get it. But you don't want to see it. And I just need you to listen to me."

She was on a knife's edge. That rage/grief edge. The enraged mother wanted to see his body. Wanted to know he was dead and how.

The grieving wife wanted to hide.

The grieving mother didn't want to know what he looked like because it could be what her daughter…

"Okay."

She suddenly felt exhausted.

"I'm going to stay. Through the end of this. Callie is going to take you home."

"Can I see… Can I see *something*…" If she didn't, she would never believe. Even with the backpack it would be hard.

"Hang on."

He made his way over to where the other members of the crew were. And said something. And someone handed him a license plate.

He brought it back over to her. And then he handed it to her. She stared at the letters and numbers. At the green pine tree running through them. She knew immediately it was theirs.

"Thank you." She handed it back to him. She couldn't look at it anymore.

But she'd seen that.

"You can see the car later," he said. "I know we can make sure that happens."

"Somebody has to identify Zach," she said.

"I knew him. I think my ID is decent enough."

"DeVonte can do it," Callie said, looking up from her phone. "I texted him. He said he would." She put her hand on Margo's arm. "You don't need to."

That was how she found herself bundled back up in the SUV. Being driven back home.

"Why don't you take a shower," said Callie. "Get warm."

"They didn't find her body."

"No. They didn't."

"I don't think she's dead," Margo said.

Callie looked at her. And she recognized that look. Like she was looking at a sad child.

"Good," she said finally. "I don't want you to think she's dead."

She went and took a shower, but she couldn't say for sure if she washed anything, or if she just stood there underneath the spray. She put on sweats and went out into the hall. And stood there next to Poppy's bedroom door.

She reached out and touched the doorknob, then let her hand drop. She couldn't bear it.

She went downstairs, and sat on the couch, and Callie came into the living room a few moments later, holding a mug of tea. "You should probably drink this."

"Why?"

"I don't know. You need something to do."

"I didn't expect this."

"I know. Nobody did."

"In my head, the whole time, he's been out there keeping her from me. But he's dead. He's been dead since before I knew he left. Just like Dane said. That's what he said. That people are usually dead before you realize they're missing, and that's exactly what happened in... I can't bear it. I need her to be alive. I need to believe that."

"Then believe it. Believe what you need to."

"Okay."

Zach was dead.

That was all she knew.

She was a widow.

But her daughter wasn't dead.

Until she saw her body, she wasn't going to believe that she was dead.

She had to believe that she was alive.

She had to.

10

THERE WAS A knock at the front door late that night.

Callie went and answered it while Margo sat, her arms wrapped around herself like she was trying to keep her body from flying apart.

She looked up when she heard footsteps. And there was Dane. Standing in the doorway of the living room.

"You can go home, Callie," he said.

"Can I?" she asked, looking between them.

"Yes," said Margo. "Go get some sleep. Thank you. For sitting with me."

"Of course."

"I've been kind of high-maintenance lately."

"Wow," said Callie, clearly not sure whether to laugh or cry. "That is one of the craziest things you've ever said. You are entitled to all the maintenance that you need. Call me if you need anything."

She didn't know whether to be irritated or not that this had clearly been a coordinated effort. That Callie and Dane had clearly spoken separately and come to a decision about who would stay with her tonight.

And neither of them had asked if she wanted to be alone.

But hey, Callie had been convinced Margo was on a short path to suicide before all of this, so of course she wouldn't want her alone. It was why they had kept her off the bridge today, too.

Margo wouldn't hurt herself.

Because Poppy was still out there.

She was.

Right then, she didn't have the energy to be upset about the fact that they had made a unilateral decision on her behalf.

She just sat there on the couch, and he stood in the doorway.

"You have tea?" he asked.

She looked down at her cup. At the string that hung over the side of the mug. It was fairly obvious that she had tea.

"Yes."

"Good."

What if they'd found more. That thought hadn't occurred to her until just now and it made her whole body seize up, her hands going right around her mug. "You didn't find…"

He shook his head. "No. If we'd found anything else we would've let you know." He moved closer to the couch. "*I* would have let you know."

"Tell me. Tell me how he was. Tell me everything."

"You weren't there for a reason."

"You know how my brain is. I need to fill this all in. If I don't have facts, I'll just have my wild speculation and that can be so, so much worse than reality. I need to… I need to figure all this out. Because I need to try to get a clear picture in my head. Because I'm going wrong somewhere. I have been from the beginning. I wanted to work on Sarah's case, because no matter how hard I tried I couldn't make any progress on what had happened with Zach and Poppy. And I was wrong about something crucial. He wasn't out there. He wasn't alive. I sent a private detective out looking for him, and didn't pull up anything. And now it makes sense to me why. Because Zach was already dead. The vehicle wasn't out there. I might not know where Poppy is, but now I can eliminate some things. There was another woman. I know there was."

"I assume that his computer has been seized?"

"Yes."

"And nobody has found anything about an affair or plans to leave on it."

"No," she said.

"Okay. Good to know. Because yeah, obviously that would be the first place to start."

"Tell me. So that I can... Please." Her mind was spinning with possibilities. For her, possibilities could spider out into all the darkest corners. She would rather know. No matter how grim the truth was. "I know that you think I'm crazy. I know. I get it. I know that you think it is completely crazy that I still believe that she might be alive. That she didn't go over in that car. You have to understand, that if she's out there somewhere, then I have to believe in her. I'm her mother. If I don't believe in her until..." She put her hand over her mouth and swallowed the scream that was rising up inside of her. "I never understood it. I've looked at a lot of cold cases. I've interviewed a lot of mothers who have been in the same position. And I never understood why they couldn't face what I saw as being completely obvious. That by all accounts, by all odds, every other example of something like this that you see, that kid is dead. I get that. I could never understand why those women couldn't face reality. But I do now. Because reality is a betrayal. As long as there's hope, even one little sliver of it. Like the end of the moon, right before everything goes dark, then you have to hold on to it. You have to. Because if I don't, then there's nothing. There's nothing left to fight for. I will fight to bring my daughter home. I will never stop. If I let myself believe that she's not out there, then the search isn't going to keep going. Because who else is going to care? Not her dead father, that's for sure."

Zach was dead. Even when she'd believed he had Poppy with him she'd thought at least…

She was safe.

Physically safe. Because Zach had been neurotic about Poppy's safety.

Zach was dead. So Poppy wasn't even with him.

Even in his twisted state, in whatever story he'd written in his head about them, she'd thought he'd had her and…

She didn't know who had her now.

And she was the only parent left to worry.

Dane pushed away from the doorway and crossed the space, came down on the couch beside her, then he reached out and pulled her to him. He had held her like this to keep her from crumbling earlier. But this was different. This was just offering comfort. She hadn't realized he was the kind of man that could do that. But there he was.

"I get it. You keep hoping. And I will keep looking. I swear to you. I will keep looking as long as it takes."

"You mean you're going to keep looking in the river."

For a body.

"I'll look whatever you want me to. But the river is where my skill set is probably best used. I'll do whatever you need."

"I just can't…"

"I know. I want you to believe that she's alive. I want everyone around you to think you're fucking crazy, okay? Because she deserves that. She deserves it. I never understood that. With my mom. I can never understand why she kept Sarah's room the same. It seemed ridiculous. It seemed morbid. Like a tomb. A mausoleum in the upstairs of our house, but I get it now. I understand why she waited to take it down. I understand why she pushed so hard. So long. She did it because like you said, somebody has to believe it with all the ferocity inside of them, so that the search goes on as it should." He put his hand on her face and she felt some tension bleed from her. Into him.

For one moment she closed her eyes. Just one. Then she straightened up and tried to think of what made sense to ask next.

She tried to think what she'd ask if she wasn't so close to this. "What stance is the police department taking?"

"Officer Daniels told me he's not assuming anything until he has a body." He winced. "I'm sorry. I need to make sure that I don't...just say things like that."

"No," she said, choosing in that moment to take a step back from her emotions. From her body. She had detached completely for a while there on the edge of the river. She didn't want to do that again. Not completely. But it couldn't hurt to hold herself at a distance. She couldn't exist with this much feeling, this much intensity and survive. "I understand how this kind of thing works. It's actually better if we can look at it objectively. Like a crime scene. I understand that. I know how to evaluate that."

"Okay. Whatever makes you feel better."

She let her head fall back against the back of the couch. "Nothing. Nothing will make me feel better. But I need honesty. Complete and total honesty. Because I can't wonder." She lifted her head and looked him in the eye. "Because my husband was such a liar. Because he was planning this. Whatever it was. Whatever it was intended to be, I know that he didn't just have an accident coming home from dinner."

"Not even entertaining the idea?"

"The passport and the money are gone. The overnight bag for Poppy, it doesn't add up. So yes, he could've killed himself." She swallowed hard. "He could've killed them both. But his actions are not the actions of a man who was trying to die. Because a dead man doesn't need ten grand. Or to buckle his seat belt. It's just...none of it makes sense."

"That's fair."

"But whatever was going on, he was lying. And I didn't pick up on what was going on. I thought he was having an affair. I believe that he convinced himself that you and I had slept together. I felt like he had probably done it to make himself feel justified in cheating on me."

"Do you have any idea who he was cheating with?"

"I would assume a woman from work? And the company that he works for is big. They're based in Seattle, and he goes up there..." She closed her eyes. "He went up there pretty frequently. I wouldn't be surprised if he did it while he was traveling. Because he would often spend nights away, and there would be no way that I could know. Also, it would be easy for him to travel with a local woman and go to Seattle, and no one would ever know."

She'd been over this before. So many times.

But not since they'd found Zach's body. So it probably bore looking at again.

"Right. So could be someone from here, but odds are the actual affair was taking place out of town."

"That's what I think. But that was such a shallow understanding of what was going on. I feel like maybe it... I don't know. I didn't want to face it."

"What was your plan?"

"To deal with it later. At a better time. When Poppy was going to school. In kindergarten. When I was done writing the next book. It just wasn't the right time to get a divorce. It wasn't the right time to have a conversation about something that heavy."

"You just never mentioned to him that you suspected he was cheating."

"I didn't start to suspect it until I discovered the missing condoms. It was just such a... It was such a shock. I kept trying to tell myself that I was wrong. It was only after he left that I really accepted it. So you have to understand that at the time I wasn't totally accepting of it."

"Right."

"So he was buckled and in the car."

"Yes. The car was upside down. He may have been unconscious before the impact. Or not. The window was rolled down. He was still buckled, but you know, panic makes people do strange things. And there's not a lot of time in a situation like that."

"Is it pretty common? I mean, for you. For what you see?"

"Yes."

"Okay."

"You don't have to think about it, you know. You don't have to try to outthink this. You don't have to try to understand it all. You're allowed to let other people find the truth. It isn't your job."

She shook her head. "But it's what I do. What's the point of having ever done it for anyone else if I can't do it for my own daughter?"

"You did it for someone else's daughters. That has to count for something. That has to have put out some good karma in the universe for you."

"Good karma." She nearly choked on that. "There is no evidence that I have any kind of good karma with the universe. Anyway, I don't think you actually believe in that."

He shook his head. "No. I don't."

"Good. I can't handle you having a personality transplant at the same time as all of this." He was way too practical for karma or anything adjacent to it.

"You don't have to be strong," he said.

"I'm not. I'm breaking apart. Why do you think I'm trying to collect all these facts? Because I need something to hold on to. Because if I don't I'm just going to... I was no help down by the river today. I lost my mind."

"Anyone would in your position."

"I just... I need to be able to feel like I can breathe. I have to be able to feel like I can do something for her."

"But not tonight. You're not going to do anything tonight."

She nodded slowly. She just leaned against him, let his warmth surround her. Let his strength surround her. It was a terrifying feeling. Leaning on somebody else. It made the distance between herself and Zach feel that much more prominent. Because she couldn't remember the last time she'd felt like she could trust someone enough to lean on them.

Had she ever trusted Zach like that?

Did it matter?

She wasn't married anymore.

Two days ago, she'd kissed Dane Hartley, and he'd told her that she was still married.

But she wasn't.

She was a widow.

She felt violently, acutely angry that she had to take on that mantle, all because her husband had had the bad sense to die before she could divorce him.

She leaned her head against Dane's shoulder and turned her face in, stifling a laugh.

"What?" he asked, sounding shocked.

"I was just feeling quietly furious that Zach made me a widow. Because it isn't fair. It's like somebody firing you when you wanted to quit."

He laughed. Short and hard. "Sorry. Maybe that isn't funny."

"I think it is." She shook her head. "This is absurd. This whole thing is absurd."

She looked up at him, and she understood. Suddenly.

Why people looked for something to grab hold of when they experienced the trauma. Why they looked for something to make them feel alive.

Because pieces of her were disparate, acting independently of each other. Because everything was wrong. And when everything was wrong, you wanted one certain thing to feel right.

Dane had always felt right.

"I don't want to think anymore."

"You don't have to."

"I don't want to talk anymore either."

"You don't have to do that."

"I want to go to bed."

He cleared his throat. "I'll stay here."

She shook her head.

"Margo," he said. "Probably not tonight."

"Please," she said.

And suddenly, she didn't have any strength left. She didn't have anything left inside her. But she remembered that night when she had decided to not kiss him. Because she hadn't wanted to use him. And she knew that tonight she would be using him.

But she needed him.

She watched him lose a battle with himself. Watched his muscles tense, relax. Give in.

He scooped her up off the couch, and carried her toward the stairs, up the stairs.

And laid her down in the soft bed. Her heart was thundering hard, and her head was swimming.

He took his shirt off, his jeans. He was standing there wearing only his boxers. And she didn't quite know where to look. At first, she was a little bit shocked that he'd gone from denial to stripping his clothes off.

But then he got in bed beneath the covers, and pulled her up against him. "Sleep. I'm here."

She turned over on her side. "Just sleep?"

"Yes," he said. "Just sleep. You need to fucking sleep."

"But…"

"Listen to me. For once in your life, listen. Go to sleep. I'm going to stay with you. I'll stay with you all night."

At first, she didn't understand how she was going to fall asleep. Not after all of that. Not with him holding her like this. But she needed to sleep.

When she opened her eyes, there was light streaming into the room. And Dane was still holding her close.

11

SHE STARTED GETTING phone calls from reporters the next day. The news had broken that Zach's body had been found.

She hadn't spoken to her mother-in-law since right after Zach had disappeared. There had been a vague hint of blame on the night it had happened. And of course outrage that Margo could ever believe that he had done something wrong on purpose.

She wasn't sure what her mother-in-law had believed. But today was the first day she'd considered calling her since. Her only son was gone.

He'd taken Margo's only daughter.

That was a spiderweb of pain and brushing up against it sent a wave of it through her body.

She couldn't call her. She couldn't hear her grief. Either Margo wouldn't be able to empathize with her because of her own anger with Zach. Or worse it would amplify her grief and she just couldn't.

There had been a rotation of neighbors and food for much of the day. Gail had come over and had been visibly shaken by the sight of Dane in the house. She'd recovered, but it was clear to Margo that interacting with the Hartleys was still something she'd rather not do.

But even with the thorny patches in her own yard, she'd shown up. It was what people did. With food.

Julie came with two casseroles and shining eyes. "I'm so sorry," she said.

Margo thanked her and took the dishes, and looked into her kitchen at the evidence that people cared. The evidence she wasn't alone.

She felt the community surrounding her. Felt her family closing in.

She felt Dane's presence, steady and comforting. And something deeper. More.

She was still alone.

Her dad called right as her brother, Christopher, came to the house.

"I can get on a plane and..."

"It's okay, Dad. Wait until we know more. Wait until we... Until we find Poppy. Because we will. And then she's going to want to see you."

She heard that same pity lace her dad's voice as she had heard in Dane's.

"Okay, honey."

"That motherfucker," said Christopher.

"Christopher," Laura said, looking over at the boys, who were in the corner of the kitchen playing on an old phone.

"Well. If they're going to hear that word, it's going to be about him, and I'm not going to apologize for it."

"Thank you," Margo said softly.

"They've identified him for sure?"

"He was in our car. But yeah. Callie's husband went down and did it today at the morgue. I'm..."

"Thank God he did that," said Laura. "You've been through enough."

And unspoken in all of this was that they believed that Poppy was gone.

Dane, for his part, was there hovering at the edges the whole time. Standing there with an air of protectiveness, but making sure not to intrude on anything too.

She wanted to touch him. Touching him would make her feel less alone.

She wasn't sure exactly what they were, though.

It was not the time to worry about it.

He had held her all night.

He had held her together. And she would always be grateful for that.

He hadn't let her use him. Or maybe he'd been afraid it would be using her. It might have been both.

"The dive team is going to run sonar between the bridge to the ocean. Going to keep looking."

"For her body," said Christopher, looking destroyed. She wondered if that was what she looked like. She hadn't been able to bear to look in the mirror since it all happened.

"You need to rule things out sometimes," he said. "If we don't find her..."

"It doesn't necessarily mean anything, does it?" Christopher asked.

"It means we didn't find her," said Dane.

"Thank you," said Christopher.

The police showed up not long after that.

"We want to ask you a few more questions about your husband's state of mind that night."

They'd been over it. And over and over. But it was the endless loop in her head and now something had changed. The loop didn't circle back to the same blank space anymore. She felt ragged and wrung out, but this was *something*.

She sucked in a sharp breath. "Our marriage had been un-happy for a while, but I would say it was stable. There were a few issues that had come up, but it had been months."

"What issues?"

She hesitated. "He'd accused me of having an affair."

"Were you?"

"We've been over this."

"Your husband is dead. Any additional party who might be involved is relevant," said Officer Daniels.

"No," she said. "My answer is the same now as it was then. I didn't have an affair."

Dane looked at them both from the corner of the kitchen. She could feel his gaze on them.

"You said back when we questioned you the first time that you suspected your husband of having an affair."

"Yes. That was three months before he left."

"And you believe that night that he intended to leave the marriage."

"Yes."

"Did he show signs of emotional distress?"

"Are you asking me if I think he killed himself to get out of the marriage?"

"It happens."

Men killed themselves, and their children, to punish their wives.

She knew that.

"I know it does, but no. Zach... I don't know how to say this so that it makes sense. He had a very intense sense of self-preservation. He always went for his physical, he worried about his cholesterol. He worked out five days a week. He was... He never seemed like the kind of person who would harm himself."

"And how was he with Poppy?"

"He was an overprotective father. Always. If anything, he was more protective of her than I was. More afraid of everything.

I just… The safety seat in the back of the car was unbuckled. And I cannot imagine him ever taking her out in the car and not having her buckled in."

"It's possible. Especially given what his mental state might've been."

"I don't think it is."

"Margo." His voice was heavy. "I'm not trying to be dis-respectful, but you didn't realize that he intended to take the child away either. You didn't realize that he was on the cusp of doing something extremely out of character. Not securing her into her child safety seat would be one of the smaller mis-takes that he made."

"I just can't see it."

Maybe that didn't make sense to him, but Margo could see how Zach might justify taking Poppy away. He would tell himself that she had neglected them both. That she cared more about her career than she did them. That she wanted Dane. That they had probably been sleeping together. That Margo losing sight of Poppy on the playground was evidence that she was an unfit mother. That the pills were affecting her. That it would get worse. That he was saving his daughter.

Because she was maybe even a dangerous parent for Poppy to be with. Yes, she could draw lines to all those things. She could see how he might justify that.

She thought of him reading *Devil in the Dark* in high school. He'd believed the story the murderer had told. Had believed the police officer was trying to ruin his life.

When they'd discussed the book, they'd all had to do com-plicated mental gymnastics routines to make their cases. It was why they'd enjoyed it. And if the case had been clear-cut, the cops would have solved it. It wouldn't have been solved by a group of eight teenagers who fancied themselves erudite be-cause they refused to wear clothing with brand logos on them.

"It's always men with power."

She could still see Sarah, perched on a cement planter ledge at the school, a silver chain hanging off her plaid pants, the striped sleeves on her shirt pulled down over her hands.

"*Why would he compromise his position?*" Margo asked.

"*He's in his position so he can take advantage of it, Margo, that's the point of the position.*"

Callie shook her head. "*He had too many ties to the town. He wasn't clever. I think it was a trucker going down the interstate. There were some similar crimes in other areas a few years before and after, and to me that says mobile serial killer.*"

"*Boring,*" said Margo.

"*Agreed,*" said Callie. "*But it always is, right?*"

"*That's my point,*" Sarah said. "*It's always boring and in my opinion the cops wanted something interesting and easy, which is why they missed it.*"

"*The police department might have missed it, but Officer Heaney was a scapegoat because she was a woman,*" Amber said. "*If she'd been a man no one would have ever called her tactics aggressive.*"

Zach made a scathing sound. "*You're wrong. She was dead set on manipulating the evidence so she could ruin Cody's life.*"

"*Cody ruined his own life,*" Margo said. "*He assaulted a girl he took on a date, it was just she dropped the charges, and that makes him a suspect, not for no reason, but because of his own actions.*"

"*There was never any proof. Just her word against his. That's all there ever was. One girl who was envious of his life—she said that herself—and a cop who made up her mind without any evidence.*"

"*How do you explain some of his behavior?*" Margo pushed.

"*When no one believes you anymore and they've made up their mind about you…what should you do? If everyone makes you the villain you have to find a way to make yourself the hero.*"

But she could not understand him justifying putting Poppy in harm's way. Not ever.

I kept them safe.

Those words haunted her. Echoed inside of her. Her own true crime book and all the dirty truth around it rising up in her mind.

You don't know how twisted Zach was. Because people can twist themselves up in all kinds of ways.

He was right back then. You'll find a way to make yourself a hero.

The Incline Valley Killer had convinced himself he'd kept those girls he'd raped and murdered safe at the bottom of a lake.

You couldn't trust what someone else might decide to do.

She tried not to let that reverberate within her, but it was a battle she'd already lost.

Panic overtook her then.

And she tried not to let it show. Because she didn't want to show Officer Daniels that she thought for a moment Poppy might be gone. Because she couldn't have him approaching this as a recovery. It needed to be a rescue. It needed to be a missing person.

She could be out there somewhere. She could be.

"He had time to drive to Seattle and back. I have suspicions that the woman he was having an affair with might be there. He worked from there. We need to start asking people at the corporate office for his company."

"Okay," said Daniels. "I can do that."

And she made a mental note that she was going to contact her private investigator, and send him there. He had already talked to the people at Zach's corporation, but now that Zach was dead, she had a feeling that people might speak a little bit more freely.

The entire tenor of all this had changed.

It was possible new information could be brought to light as a result.

By midafternoon, the extra people had cleared out of the house. She no longer considered Dane extra.

"How are you feeling?"

"I'm fine."

"In context?"

"Obviously."

"Do you want me to go home?"

The way that he was rooted firmly in that kitchen chair suggested to her that he was not going home. She looked across the table, where there were still case files for Sarah.

"No. I don't want you to go home. I want you to stay with me."

He nodded. "I can do that."

"Anyway, we only got halfway through these case files."

"What?"

"I want to go through the rest of these."

"Margo, you're hardly in a fit state to…"

"What else am I supposed to do? I had a private investigator talk to everyone at Zach's office, just in case the police missed something. I messaged him because I want him to go back now that Zach's dead and just…make sure. The police have all of Zach's things. It's an active investigation. Your team is going out with sonar and… I don't know what else to do. I don't know what else to do except keep looking into all this. What else am I supposed to do?"

"I'll make you some coffee."

She didn't know whether it was a victory or not that he had simply embraced her brand of insanity. She decided to go ahead and take it as something of a neutral victory. In this moment, she would take whatever she could get. They pored over the records, until her eyes were scratchy.

"I don't know. Nothing makes sense right now."

"I don't see why anything would," he said.

"We need more. We need…something. I wish that we still had your sister's room."

Dane frowned. "There's a storage unit," he said.

"What?"

"There's a storage unit. My mom put most of Sarah's belongings in storage when she finally moved. She couldn't really part with them."

"I thought she got rid of everything at the yard sale."

"No. Never Sarah's things. Everything from her room went into the unit. The police looked through Sarah's things, though."

"Still. We should."

She didn't know what she felt. It was something. Something to latch on to. And Sarah's things might...at least make her feel closer to her again.

But everything felt like it was just the aftermath of a bomb blast. Everything felt wrong. But she needed to find something to look forward to. Something that would bring her some hope.

God, how sad was her life that going through her missing friend's old things felt hopeful?

"I'm going to order some dinner," he said.

She didn't want to eat the sadness casseroles that had come her way today. It was too grim.

"I have Hot Pockets in the freezer."

"For God's sake. I'm going to order some dinner."

Forty-five minutes later, they had Thai food, and she was surprised how hungry she was.

"I'm going to run back to my place," he said. "I'm just going to get a bag. Bring some things over. That okay?"

She nodded. "I'll be fine."

"Good."

He loaded the dishwasher, and she wanted to ask if he was real. But that seemed like the kind of thing you'd say if you were flirting with somebody. And she wasn't sure she was allowed to flirt with him right now.

There were no rules in this present moment.

Nothing made sense. But he left to go and get his supplies, and she found herself pondering the whole situation.

She felt like there were all these pieces and she needed to take a minute to examine all of them.

Zach.

Zach was dead.

There would have to be a funeral.

She was his wife. But not really.

She decided that was something she couldn't examine right now.

Poppy. They had not found Poppy's body. Poppy was still alive.

She repeated that to herself. Over and over again.

And she found herself heading upstairs. Stopping in front of her daughter's bedroom door.

She hadn't been able to open it. Not for all these months. Not after she'd searched to see what was missing. Not after she'd accepted she was missing. Not when she thought she heard Poppy cry. Not ever.

Zach was dead.

She opened up the door, and felt all the air exit her body.

It was so beautiful. She'd always been proud of that. The room that she'd been able to put together for Poppy when they'd moved into this house. Delicate lavender with little butterflies on the wall. White lace curtains.

It looked so serene. So safe. Like nothing bad could possibly happen here.

"I'm sorry," she said, her chest contracting so hard she could barely get words out, let alone take a breath. "I'm so sorry. I wanted everything to be perfect for you. I wanted it to be safe. But I missed things. I missed so many things. And I screwed it up. I made too many mistakes. And this wasn't safe. You weren't safe here. I'm going to find you. I'm not going to give up. I swear. I'm going to be that last holdout. I'm going to be that crazy lady. For you. I will fight until the end. And then I will fight after that."

She sat next to the bed, and drew her knees up to her chest, and then she cried. It wasn't the same animalistic wailing she'd done down at the river when she believed that that body was in the car.

No. This was just sorrow. A deep, unending wave of sadness over not knowing where her daughter was. Over being separated from her. Six months.

No songs. No smiles. No jam fingerprints on the counter. No backtalk from a child who was far too smart for her own good. Opinionated like Margo, with her dad's charisma.

She had carried the child in her body for nine months. And now she'd been away from her for six.

She may never see her again.

She doubled over, wrapping an arm around her stomach as she sobbed until there was no more sound left inside of her.

She heard the door, and looked up. Dane was standing there, and the raw sadness on his face would've stolen her breath if she'd had any left in her body.

He moved to her, gripped her by the arms and lifted her up. And then he kissed her cheek. Her forehead. Kissed the tears away from her skin, before he found his way to her mouth. And this was what she had been missing last night. This desperation.

Because her body was a hollow, yawning cavern of need. And he was here. He wasn't missing. He wasn't dead. He was *here*. They were both here.

She needed him. She needed this.

She wrapped her arms around his neck and she kissed him. Kissed him deep and hard.

Kissed him with all the feeling that she tried to deny the other day.

That she tried to turn away from.

There was no running from it.

There was no rationalizing. And she was so damned wedded to trying to rationalize.

She just wanted to think her way out of everything. But right now all she could do was feel.

She had exhausted her despair.

She wanted to feel alive.

Maybe she was using him. Maybe people always used each other.

Or maybe she just needed someone to hold on to. Maybe she'd always needed *him* to hold on to.

So she kissed him, because it ignited something inside of her. Because it made her body feel electric.

Because it made her feel as if there was something beautiful left in this world. A trail of sparks left behind by his hands.

"Please," she whispered against his lips. "Please."

They walked out of the bedroom together, and closed the door.

And then they went into her master bedroom. He took her hand and led her to the bathroom. He turned on the water in the shower, and stripped her clothes off her while it got hot.

Then he pulled them both in beneath the spray. She could feel that he was aroused, hard and glorious against her.

It felt good to be wanted. It felt good to not feel like a failure.

It felt good to feel alive.

To feel everything in the moment.

To shut everything out and focus on his hands. On the hot water. On the firmness of his kiss, and the scratch of his beard against her face.

His hands were rough, and she hoped he left her bruised.

She wanted to be bruised, because she wanted to be marked by this.

She couldn't get out of it without evidence that it had happened.

She needed it. Needed this. Needed him.

They stayed together like that for a long time, water-slick skin, heavy breathing punctuated by deep kisses.

A carnal baptism that made her feel new.

Finally, she couldn't wait anymore. Finally, he turned the water off.

Finally, they stepped out and into the shocking cold dry air.

He toweled her off. She forgot to be embarrassed. To have any thoughts at all about him seeing her naked.

Because everything right now, everything with this, was okay.

And nothing else was. Outside of this space they'd made for themselves, everything was broken.

She wasn't borrowing trouble here.

This was her grave sin, after all.

The excuse that Zach had used to pull the pin in the grenade.

And she hadn't even ever done it.

It felt right, to do it now.

She'd already been punished for it.

If it was her sin, she deserved to commit it.

He brought her back to the bed, and moved over the top of her, kissing her, driving inside of her, driving her wild.

She couldn't relate it to the teenage fantasy she'd once had.

Because this was something new altogether. Perhaps because she was someone new. Because she could never be the person she'd been six months ago.

And somehow, he had met her here.

Didn't treat her like she was too much, and even when she was, stayed.

She came apart in his arms, and he was still there to hold her together when it was all done.

She was breathing hard after, her hand on his chest, taking a visual inventory of his body in a way she hadn't managed to do before, because she'd been so consumed with all the touching.

"What does the tattoo mean?"

He laughed. "That I was drunk one time near a tattoo parlor when I was in the military."

"No," she said. "I don't believe that."

She reached out and touched the red dragon, surrounded by other intricate designs.

"Protection," he said. "Because there was a certain point where I realized I didn't actually have a death wish, because maybe I needed to stay alive for my mom. Because maybe we needed some protection. It was dumb. Kind of a youthful, impulsive thing."

"I get it. And thank you. For not getting yourself killed. Because I needed you."

"I might've caused more trouble than I've ever solved."

She shook her head. "Whatever the situation with that, it wasn't you. I mean, even if I'd slept with you like he said, he had no right. None at all." She lay on her back, and he moved his hand, holding hers beneath the blankets. It was such a simple, nonsexual gesture, and yet it felt like everything.

She felt…she wasn't healed. She wasn't okay. But she felt like maybe she'd exorcised a demon. That it helped her accept something that had been circling inside her for a while that she hadn't been able to put into words.

"Zach was looking for an excuse," she said. "That's the thing. Whatever all this was about, he was looking for an excuse, and he needed to make me a villain. So he did his best to accomplish that. And…people can tell themselves whatever they want. We aren't in charge of what they tell themselves."

She wished she could fully believe that.

But it was hard.

Because mostly, she just felt guilt. But when she rolled up against Dane, she felt…

Not alone.

The storm had passed. The pain he'd eased with his touch started to creep back in.

But she wasn't alone.

And after everything, she was grateful for that.

12

SHE ENDED UP falling asleep at a reasonable hour for the first time in months. And Dane had made her breakfast, and brought it to her in bed. She felt soothed by it. This wasn't normal. It was like a different life had been created in the middle of this crater she'd been living in. She would take it.

"You have a key to the storage unit?"

"Yeah," he said. "I thought it would be easiest if I was the one that held on to it. My mom wants the stuff but… And you know sometimes my dad might want to go see it."

"I thought your dad was pretty detached."

"He's not," said Dane. "That's the thing. He either pulls the plug completely, or he's somewhere drinking himself into a hole and having a breakdown. And sometimes he would go to the storage unit and look through her things. Because he's not… He had to leave because it broke him."

"I understand that," she said.

"I know you do."

"I can't even say that I don't want this to break me, you

know. Because it should, right? Shouldn't it? Going through something like this should do something to you."

"Well, you're not broken."

"I'm not okay."

He put his hand on her cheek. That touch, that intimate touch, after being without for so long, felt like it caused a soul-deep shift.

"That's fine. You don't have to be."

She leaned in and pressed her forehead to his chest.

"I should have been here the whole time," he said, his voice rough.

"I wouldn't have let you. Because I wanted you too much and I could never have let myself have something I wanted."

"But you can now?"

She let out a long breath. "I…can't let myself go without you anymore. It's not about what I deserve, but I can't keep going like I have been. I need… I need you."

He traced her lower lip with his thumb. "Margo Box needs someone. Now, that's something."

"I don't know if you've noticed but I'm not doing great by myself."

"You're doing amazing."

"Well. I could keep going like I was. But I just want you. And now that's stronger than whatever held me back before. How about that?"

"Works for me."

Before they left for the storage unit she heard back from the police and her private investigator. Both reported that there were no leads suggesting that he'd been having an affair with a coworker in Seattle. None of the women in the office reported having a connection to him. Not that they would, but the private investigator told her that there was no indication any of them were particularly upset by his passing. Of course, a woman who was involved with him might've suspected…

She didn't know what she was thinking, trying to rationalize this. There wasn't actually anything sane to trace here.

If there was another woman, who knew what she'd been told? Margo had no idea what kind of man he'd been with another woman. He'd been lying to her about who he was, and his every action, everything he did.

What made her think he would've been more honest with the other woman?

The dead end made her feel edgy. Upset.

She was glad that they had something planned. She was glad there was something that was going to get her out of this house, which felt increasingly like a tomb. Or perhaps just an altar upon which her entire life had been sacrificed.

What good did it do?

The gate. It was useless. A reinforcement of every lie the people in this place told themselves.

The monsters were inside.

She stood up, her morning cup of coffee still in her hand, and Dane moved to her, lowering his head and kissing her.

"Worst timing," he said.

"Necessary timing," she said.

"You think so?"

"I don't know. I don't know what my life looks like on the other side of this. I don't really know what's happening now. I do know that I've always had feelings for you. Always. I wasn't at your house that day after you thought you saw Sarah because I'm such a nice person, and… You must know that."

The one good thing about starting this when her life was so messy was that…she wasn't afraid of anything. Wasn't afraid of pushing him away.

And life was too strange and short to not grab hold of this with both hands.

"Well, at first you were just my sister's annoying friend. Later, after Sarah disappeared, and you checked in on us, on me, all the time, I felt differently. But I also felt myself spiraling. I knew I couldn't... I knew I couldn't have you around for that. You have done remarkably well, you know."

"What do you mean?"

"You haven't lost your mind completely. I can't say the same for myself. When Sarah disappeared, I... I went over the edge. Completely. I started drinking. A lot. Then there were other drugs when alcohol wasn't enough. I got arrested."

"I remember that."

"Drunk driving. Vandalism. I was just so angry. So, so angry. And you haven't done any of that."

"Well, it's not my sister. It's my daughter. And I need to believe that she's going to come back to me. And that means that I need to be...whole when she does." She ground her back teeth together. "I was unraveling before they left. There were things I was doing that weren't healthy."

"Like?"

"I didn't sleep."

"I know that."

"I used to take Adderall to stay up." She watched his face closely.

"I knew you were using, Margo. One person who copes with substances recognizes another."

"It wasn't...like that. I didn't take pills so I wouldn't feel. I needed them to stay focused."

"You needed them so you could forget you were human. You used them to avoid quiet moments. To avoid having to make choices about what you did with your time. Am I right?"

She tried to laugh. But it wasn't funny. "Okay. Yeah."

"It's okay. I've spent a lot of time running from my life."

"But I loved my life. Or a lot about it. I just wanted to be... the best at all of it."

"Did he try to be the best for you?"

This time when the breath left her lungs, it wasn't a laugh. "It wasn't important to him like it was to me. He's easy, gregarious and funny, and I'm intense. People have to tell me to back off all the time and I need to be…indispensable. Or people will just be done with me, won't they?" She felt a tear slide down her cheek. She hadn't even been aware of tearing up. "He left anyway. It wasn't enough." She let out a jagged breath. "I wanted to be a good mom. I wanted to be the best. I wanted to give everything to all the parts of myself so I could prove my intensity mattered. Maybe that's my problem. I want everything. And I know I can't have it. But from the time I was sixteen it just felt like…there was never going to be enough time to have all the things I felt like I needed."

He was silent. Watching. Listening. How long had it been since she'd felt like Zach would listen?

She'd never told Zach this. She'd never thought he would understand, and until she'd stood there looking Dane in the face, pouring out this deep part of herself, she'd never even realized that.

"I just… I needed to be the best to keep my family together. And I needed to do everything all at once because there isn't *time*," she said. "Sarah disappeared when we were sixteen and I hope…she's out there living dreams. All the dreams. But I don't know that. As far as I can see, she's just gone. It was the first time I felt like…there was a clock ticking. Then I started studying disappearances, murders, for my hobby and…then my mother died. And I… I was never going to create a life with a space to have you. And that hurt maybe the most. You got your shit together and I'd already made my choices." She blinked, trying not to shed any more tears. "So no matter how much sleep I sacrificed I was never really going to have it all." She cleared her throat. "I thought about it, though. I was a mom during the day and a writer at night. A wife at home… I thought about being yours while we were away."

"I wouldn't have let you," he said. "If you'd have touched me, you'd have been all mine."

Maybe that was what scared her most. Maybe that was why perfection was her job and not anyone else's. So she wasn't the one who needed anyone. All the intensity was usually in her, but with him...it was mutual. And she couldn't contain that or harness it, or beat it into submission.

That had been the frightening thing about having a child. It had been love that was bigger than she was. Maybe Zach had realized that. Maybe it was why he'd done this. Because he'd known that Margo loved Poppy more than anything. More than writing. More than him.

Why had she married Zach?

She'd loved him, but why?

Maybe because he was the one thing that hadn't required intensity.

Maybe that was why she'd missed all of these important clues. Maybe it was why she hadn't asked about the affair. Maybe it was why all the rot and darkness had been able to grow. In the silent spaces she'd left unexplored because she'd wanted one easy thing, and it had been him.

"I want this to work," she said. And because she did want it to work, she knew she couldn't hold back. She wasn't afraid of very many things anymore. How could you be when you'd lost everything? She could have this though. She could try it. So she put it all on the line. "Because I have loved you for a long time. But it terrifies me. I couldn't have you, and I hated that, but maybe there was some safety in it too. I know I could never have been...living like I was if I was with you. So I have to be different. I'm not sure I know how to be."

"I'm not asking you to do anything right now, Margo. The truth is, this changed you. It'll keep changing you. We don't know when we'll find Poppy." He didn't say *if*. "We don't know what life will look like six months from now, and I don't think there's much point wondering. But I'm here. As long as you want me. I don't need you to make a decision on how you're going to change for me. We're here together. We'll change together."

She swallowed hard. "Thank you. I wish…" She breathed out. "It is so hard to remember now, why I was ever with Zach and not you."

"I get why it's hard for you to remember Zach clearly. But I'd think it wouldn't be too difficult to remember how I was. I hurt you."

"You weren't abusing me."

"I was acting like a toddler. Who was out of control."

"No. You were acting like someone who was drowning. I read somewhere that helping a drowning person usually kills you too because they're so panicked they cling on to you and pull you down, they hurt you. You were in the throes of that kind of pain."

He cleared his throat. "And to follow the metaphor through, I would have drowned you."

"We didn't see each other for a long time after that, and it was probably good in some ways. It didn't change the way I felt. None of it did. Not the way that you grabbed me, not distance, it didn't change that. And when we brought the dive team in on the case, I knew that I was just in so much trouble. From the beginning, I knew that. If I'd invited you in that night, we would've slept together."

Just as old, familiar guilt took hold, Dane reached out and touched her, his voice hushed.

"It's not failure, to want out of your marriage. Especially not when it's clear that yours was actually damned unhealthy. You can blame yourself all you want, but this is like you needing to do it all. You're taking all the blame too."

"Listen, I know that in the end our marriage wasn't healthy. I wasn't in it for us, it was more…our family. The life we'd made. He was a good father, though. That's the thing that gets me. He was not a great husband. Not in the end."

"He was in the beginning?"

"I wouldn't have married him if he wasn't. He was great, actually. He was what I needed. Or what I wanted. I knew I couldn't have you. I'd let that go. I thought. It felt good to want someone who didn't take everything to heart like I did. Who didn't need to be everything all the time. At first I felt like I could breathe a little better around him. He knew me. He'd shared that same loss in high school, but it wasn't as close. He was a lighter person than me. Not as intense. He was never lost in his own head like I was. He was good for me. He pulled me out of myself. I really do think that he loved me. I know I loved him."

She let that sit between them, and in her. This whole complicated truth. The choices she'd made and why, the ways she'd tried her best and the ways she'd failed. The ways Zach had failed her. The complication of wanting an easy life with Zach, when she herself had never been easy. When her first love had been directed toward a hard, complicated man and she'd wished for something simpler.

Here she was. Nothing was simple.

But her feelings for Dane had never gone away.

"I did love him," she said again.

"Just not exclusively," said Dane, his eyes on her.

"No. Not exclusively. Maybe a lot of people feel like that. There's an impossible person you know you're never going to have, but the feelings don't go away. You were just…a part of my heart. Always. But I married him. I regretted it sometimes, but not most of the time. But it was…it was different in the beginning." She frowned. "I thought I changed. Because I got more and more into the writing. I started… I did start using pills. But that's not…entirely true."

"He changed."

"Yes." She searched her mind now, cast it back and tried to reframe the past two years of her marriage. What had she missed?

She remembered the Zach she'd first loved. When they were twenty-three and she'd wanted something other than pining for Dane and being lost in the murky water of her own obsessions. He'd smiled all the time. He'd thought her weirdness was endearing.

But it had changed. Slowly.

She frowned. "It was really more like the last five years. He changed after Poppy was born. He was more tense. He was always someone who was very in the moment, but that was less true after she was born. He worried a lot. He got...very protective. And I kind of liked it. He found a little bit of intensity. He used to check on her multiple times a night. Make sure she was okay. But I liked it, because of course having him be a dad who loved her that much was... It was attractive, it was good."

"But that was a change for him," said Dane.

"Yes. People change when they become parents. It's normal. A trigger."

"Yeah. True." He let out a long breath. "At least, that's what I've heard. Not being a parent myself."

"Well, I guess I didn't think it was strange. I'm still not sure if it is. Our relationship changed when we became parents. Then it changed again when I was doing research for the book. Because it became clear that it was different. That it was going to be more important. It became clear that it was possible that we could solve a cold case with my research. The publisher treated it differently. I started treating it differently. Not because it was more important, but because I was closing in on something. I wasn't just writing about broken things, I was on the verge of fixing something. Zach resented that. I viewed that as me messing things up. Making mistakes, him reacting to the changes, and me not having the time to fix them. Because I didn't yet. I had to finish the job. I had to finish the investigation, because it felt so pressing. Because we were going to find those girls. And we did. We did find them."

"Yes," Dane said gruffly. "We did."

"The Zach I married wouldn't have accused me of having an affair," she said. "He would never have been that suspicious. That was part of him that came out later. But I didn't realize. I thought of it as him being a dad, but that was an overall change to who he was. So I felt…blindsided, I guess, by his accusations, but then just guilty because…he wasn't making things up. So how mad could I be? It wasn't until I suspected him of having an affair that I really realized he wasn't the same. It was just…hidden."

By the story she'd told herself.

She'd told herself she just couldn't deal with Zach. The truth was, she hadn't wanted to.

She was the kind of woman who tracked someone down to check on them when she loved them, whether they wanted her to or not. She was the kind of woman who was willing to be yelled at for just not going away because her love was persistent and intense, like the rest of her.

But she hadn't been persistent or intense with Zach.

She hadn't been in love with him anymore.

She'd wanted to be.

She'd been attached to their life.

She'd wanted to keep that perfect house. The perfect bio for the back of her book.

Margo Box lives in the rainy Pacific Northwest with her husband and daughter.

She'd been attached to that. The security of it. The safety of it.

When had she changed?

She was trying to unpack all of this. But it was so hard. What was her? What was him? What was them?

What was the truth and what was a lie?

A story she'd told to make herself sleep better at night.

"I don't know whether I'm happy or sad that he ruined everything before he died. Because I'm never going to be able to grieve him like I would have. That man was my partner for all those years. For more than a decade. I loved him. For a few years I loved him uncomplicatedly. And then it got a little bit tangled up. But now… He took my child from me. I can't even mourn what we were."

"You can do whatever you want."

He was looking at her, unwavering. She couldn't remember the last time someone had looked at her like that. Like they weren't afraid to see all of her. Or to have her see all of them. "Why are you so perfect?"

He laughed. "Well. First of all, I'm not. So please don't think that I am, because that's just going to lead to disappointment. But second, because that day in the apartment, I didn't pull you up against me and kiss you. I wanted to. I pushed you away instead. And that was the best damn thing I could've done. For us. Obviously it led you here. I don't know. But I ended up where I needed to be. I needed to sort my shit out, big-time. I needed to figure out what kind of man I was going to be if I was going to live."

"If you were going to live?"

"I hadn't decided if I was going to yet. At that point, I'd definitely found out how I could die. How to kill myself slowly. If I'd kissed you then, I would've dragged you into that, and it would've been toxic as hell. So here we are, and I'm older. I've been through things, but things that I chose. I went to battle. I decided to live. I decided that I was better off figuring out how to help people, instead of just self-destructing. Because what a fucking waste. I accepted on some level that Sarah is probably gone. And when I accepted that, I found a new kind of purpose. Because if my sister can't be here living her life, what kind of a tribute is it to give up your own? You've got to do something with the time that you have." He sighed heavily. "But that's the man who finally kissed you. I waited. Until I could back up what I was offering. Until I was offering more than something physical. So if I seem anything like perfect, it's just the passage of time. It's just not being a dumb kid."

She took his hand in hers. "Just the simple and impossible work of walking through fire and coming out the other side forged into something stronger, rather than undone?"

He smiled. "Yeah. Simple as that."

"I'm glad that I have you with me."

"Me too." He cleared his throat. "To be clear, I didn't give a shit about your husband. I was completely happy with the thought of taking you from him. I waited so long to feel like I was enough for you, and once I made it there… I wasn't going to let him stop me. I wasn't going to just let you go. Not on his account." He put his hand on her face. "I was going to fight for you."

"Were you?"

"Yes. I would've done everything I could to convince you to leave him. You were out there making moral choices. I wasn't about to."

"What stopped you?"

"At that moment? You. Because I didn't think it was what you wanted."

It hadn't been. It had been too. She'd wanted him, she just hadn't wanted to blow up her life.

But what would've happened in five years? He hadn't pushed then, but he might have someday. And if she'd been just a little bit less distracted by the job, a little more unhappy with Zach… She didn't think her morals were an unbreakable fortress.

Zach hadn't given her the chance to find out.

"We should head out to the storage unit."

"Yeah," he said. "Let's go."

13

THE STORAGE UNIT was out near Astoria, closer to the ocean. The salt air was acrid and intense, and a welcome change. Because being able to breathe air somewhere new felt necessary right now. The house felt stagnant and more than a little bit oppressive. But so did the whole town.

At least when she wasn't sitting at home, she could try to forget for a second that she still didn't know where her daughter was.

It never really went away, that feeling. But being focused on the other case helped.

It helped her find some sense of normalcy, rather than allowing her to sink into despair.

The depths of despair wouldn't make her useful to anyone.

Maybe she didn't need to be useful.

But she needed to be able to breathe.

It made the salt air feel medicinal.

The storage units had bright orange doors. They were garish, and there was something about the endless rows of identical flat-topped units that made her feel a little bit claustrophobic.

A little afraid she wouldn't be able to find her way out. She wasn't sure if her vivid imagination popping up right now was evidence she was worse off than she'd imagined, or more herself.

Wild fantasies about being lost forever in a storage unit maze were definitely vintage Margo. She'd been the cautious one in the friend group, always. No drugs, no alcohol. She liked to be in control.

Even her pill use over the past few years had been done with the strict idea that she was in control of it. Using it for a very specific purpose.

It said something about her, she imagined, that she could justify drug abuse as long as it was to support her punishing her body, working more, depriving herself of sleep and not for relaxation or to feel good.

"I think this is it," he said, looking at the numbers on the side.

"How could you tell? It's like a maze."

It was the sameness of it. The fact that there were no iden-tifying markers.

"I think it's the third row in." They drove down the aisle, and then she saw the number. Dane stopped right in front of it, unerringly.

He got out, and she followed suit. Then he went over to the unit and put his key in the lock.

He pushed the door open, and she saw an array of boxes laid out before them.

"A lot of this is Sarah's. This box is her baby stuff." He moved over to the middle. "This was her room."

The way that he knew, she wondered if he had helped pack all this up. If he had put it in here. Helped organize it.

She wondered how much of the preservation of everything his sister was had been his effort.

"I know she had journals and things like that. The police looked at them."

"Right. Of course they did."

So many of the notes had been vague.

Because they'd made assumptions. Of course they had. That whatever was in Brian's belongings were more important.

And anything short of her journaling about a love affair with the teacher wouldn't be useful from Sarah.

She didn't get the impression that Officer Daniels thought of Sarah as being the aggressor. Even thinking that made her want to claw her own skin off. Thankfully, she had the impression that he saw the power balance and age gap for what they were.

But that didn't mean there weren't biases that had gone into looking through all of this.

"Okay. Let's take these boxes back."

"All right."

She put her hand on his. "You know that I'm going to make sure that everything is well preserved. And brought right back."

"Of course. I trust you."

They started to move the boxes out to her car. "So you thought you were going to steal me from my husband?"

"Why do you think I've been such a standoffish asshole?"

"To be fair, it is part of your personality."

"Yes. But… I want you. And I felt like you made your decision. And then when they disappeared… Margo, I didn't want to take advantage of how you felt. I didn't want to take advantage of you being lonely or sad. And I really hope that…"

"No. I know what I want. As far as all that goes… As far as sex goes, I… It wasn't because I was sad. If I had opened the door in Tahoe, we would've been in bed together. If I had lingered in the hall in New York, we would've been in bed together. If we'd gone to breakfast in New York…"

"Even unto morning sex," he said, humor in his voice.

She nodded gravely. "Even then. I was stopping myself. I just quit holding back."

"Okay. That's good to know."

"I knew what I wanted." She laughed. "I just wanted… to keep holding on to what I had too, and I knew I couldn't. There wasn't a pill for that."

"Just a double life, and that's not you."

She blinked. She'd sort of felt like she'd had a double life, but she…she hadn't. He was right. She was herself, in all things. That was the funny thing about the pills. She'd never taken them to be less herself; she'd taken them to be more herself.

She had never been lying about who she was.

She'd assumed Zach wasn't.

He had been. And that's what made it impossible to figure it all out now.

"It's not me," she said. "I wish it were. Maybe I'd compartmentalize better. But it's just…all the feelings all the time."

"Margo," he said. "I can handle it."

"Thank you."

"Yeah. Well. Let's head back."

The reprieve was over. He didn't say anything, but drove them out to a fish and chips place on the water. Gave her a few more minutes of being away from the house.

He didn't visit his mother. Didn't even mention it. They enjoyed their food.

It was a moment of being detached from all the heaviness.

Of just being together in a place that felt separate.

For just a second, she felt like maybe they were Dane and Margo if he hadn't lost his sister. If she had never married Zach.

And instead of turning away from that, she let herself have it for just a moment. Maybe this was the closest thing to a double life she'd ever get. She needed it right now.

So that she could face the rest of the day. So that she could face the house again.

The burning fury inside of her. The hollow grief.

It was with her all the time, so she took this one moment where it wasn't the most pressing feeling.

When they got back on the road, heaviness descended over her. She almost welcomed it. Because it felt right.

If she really let herself she could feel guilty for not having that heaviness on her for the past hour or so.

But she was the one who had to keep on moving through all this. And Dane had said it himself. She needed to keep hoping.

The dive team was going out tomorrow. Canvassing the whole of the river.

She needed to be able to survive tomorrow.

And that meant clinging to a little bit of joy today.

She looked out the window as they drove down the winding two-lane highway, trees on either side of them.

They were nearly back to the gated community when she looked into the woods and saw something that made her heart jump. The flick of blond hair, and a flurry of movement.

Poppy.

14

THE WOODS WERE thick, tall imperious pine trees creating a near impenetrable canopy, thick devil brush winding through those trees creating an impassable labyrinth, with fallen, moss-covered logs and large ferns only adding to the tangle.

But through those trees, she'd seen her.

She'd seen her daughter.

"*Stop*," she shouted.

"What?"

"Stop the car." She started to unbuckle even before he pulled over. "Stop."

He pulled quickly off onto the narrow shoulder, two tires in the dirt.

And she stumbled out of the car without pausing to think.

She ran straight into the woods, toward the place she'd seen her. That bright pop of cover in the inky green.

"Poppy!" She shouted her daughter's name. Looked for more movement.

She couldn't see anything. So she kept on running. In the direction that she'd seen that blond hair.

That's what she'd seen. Part of a little girl, obscured in the trees. Blond hair. A blue coat. Rainbow tights. A black shoe. Poppy had been missing all those things.

She wasn't crazy. She wasn't.

"Poppy!" she yelled again. And she kept running. Running until her eyes were dry and there were tears on her cheeks.

Running.

Sticks gouging her legs, branches whipping at her face.

There was nothing. There was no one. She was covered in the oppressive darkness of the canopy of trees.

But she knew what she'd seen. She knew.

She wasn't crazy.

Be crazy.

Dane had told her to go ahead and be crazy. Someone had to be. For Poppy.

At least she was hoping.

At least she'd seen something.

She *had*.

She looked around, her heart beating wildly.

She heard crashing behind her, and Dane came through the trees. "What the fuck?"

"I saw her," she said.

She saw it. A flash of pity.

She hated him for that. Hated that this was the real, honest reaction from someone who cared about her. Didn't patronize her.

He was a better barometer than her own heart. She hated that she knew it.

She chose not to believe it.

"Remember, I was sure I saw Sarah," he said.

"*No,*" she said, shaking her head. "I didn't see a different person on the trailhead. These are the woods. And she's a little girl. What other little girl would be here? I saw *her*."

When the words came out, she realized how ridiculous they sounded.

That anybody would think she was hallucinating.

That there was no way she'd seen what she believed she'd seen.

But she had.

"I know she was there," she said.

"Then let's call the police," said Dane.

And she didn't know what was worse. The very obvious truth that he didn't believe her, or the fact that he was indulging her anyway.

But she needed to call the police.

"You can go back to the truck and call," she said.

"I have my phone," he said. He pulled it out of his pocket. "Yeah. Daniels, I'm with Margo. We're out on Highway 62. The truck is parked right where we're at in the woods. I think somewhere past mile marker nine. Yes. She thinks that she saw Poppy. In the woods."

He said nothing for a moment.

"I think you should come look. It's as credible as anything else. At this point, we might as well look at everything."

Because tomorrow he would be diving for Poppy's body. So why not look now? Why not look in the woods now?

Because that child had been alive. Alive and running. Running in the woods.

But there was no evidence there had ever been a child.

The police did come. They canvassed the area.

They didn't see a thing.

Margo stood there, as the darkness descended around them.

"I saw her," she said.

"Margo," said Dane, taking hold of her arms. "Maybe you did. Or maybe you really wanted to. Either way, you know there is no shame in that. That's how much you love her. Because if you could bring her up out of thin air, you would. And your mind basically did. Your heart."

"No. Don't. Don't. You think I'm insane."

"I think you're normal. I think you're like all of us who have ever wanted more than anything to look into the darkness and see the person we love looking back at us."

"What if it was her?"

"Then you'll see her again. But she's not here right now."

She held on to that. *You'll see her again.*

That was how he finally got her to go back to the car.

She buckled in, and started shaking.

"Did I just make it up?"

"Odds are? Yes."

"But I want it to be true."

"I know you do."

"I want to just make it true. I can't... I don't know where my daughter is. I can't do this anymore. I can't. I keep trying. I keep trying to take a minute. To take a minute to breathe. To take a minute to remind myself that I'm alive. Eating fish and chips with you, and having sex with you. Kissing you. I keep trying. But then it's reality again, and nothing's okay. And I'm not okay."

"That's okay. You don't have to be."

"I'm so tired of this. When I lost sight of her on the playground for just two minutes, two minutes, it was like the whole world caved in. And I am just in that hell, all the time."

"I know."

"What if I unravel completely? What if I never see her again? What if I lose my mind?"

"That won't be you. Not ever. Because you don't give up. Because you are tenacious. Because you are you. And that's what Zach didn't take into account when he did all this. Margo Box doesn't give up. You're the one that's always there. Shining a light. Turning over rocks. Running through the fucking forest after an apparition. You're the kind of person that solves the mystery. You will."

And unspoken under all of that was the truth that sometimes it was a sad ending, even when you did all the work to solve it.

That sometimes all you were doing was finding the underwater garden of the serial killer. Reuniting parents with their children's bodies.

But she knew one thing right then.

It really was better than not knowing. She hadn't believed that. Not until right then.

"I will find out. I will."

"So keep seeing things."

15

THE NEXT MORNING, Callie came over. Dane was up at dawn, and headed out to help with the dive team, and she was doing her best to stay…sane. Such as her sanity was.

She already had coffee on when Callie got there.

"Did Dane make this?"

"Yes. He did."

"Do you want to talk about all the terrible things going on, or do you want to tell me about the sex you are having with the hot boy?"

And she laughed, like a dam had burst inside of her chest. She really did love her friend.

"Well," she said. "It's going to be a long day. So I have a feeling we have time to cover all of it."

"I'm happy for you. In the most bizarre way."

"Thank you. Because really, there's nothing to be all that happy about right now. So I will take this thing with him and just…be grateful for it. Because otherwise everything is terrible."

"I know."

"I have a bunch of Sarah's things to go through. He said I

could do it while he was gone. And he said it was okay if you were here."

Callie looked haunted. "Really?"

"Yeah. Would you be okay with that?"

She nodded slowly. "Yeah. I would be. But you know… It's all very weird."

"I know. I was a little bit worried that my being with him was going to be a problem for us."

She shook her head. "No. It's not. Not at all. Listen, I know the whole thing is complicated. But I'd rather have Sarah back than my dad. Do you ever wonder, though, if they really did love each other?"

Margo sat with that for a second. "Not usually. But I wonder about everything. People are complicated. And even if I believe that there was a fair amount of manipulation involved, I guess that could've been something she really felt."

"People get so lost in their own…stuff, you know?"

"Yeah. I do know."

"Anyway, I have always felt…upset. At my dad. Never at Sarah."

"I talked to Sarah's mom, and she said she struggled with being angry at Sarah. If you were, it wouldn't be a moral failing. It just makes you human."

"Well, I never was, because I really knew her. I'm not saying I was fully in the Me Too era prior to it happening. She just wasn't that person, you know? She wasn't edgy. She wasn't drinking, she wasn't sleeping around. She wasn't like some of us. Even me. I was in more trouble than she was. It never made sense. And I could never reconcile what they said about her with what I knew. I know people keep secrets. Because the whole thing was obviously a big secret. But in my mind, it could never be anything but abuse. Even if I do sit there and try to reframe it. Try to ask myself if she could've chosen to go off with him—you know, think that she chose it. Whatever. When you're sixteen, you think you're an adult. And you could be so easily manipulated into thinking it was your choice. And that it was something that you wanted. I just don't think she did."

"Neither do I."

She nodded. "Yeah. It's like I know things are complicated for my mom…"

"Is your mom angry at Sarah?"

"No. But I think she feels responsible. I think she doesn't like to be around the Hartleys ever because she feels like she probably should've known. I don't know. My mom has always been completely nonjudgmental of Sarah. Completely."

"Your mom is great."

"Yes."

She started to open up the boxes. There were diaries in there. They kept rummaging around. There was a stack of books. It made Margo's mind flash back to the Little Free Library.

"You remember when we all read *Devil in the Dark*?"

"I've been thinking about it since you mentioned finding the book. Because I'm haunted by what Sarah said. About it always being the powerful man. I wondered if she was trying to tell us something."

"Maybe. You thought it was a stranger. Why?"

"I don't know. Maybe I needed to believe those things are random. God knows I could never have believed… I guess I could never believe someone I might know was the bad guy. How's that for a blind spot."

"Well, I doubt most people think their normal-seeming father is a sexual predator, Cal."

"Fair enough."

Then she spotted it. The computer.

"Oh, thank God. I really wanted the computer. I have no idea if I'll be able to start it up or get anything off it…"

"My husband could."

"Really?"

"Yeah. He does this kind of stuff for work. He could get everything off the hard drive and put it onto a different computer. I mean, if we need to."

"Well, that would be amazing."

She took a cord out and plugged the computer in, hoping that eventually it would start up.

But then, after all this time, the battery could be completely corroded.

There were little photo albums inside, and she took one out, surprised at what a gut punch the first picture was.

Herself, Sarah, Callie, Amber. Young and carefree, smiling into the intense flash of what was probably a disposable camera.

"I think that was on the trip down to Magic Mountain," said Callie. "Remember that? We didn't go on any rides, we just walked around and shopped at the Roxy store."

"I remember. And I remember the angst, coming back and wanting to get the photos developed, and them telling us we were too late in the day to do one-hour."

"Nothing has ever been so torturous."

She flipped to the next page.

There was a picture of Zach, hanging from his knees on the monkey bars at the elementary school. They'd gone over there one day to play after school. Feeling grown-up and like everything there was so small, because they were high schoolers.

It was so funny how mature they'd all thought they were.

Callie was right about that. A sixteen-year-old didn't have a real idea of their actual age.

They thought they were grown. They thought they knew exactly what they were doing all the time.

But all the kids in these pictures looked so carefree. She scrolled through page after page. Of them eating ice cream sundaes, of the boys half buried in sand on the beach, and the girls wearing prom dresses for fun in a teen store. On the verge of getting kicked out by the sales staff.

Because it wasn't like they were going to buy anything.

She flipped to the next page, and her heart squeezed. It was Dane, giving the camera a scathing look.

She touched the photo. "I loved him so much."

"Zach?" Then she looked down at what Margo was actually looking at. "Oh. Him. I know you did. You do." Callie moved over to where she was standing and looked down at the photograph. "Everything is really messed up. Things have been messed up here for a long time. There are people who are gone who should be here. My dad, because he should have to at least answer for what he did. He should have to face my mom, and Debbie Hartley. He should have to face justice. Sarah, because it has never felt quite the same without her. Your mom. She would've been a good grandma. You deserved that."

Margo felt her throat get tight.

"Yeah." She couldn't think about her mom right now. That was just one of the many painful things that couldn't be fixed.

One thing about losing her mother to cancer, though, was that it hadn't been a shock. And in the end she'd known exactly how it would wind down, and she had never spent a day wondering where her mother was.

She was safe.

Poppy wasn't.

"It's just, we've always got people missing from us. We have. I'm really glad that somehow in the tangled maze of all of this, you've got him."

She tried to smile. "Yeah. I mean, of all the things, it's a little bit of a miracle."

"I would say."

The computer made a noise, and the red light next to the cord went green. She opened up the laptop, and got a logo.

"And of course there's no password," Margo said, as the computer groaned and then booted up. Slowly.

"Wow," Callie said. "It's actually…going."

"Yeah," she said. "That's the thing with old technology. It just keeps on going, even when it should be dead. Unlike my cell phone which I find myself having to replace every eighteen months because the battery is toast."

"Well, the less said about the battery life on a computer this age the better."

"Fair."

She moused around the device, unfamiliar with the layout of the operating system. Unfamiliar with everything on something this old now.

She opened up the internet, and saw that the browser history had been wiped clean.

"I mean, we could maybe forensically find it? I don't know." Callie shrugged. "I'm not sure if that's something that someone must've done manually, and if so if it can be recovered, or if it's just been too long."

"Eighteen years is a long time to hold on to a browser history. Whatever websites she was visiting may not even exist anymore."

"Oh, everything exists on the internet still," Callie said. "Haven't you ever heard of the Wayback Machine? You can go look at all kinds of things people tried to delete. But it's there. In a vault of shame."

"Well, that's good to know."

Callie took another photo album out of the box, and started leafing through it. "She really kept everything. I just wonder… I wonder how different things would have been if she would've still been around. We would've definitely all stayed friends."

Margo didn't agree.

"The thing is," said Margo, "I'm not sure that it's worth being friends with Amber. I think she's a bitch."

"Wow," said Callie. "I mean, say more."

"Oh, she was just being snotty when I was down at the station getting files. But then, maybe she wouldn't be the way she is if we hadn't… It's really hard to say. I think collectively we all kind of went through trauma losing her like that. But you know, you went through a bigger one, because it was actually connected to your dad, and people were shitty to you."

"Yeah. They were. But it is what it is. I don't know how I would've handled it. But you handled it by being a decent human being. Except you know what annoys me? So did Zach. Zach was really cool afterward. And so I guess maybe that can't be the mark of whether or not somebody's a good person."

Margo went back to the computer and opened up a word processing program. She looked at all the most recent files. The last thing that was typed on the computer was the note. She pulled it up.

"Wow."

"What?"

"I just read this letter. In Sarah's case file, but it's… It's chilling. To see it here. On her computer. This goodbye note. 11:03 p.m. It was the last thing she did before they left, probably."

"I've never seen it," said Callie.

"You don't have to."

"No. I want to."

Callie stood there and stared at the screen for a long moment.

I'm sorry. For any pain that I might've caused. We are running away together, because we are in love. We didn't expect for it to happen. We didn't want it to happen like this, but it did. I hope you can all forgive us. Just know that we're happy. Don't come looking for us.

"Fuck," said Callie. "That's… Do you really think she believed that?"

"I don't know. It just sounds… Maybe. Because she was sixteen. And who doesn't want to cast themselves in the center of a dramatic novel, right?"

"I guess. But it's just kind of hideous."

"Agreed."

"My dad, though," she said. "Couldn't she have fun off with somebody... I don't know. I've never been able to understand it."

"I don't think anyone can."

She went to open up some other documents. To look at the file folders. There were some school reports and some other things. And then she saw a folder that said autosave.

She opened it up, and saw a catalog of unlabeled documents that were classified by date.

She opened up the first untitled document.

The potential impact of the EU expansion on the rest of the world—

She closed that document. She opened up the next one.

The hourglass turned for a moment, and then the next document appeared.

March 11th
Dear Mr. Spinner,

I read all your books. I love how brave your characters are, and that they always try to do the right thing even when they're scared. I'm like one of your characters, but I'm not brave. And I'm not like you. I know you wrote your new book about real people, because you wanted to help them. I know he's hurting her. But I don't know what to do. I can't tell anyone.

I thought I would tell you.

Sincerely,
Your Biggest Fan

16

MARGO HAD NO idea what that meant. She had no idea how that document had gotten on this computer.

One thing she knew, it confirmed the connection between Sarah and that note.

But she'd been certain that someone else had been writing about Sarah. How could...

How could it be on Sarah's computer?

She stared at it, trying to grasp exactly what she was seeing. All those letters that she'd seen printed inside the book, right there in front of her.

"Callie," she said. "It's the letter. The letter to Jacob Spinner. It came from this computer."

"What?"

Callie moved over to the computer. "How is that possible?"

"I have no idea. It means... Sarah must've written it? Unless somebody else used this computer."

If Dane had written it, he would've said. Also, it would have been a strange thing for him to use his younger sister's computer when he presumably had his own.

Kerrigan. The younger sister. She might not have had her own computer.

It was possible.

"I need to find out from Dane if their younger sister ever used this computer. If Sarah wrote it, then that means that she knew of somebody else who was being abused. That's a whole other dark pit."

"Yeah. Definitely."

She texted Dane. She knew that he was out diving. And yet again, that icy fear overtook her. Because he might find her.

She wanted to find Poppy.

Not like that.

You saw her.

"Why don't we eat something?" asked Callie.

"I don't know if I can stand it."

She hadn't told Callie yet. That she was sure that she'd seen Poppy. She decided to keep it to herself.

It was one thing to have Dane think that she was losing her mind.

She didn't need a whole host of people thinking that.

So she decided to focus on lunch, and not on what Dane might be doing right now. And not on that letter. For just a moment.

Her phone vibrated, and she picked it up immediately, her heart hammering.

Didn't find anything. And you got my sister's computer to work?

Yes. The letter is on there. Letter to Mr. Spinner.

I'll be there in a half hour.

"Dane says they didn't find anything."

"That's good, right?"

She saw that image of Poppy's golden hair in the woods.

"I don't know. Yes. Yes, because I want to keep hope alive."

"You want to know where she is," said Callie. "You want it to be over. That's okay."

"Is it?"

"Yes. Whatever you think, however you respond to anything during all of this, it's all okay. There's no guidebook to how to handle these things."

"Yeah. I get that."

She thought, absurdly just then, that maybe she should write it.

Dane got there a half hour later, and he hunched over the computer, tension lancing through his body. "This is wild. Just…seeing her computer like this. Well, and the letter."

"Did Kerrigan ever use the computer?"

He nodded. "Yes. I think she did. There was a family computer, but sometimes she didn't like to use it. So, when Sarah was out, she would use Sarah's. Sometimes she'd get in trouble, but she did it anyway. She saved this document on the computer?"

"It was in an autosave file. So, it definitely speaks to somebody who didn't want the document to stay on the computer, but who also didn't know very much about technology."

"Kerrigan was only ten. I feel like that's entirely possible."

"Well, can we call her?"

"Yeah. I guess so. We have to find out if she's the one who wrote the letter."

Dane took his phone out of his pocket, and called his sister, who lived on the East Coast. "Hey, Ker," he said. "I have kind of a weird question to ask you."

There was silence. Margo heard Kerrigan's voice, but not what she said.

"Can I put you on speaker?" Dane asked. "Callie Archer. And

Margo Box. Margo found something," he said, switching the phone over to speaker. "A letter, in a book a couple of weeks ago."

"Didn't her husband just die?"

The voice was harsh over the speaker.

"Yes," said Margo. "He did. But I was already looking into this, and I want to keep going."

"Hi, Margo," said the voice, sounding apologetic. "Sorry. I didn't realize I was on speaker yet."

"It's okay. I'm okay. I found a letter in a book written by Jacob Spinner. In the Little Free Library outside the gated community." There was silence on the other end. "I thought that it might connect to your family. I kept it. We just got Sarah's computer out of storage, and I found the same letter in the documents on the computer."

There was a pause. "Oh."

"I was talking to Dane and he said you used the computer sometimes. I was wondering…did you write the letter?"

There was nothing but silence.

"Kerrigan, if you didn't write it, maybe Sarah did. The letter indicates that the letter writer knew that someone was being abused. If Sarah wrote it, that means maybe someone else was being victimized. We just want to know who wrote it so we can figure out how to proceed."

"Why?"

"I'm investigating your sister's disappearance. It was the letter that brought me back to this and I think it's important."

"Dane," Kerrigan said. "I'm sorry. I'm so sorry."

"Hey," Dane said, taking the phone out of Margo's hand. "Ker, just tell us what happened. You don't need to be upset."

"I should have told you. I should have told someone. I…"

"You wrote the letter," said Margo.

"Yes." She paused. "I did."

Kerrigan started to cry. The sound was jagged, cutting Margo deep.

"I… I never told anybody, because I… She disappeared. I couldn't… I didn't know what to do. I felt guilty. Because I never sent that letter. I never told anybody. She told me not to."

"Who?" asked Dane. "Who asked you not to say something?"

"Sarah did."

The words landed heavy all around. Dane's face was unreadable. Like he was forcing his expression to stay neutral so that he could handle the situation. He looked like he did when he'd come out of the water to tell her that he'd found her husband's body.

"Kerrigan," he said slowly. "I think it might be better if we had this conversation on video."

"I don't know if I can," she said.

"It's been a long time coming."

"I'm scared," she said.

"You don't need to be scared," Dane said. "I'm not going to be angry, I…"

"No, not of you. Zach is dead," she said. "Zach is dead and… What if it's related?"

"Why would it be related?" Margo asked.

"Because Zach knew too. Zach knew what Brian was doing to Sarah."

17

MARGO WAS DIZZY by the time they sat down in front of the computer. Dane called his sister again using a link that they'd established for the call, and the three of them sat there in front of the screen waiting for her to answer.

Callie had her hand resting on Margo's shoulder. Dane was holding on to her hand.

When Kerrigan appeared, her eyes were red. "We didn't think… We didn't think there was any point telling if she didn't want us to."

Margo's brain was racing. Why did her husband have a secret with Kerrigan Hartley? Kerrigan would've been ten years old. On some level, she didn't find it too surprising that Kerrigan had been reading Jacob Spinner books. In her head, Margo had imagined the letter writer had to be older. But the letter writer could also be a very precocious kid, and that had been Kerrigan.

"But you didn't tell the police? Even when questioned?"

"I felt too bad," she said. "I was just so ashamed I…"

"What happened, Ker?" Dane said, his voice soft. "What did you know?"

"I was supposed to walk from the elementary school to the high school after my clarinet practice. But it got out early. I went down to the history room. Zach was standing outside, and everything was dark. There was a piece of paper taped up over the window, but you could see just through it a little bit. We saw them. We saw him...doing things to her."

"You both...watched?"

Kerrigan had been ten. The image made her stomach twist.

"He was shocked. He was in shock. I don't think that he really understood what he was looking at at first. I know I didn't. I didn't even understand what it was."

Her husband had to have known what he'd been looking at. He'd been sixteen, not ten.

Maybe that was unkind. Uncharitable. Sixteen-year-olds were only kids. And that was the problem. All these adults around them who simultaneously treated them like toddlers and adults.

The same kinds of people who would say they were too immature to choose their own movies, to make their own decisions about their sex lives, also thought that Sarah should be responsible for what had happened between herself and a grown man.

It was absurd. All of it.

Zach had *known*.

He had never said anything to her. All those years.

All those years and he had known.

You never knew him.

Maybe he didn't change.

Maybe he just started showing his face.

"We waited for Sarah after, and Zach...he was really angry. He was like... 'What the hell is going on?' And she got really angry and said, 'My little sister is here, I don't want to talk about it.' He said, 'Your little sister saw you...'" She winced. "He said, 'Your little sister saw you sucking his dick. So, maybe you should come clean about it.'"

"*Fuck* him," said Callie, standing up and moving away from the desk. "Fuck Zach."

"He was upset," said Kerrigan, clearly defensive. "And I don't blame him. Unless you were there… Don't judge him. I think actually he felt protective of me. He was mad that I'd seen all that. And I think maybe he didn't realize how confused I was, so he was blunt. Because he figured if I saw it, I'd seen it."

"There was no excuse for him to talk to her that way. To talk like that in front of you." And then it was like all the ferocity drained out of Callie. "I'm sorry. I have a ten-year-old. That shouldn't have happened to you, Kerrigan. None of it should have happened to anybody. And it's my dad's fault."

"It's not your fault," said Kerrigan.

"But someone has to be sorry. My dad's not here. And someone has to be sorry. So if it has to be me, then I guess it has to be me. I'm sorry. I'm sorry that any of you went through that."

"It's okay," Kerrigan said. "I mean… I'm here."

"What else happened?" Dane asked.

"She got really upset, she started crying. She told us that we couldn't say anything. She said it would ruin her life. I wanted to tell. I wanted to tell Dane. But even after we separated from Zach, when we got home, she said… 'You can't tell anybody. You have to promise. Because if you do, he might hurt you. Or he might hurt Mom.' She said that all of her dreams of getting into college, of all the things that she wanted, would be ruined. That if anyone knew, it would destroy her life. And I was scared. So I just said okay. I just didn't say anything. I was such a coward. I wrote that letter, one night when she was out. One night when I knew that she was with *him*. I sat down and I wrote it, and I printed it off. I was in the middle of Jacob's book. I stole it from her room. And I felt so sick about it all. About how unfair life is, and I felt like he understood. I ended up sticking the letter between the pages. I never sent it. I'd forgotten about it. When she disappeared… I didn't know what to say. It wasn't any information the police didn't have. Sarah and Brian Archer were…having sex. And I could never figure out from her if it was something that she wanted."

It wasn't just any book. Not just a book that made her think of Sarah. It had been Sarah's book. Someone from the community might have bought it at the yard sale Sarah's parents had. Left it unread and discarded it years later. But it had ended up there. With Kerrigan's letter.

Margo didn't put a lot of stock in the universe working in mysterious ways, not when the universe had left her feeling so profoundly alone for all these months, but this…

She'd been meant to find this book.

"You know she was sixteen," Dane said, his voice hard.

Kerrigan seemed to curl in on herself. To get younger. "Yes, now I do. But I was ten then, and she seemed like an adult. Okay?"

"Yeah. I'm sorry."

"I know it was stupid. I get that now. I get now that the way that I thought about it was wrong. And I have to live with that. Like I said, it's just I didn't think… I didn't think that there was any new information. And Zach told me that we could get in trouble. For knowing and not telling before. He said we didn't know anything the police didn't know, so we needed to keep it between us."

"My husband said that to you?" This changed everything for her. Zach was capable of keeping secrets. Deep secrets. And had been since high school. He had asked a ten-year-old girl to do the same.

"He wasn't your husband then. He was just a kid." She couldn't tell if Margo's defensiveness was for Zach, really, or for herself. A need to make their choice the only right choice to help minimize her guilt. "I've gone over and over all of this since I heard about Zach's body being found. We were kids.

We did the wrong thing. I *know* we did. But what if... What if that's why Zach is dead?"

"No," said Margo. "You said yourself, you didn't have any information that the police didn't already have. You didn't know anything that they didn't already know. Why would Brian come after Zach?"

That seemed to calm Kerrigan. "I don't know. You're right. You're right. That doesn't make any sense."

"Kerrigan," said Dane. "You've really been holding on to all that this whole time?"

"I forget sometimes. I can convince myself that it was a dream. Or that I got it wrong. I can convince myself that it's actually wishful thinking that I knew something, that I like to think that I could've saved her. If I'd told," she said. "If I'd told, he would've gone to jail. He couldn't have taken her away. I didn't understand that what was happening was a crime. I didn't know that, I didn't... I just thought she would get in trouble. I didn't think that he would."

She could feel regret emanating from Dane. Could feel sorrow from Callie. She had no idea what she felt.

Zach had known. And whatever she'd just said to Kerrigan, she couldn't help but think it felt significant.

But maybe that was, again, her being a writer. Her wanting everything to connect up nicely, when the reality was it rarely ever did.

Reality was messy.

Things felt connected when they weren't.

People always wanted to make a story clean. Clear and concise.

But it was possible there was nothing clean, clear or concise about this.

It was more than possible.

"You need to talk to Mom," said Dane.

Kerrigan looked bleak. "Why?"

And Margo could see, so clearly, the futility of a secret like Kerrigan's. She had known. She hadn't told.

She'd been a child.

Zach had been a child.

The only person truly in the wrong was Brian Archer.

And Kerrigan felt responsible.

Of course she did.

"Never feel more responsible than the perpetrator," she said.

Because it was something she'd heard a police officer tell a parent when they had found the bodies of the victims of the Incline Valley Killer.

And it had stayed with her.

Ultimately, the only person responsible for victimizing someone like that was the person who perpetrated the crime.

Good people could drive themselves crazy regretting it. Asking themselves what they could've done. Asking themselves why they hadn't seen a predator in their midst, when the truth was, it was what predators did. They disguised themselves.

"This whole time that Zach and Poppy have been missing I've been asking myself what I missed. How I could be so foolish. The truth is, when someone has decided to do something that would shock a normal person, it's impossible for you to have guessed it. It's not your fault. You were ten years old. You were shocked by what you saw, and your older sister told you to say nothing. You listened to her. Because of course you did. She was your big sister."

Kerrigan nodded. "I thought she knew what she was doing. I thought she could handle anything. It seems so stupid now that I realize how young she was."

"I need to go," said Callie. "Margo, will you walk me out?"

She had a feeling that this was all in aid of allowing Dane to have a moment alone with Kerrigan. And Margo followed her friend's lead.

She walked out the front door, and suddenly, Callie crumbled. She rested her head against Margo's shoulder, and started to weep. Great, gulping sobs.

Margo wrapped her arms around her and held her steady. Held her until she could speak. Until she could breathe.

"I'm sorry," Callie said. "Because I know everything is worse for you than it is for me right now. I'm sorry. This is just... It's so damned painful. My father was such a creep. And I love him."

Callie looked up at Margo, the helplessness in her expression echoing in Margo.

I love him.

She understood.

She understood that it didn't just go away. That love like this was a curse, not a blessing.

Callie wiped her cheeks. "I miss him. He took us out to ice cream the day before. Like everything was normal. Then he was just gone. And he didn't get to see me get married. He didn't get to meet my kids. And I shouldn't even want him to meet my kids because he is a horrible pervert. But everything is just...so *hard*."

"It's okay to let it be hard," said Margo. "I wish I didn't understand. I do, though. I do."

"I can't believe Kerrigan saw that when she was ten. I'm so... I'm so angry at him, Margo. And he's still my father. I'm on this earth because of him. His DNA. He was... I hate him."

She knew both things were true. That Callie loved her father and hated him. But Margo was familiar with feeling things one hundred percent, even if they were contradictory. She understood.

They stood, silent. Holding each other together.

"Why is life such a mess?" Callie whispered.

"I wish I knew."

Callie wiped at her tears. "Sorry. I just needed to have a breakdown. Today was a lot."

"I know it was. I'm sorry. I really am."

"Well. None of it was your fault."

"I'm the one that dredged it all up," Margo said.

"It feels like it floated to the surface. More than anything."
She pulled a face. "Sorry, bad choice of words"

"It's true. We brought it up with a crane."

Callie looked at her. "Anyone could've grabbed Jacob's book.
You did. Maybe there's something to that."

Margo stood on the steps for a long moment after her friend
left. She had quit thinking that there were signs a long time ago.
That anything meant anything. She looked across the street at
her neighbor's house, and watched as the lights flickered off.

She looked next door, and saw an upstairs light go out. Then
she looked at her watch.

It was after eleven.

She sighed and walked back into the house. Dane was sitting in front of the darkened computer screen.

"Go ahead. Say it."

"Say what?" he asked, looking shell-shocked.

"All the complicated things. The dark things. The horrible
things. Because you're entitled to them. Right now especially,
you're entitled to them. Because this was a lot."

"She was so stupid," he said, putting his hands over his face.
"Why didn't she tell anybody? She saw him... Why didn't she
tell anybody?"

"Why didn't Zach?"

"It wasn't Zach's sister."

"And Zach wasn't ten."

"Are you going let me say the complicated thing, or are you
going to defend my sister?"

"I'm sorry. Go ahead. Say it. All of it."

"She could've stopped it. She could've saved her. This is
going to kill my mother. Just fucking kill her. My dad... Why
would she write a letter to an author? Why would she... Why
didn't she tell us?"

"Why didn't Sarah tell you?"

"*I don't know.* I'm so mad at both of them. And your dead husband."

"Well. There's a lot of reasons to be mad at him."

"He never said anything to you?" he asked.

"You know he didn't. If he would've said something to me, the first thing I would've done is come to you. Well, probably the police first."

"Yeah. I know that. I do. I don't get it. I don't get why…"

"She is right, though. There's no new information there. She and Zach knew. They knew something that we found out eventually. You are right, though. Telling would've stopped them from leaving. That's really tough to swallow."

He breathed out, hard. "What if you knew that there was a trigger point for Zach? And someone had seen it. And they didn't tell."

"I would be angry. But she's your sister. And she was a child."

"Yeah. I know. I'll get over it."

"I'm sorry."

It was her turn to kiss him. Her turn to be there while his world imploded. His hands were rough and ready, and he didn't wait for them to get upstairs.

He had her on the couch, no foreplay, no romantic words. Just desperation. The desperate need to connect with another person.

She understood it.

She felt it.

She clung to his shoulders after, stroked his hair. "I'm really glad that you're here," she whispered.

"Me too."

They went upstairs after, and he went to bed.

She stood in front of the bed for a long moment, wearing her pajamas.

And then she walked back down the hall to her office.

She sat in front of the computer, and started typing.

Zach was already dead when I found out that he knew about Sarah Hartley. That he knew that there was a teacher abusing her. My husband's legacy will always be complicated, because I think he abducted my child. And this adds yet another complication. Another piece to the story that I didn't know.

What did he tell himself? I have no way of knowing.

This thing cast such a shadow over everybody. And the connections. They're everywhere.

It's like there's a big tree, growing at the center of this neighborhood. And the roots spider outward. And you might think that you're looking at a single root, but it has to grow from somewhere. And all the roots all around, seemingly unconnected, all grow back to a source.

You just have to find it.

Maybe that's why I'm sitting up in my office at midnight, when the man I love is asleep in bed. When I should be there taking care of him. Should be there holding him, because everything about today was terrible.

We figured out who wrote the letter to Jacob Spinner. And it feels like it's broken more than it's pieced together.

18

THE PHONE RANG early the next morning, while Dane was getting ready to go out with the dive team again.

It was the sheriff's office.

"We have the coroner's report. For Zach."

"Oh."

She didn't know why it felt shocking or out of the blue. She'd been expecting it. But after last night it was like time didn't feel real. And in last night's conversation they'd been talking about teenage Zach. So for some reason she'd been imagining him then. Cocky and handsome and not dead.

"Preliminary findings are that it's very likely he drowned. There is no other sign of trauma."

"Surprising, since the car went over a bridge." It was a weird thing to say. It was the investigator in her. She was more stable than the wife and mother in her.

"Yes. But we can confirm from that that he was alive when he went into the water."

What a terrible death. She wished she could feel sorry for him. Instead she wondered what he'd thought about. Had his life flashed before his eyes? Had he regretted the way things had gone with them?

Had he thought about Sarah?

And what he'd known.

"Would you like a copy?"

She had a feeling it was a weird thing to offer most family members. But it was about right for her.

"Yes. I would."

"I can have that over to you today if you want."

"Yes."

She hung up. "No surprises. He drowned."

"Were you expecting to hear anything else?" Dane asked.

"I wasn't expecting anything. I forgot that they would do this. I know the process. I just… Of course there had to be an autopsy. Thank you, by the way, for telling me not to look at his body. I really appreciate that."

"Yeah. You should listen to me sometimes. It's almost like I know what I'm talking about."

"I probably listen to you more than I listen to anybody else." She tried to smile. "Of course, my track record for taking advice isn't great." She wrinkled her nose. "So it's possible that it doesn't feel like I listen to you all that often."

He nodded, and the grim heaviness was back. "You know it's okay if you can't dive today. Maybe you should go talk to your mom. Or…maybe you should go visit your sister."

"I'm not leaving you right now. I'm not flying across the country while you're…"

"Living in the same hell I've been in for the last six months?"

"With the addition of your husband's body being found, and what you think was a sighting of your daughter."

"But nobody else thinks that it was a sighting of my daughter," she said. "I'm figuring out how I feel about that."

"What do you mean?"

"Well, I prize your honesty. I wouldn't want you to tell me

something that wasn't true. But I'm also kind of furious at you for not being able to believe me. But maybe this is what I need."

"All I can tell you is what I've been through. I know that the desperate hope eats at you. And that your desire to see something, to find something new, can get so intense that you really would believe that they were right there. In the woods. In the next aisle at the grocery store. I'm actually one of the few people who could understand why that could happen, and why it doesn't mean you're losing your grip on reality. It's existing in that state where somebody that you love is in a place that you can't imagine. They're gone from you. There's no sign of them. There's nobody. There's nothing left but a memory. And your hope."

"Yeah," she said. "I guess that's true. But I haven't seen her. Six months and I haven't seen her. I wish I could have hallucinated her. In a mall. In a department store. On the street. But I never did. Seeing her would've been a balm for my soul. But I never did."

"It might have something to do with finding Zach."

"Yeah. It might. But why not the day that it happened? I was completely messed up that day."

"I don't know. I don't know why the strongest hallucination I had of my sister was four years after she disappeared. Maybe it's because it was unbearable. What was impossible became so horrendously possible that I just couldn't deal with it anymore. I had to see her. I had to make a picture of her. I had to... I don't know if it makes any sense. But maybe there is no making sense of this."

"That's what I'm afraid of. That everything I know, every rule to everything, just doesn't apply here. Doesn't count. How can you rationalize any of this?"

"You can't. Because nothing about it is rational or reasonable."

"I don't like it."

"I know."

"I'm serious, though. You have your own stuff to deal with, you don't need to fling yourself exhaustively at mine."

"I was under the impression that was kind of the point of a relationship."

"Yeah. I realize that what Kerrigan told you last night changes things. That it makes things really difficult. I'm so sorry."

"It's always been difficult. I want to help you. Because yes, that changes the way that I feel about some things, but it doesn't change what happened. It doesn't bring me any closer to finding Sarah than I was. Just like diving in the river didn't bring us any closer. It brought you Zach. And I'm glad for that. But that means the urgency is on your situation. Not mine."

"Okay. If you want to go… Thank you. Just thank you."

"I'd do anything for you. You know that."

"I do. It's very strange. And amazing."

Callie texted her about a half hour after Dane left.

Coming over with mom, is that okay? She wants to talk about last night.

Sure.

Margo ran upstairs and changed quickly, because she didn't exactly want to meet Gail in her bathrobe. And then, because she was dressed, she went out to the curb to get her mail. She happened to be walking down the driveway at the same time as Julie.

"Good morning," Julie said.

She was wearing pink scrubs, cheery like the rest of her. "Morning," she said.

"How've you been?"

It was like *Groundhog Day*. How've you been. Just bad. Always bad.

"I'm okay," she lied.

"I'm glad you aren't by yourself," she said.

Nosy. But then, she supposed that was theoretically a feature of living in a neighborhood like this. You knew what your neighbors were up to. You knew their business.

You didn't know what was going on in your own house.

It was such a tired refrain, and it was one that ran through her head all the time. Because try as she might, she couldn't stop blaming herself.

All these bright cheery streets hiding shadows inside the houses. It was just such a desperate cliché. But it was her reality. So it did no good to complain about it being a cliché. It was what it was.

"See you later," said Julie.

"Yeah. See you."

She went back inside and went up to her office. Callie texted her and gave a thirty-minute ETA. She went to her computer and she started to type.

Connecting all the things that'd happened in the past few days.

I'm a writer. So I'm always looking for a story. I used to drive my husband nuts speculating on strangers we passed on the street. *She's in a hurry. Maybe she's meeting a lover?*

I like to construct stories out of pieces of everyday life.

My husband's take would be: maybe she's late for a doctor appointment. He was never curious about people the way I was.

But that doesn't mean he didn't tell himself stories. I thought I knew what they were. When you're married to someone, you know them. Or you think you do.

Gail Archer went to bed with Brian Archer every night, not knowing he was sexually abusing a student.

I thought I knew my husband. I thought I recognized when he changed.

But that was the story. That I married this man who was easygoing and fun. That I married a man who didn't think deeply about things, but who saved me from drowning in my own thoughts.

It never occurred to me that maybe he wasn't uninterested in my deep thoughts on strangers on the streets. It never occurred to me that maybe he wasn't ambivalent to my curiosity, but afraid of it.

Afraid I might look at him one day and ask myself what he was really thinking.

I made him into the man I needed. Maybe his facade was never all that convincing. I told myself the story I wanted to believe in.

Maybe he was never that man.

Just like my neighborhood was never safe.

Brian Archer was a predator living in this suburban paradise of manicured lawns and well-kept hedges.

My husband was a man on the brink. A man who kidnapped his daughter to exit his marriage.

He was always closer to Brian Archer than I realized. The keeper of a terrible secret that allowed Brian to get away with taking Sarah away.

There were signs that Zach wasn't who I thought he was. But I couldn't guess what they were pointing to because I was telling myself the wrong story. That my husband was a good man who had done some bad things. That what he'd done was because of me.

It never occurred to me that he might have been this man all along. The one who would take his daughter to hurt his wife.

The one who hid a monster's secrets.

I'm no different than Gail Archer. I went to bed next to a man who was capable of things I couldn't imagine. And I didn't realize, because all I saw was my husband.

She stared at that and felt a growing anger burning in her chest.

She had been telling herself a story.

She wasn't smarter or more insightful than anyone around her. She was the same sort of sad person who turned the world into the most comfortable version for herself.

She growled in frustration and pushed herself away from the desk, heading downstairs and going into the kitchen. She stared at the fridge. She had enough things. To offer guests. It was just that she had forgotten how to be a hostess. She had forgotten a whole lot of things. But she should be prepared to offer Gail something to eat.

Everything felt complicated. So much more complicated than she would like. Her personal relationships right now were a mess.

She was still grappling with everything that Kerrigan had told them. Every time she felt like she found a foothold in this current situation, something came along to make her feel like she was unmoored.

She reached into the fridge and started getting out blocks of cheese.

People had brought cheese. It was kind of a strange thing, but she was appreciative of it. Because a lot of it was gourmet, and it was pretty nice to have.

And she could put out a tray, or something.

We're discussing your long-lost sexually predatory husband, and the fact that somebody witnessed him engaging in sexual activities with a minor. Have some Brie.

What was the point of any of it, really? She had wondered that. On long, sleepless nights with her husband breathing easily beside her.

Why did humans pretend to be civilized? Why did they have these rituals? When the truth was, at their very core, people were capable of such horrendous things. And even when they were good people. Reasonable people. People who conformed in the ways that they were supposed to, in the dark of night, in the privacy of their own heads and hearts, they were something else entirely.

She began to assemble the cheese tray.

The truth was, she had slept with her husband, and thought about Dane.

The truth was, she'd plastered a smile on her face and gotten her daughter ready for school, and thought about the last moments of a young woman's life who had thought that she was saving a stranded hitchhiker on the side of the road, but was in fact encountering a serial killer.

She'd thought about violent deaths and sexual assault. Over dinner.

She'd fantasized another man's hands on her body in the darkness while her husband gripped her hips.

She was a good citizen. A productive one. And even she had a dirty, secret soul.

And she could still arrange a glorious cheese platter.

With a missing child. A dead husband.

Possible hallucinations.

She decided to put the crackers in a spiral pattern.

She was pretty satisfied with that. She got a bottle of wine out of the cupboard. It was untouched, because she didn't drink wine.

What a weird, arbitrary thing she'd chosen to not do. People were just so very strange.

She put the platter out on the table, and went to go answer the door.

Callie was there with her mother, and Jaden was behind them.

"I had to go get them from school," Callie said apologetically. "He's in a mood. The aide was having trouble with him. And mostly, I'm just not interested in having him somewhere where people act like he's dangerous when he isn't." She was smiling, but Margo could feel her friend's stress radiating off her.

"Hi, Jaden," said Margo. "How are you?"

He grinned widely and gave her two thumbs up. "Great."

Then he reached into his pocket and pulled out his phone.

She knew that Callie got a lot of crap for having a kid on his phone all the time. Those people had no idea how grateful they should be that Callie had Jaden on his phone sometimes. Because it allowed her to get her errands done, it kept him engaged, and helped him block out some of the sensory things going on around him. They were the same people that would judge her if he had a tantrum.

People really were something else.

"Jaden?" Callie asked. "Can you sit in the living room?"

"Yup," he said, nodding, and not looking up from his phone.

"You can turn the TV on," said Margo, as Jaden walked past them, and then Margo turned her focus to Gail. "Hi, Gail. Come on in."

They walked into the dining room, and Margo gestured to the wine and cheese. "Wine?"

"Yes, please," said Callie.

"I'll take some," said Gail. "Thank you."

She poured them some wine in glasses and sat down at the table. She realized that looked a little strange that she didn't have a drink. But she didn't need anything.

"Callie tells me that you're seeing Dane Hartley," said Gail.

As openings went, she hadn't quite expected that one.

"Yes," she said. "I am. We got close on that case. Reconnected, I mean. And then with everything he's done to help with Zach and Poppy..."

"You don't have to justify anything to me. I understand."

Gail looked at her, her eyes level, and deeply knowing.

"I imagine you must."

"Do you know why I've been single all this time, Margo?"

She shook her head, unsure where was going.

Gail took a drink of the wine. "I've been single for so long not because I miss my husband, or because I'm mourning him in any fashion. It's because I don't know what to do with all the guilt. I was part of the cover for a sexual predator. He had a normal house. A normal life. A normal family. I was part of that. Part of protecting him."

"You didn't enable him on purpose," said Callie.

"It doesn't matter. How can you ever trust yourself to choose again? No. I feel very strongly that much of the grief that Brian caused is on my head as well. It tortures you. What you think you should've seen. I'm glad that you're with Dane Hartley. Because I'm glad that you're not stuck."

"Mom," said Callie. "The only people that blame you are the kind of people who don't know how to blame men for their own actions. You haven't done anything wrong." Callie looked apologetically at Margo. "It just all opens old wounds up, you know? And the whole thing with Kerrigan really has."

"Yes. I am… I'm very sorry for her. I feel like I should call her. She was ten years old, she never should've seen anything like that. She never should have… I'm afraid," said Gail. "Always. That someday we're going to unearth more of what he's done."

"If he changed his identity, and he must have," said Callie, "it's entirely possible he's falsified information. Got another teaching job. That he's…just victimizing people over and over again."

"I just want to walk back through the days before the disappearance," said Margo. "Because it turns out a couple months before my husband, Zach, and Kerrigan Hartley were aware of what was going on. I can't ask Zach what he did in response. We know for certain that Kerrigan did nothing. But I don't know if you can remember… If you can remember any change in Brian's behavior in those two months beforehand. Because I have wondered…if maybe Zach put pressure on him. On them. I have wondered if maybe this is a catalyst that we didn't know about. The thing that made them decide to leave. I found the note about their leaving on Sarah's computer. That means that she typed it. He didn't do it on her behalf. Now, he might have coerced or forced her into it, but that it came from her computer I think is an interesting thing."

"I don't know," said Gail. "That's the terrifying thing. And that, I think, is the most difficult thing to accept about this sort of thing. If you are married to a sociopath, then you can't tell when he's done something that a normal person would feel guilty about, because he doesn't feel guilty. He doesn't feel worried. He thinks he's smarter than everybody, he thinks that he, with his lack of guilt and remorse, has somehow hacked the human condition. Everything that I've read suggests to me that the man I married was a narcissist. That was how he got it past me. For all I know, there were many other girls like Sarah. So many. You know me. I was a teacher too, I just wanted to protect children. I would never have wanted them to be hurt. It kills me. Sarah was in my fourth grade class. I could never blame her, because I knew her. Not just as Callie's friend. As a child that I used to teach."

It gave Margo goose bumps.

He doesn't feel guilty...

She didn't think Zach was a sociopath. She didn't think he'd faked his concern or love for Poppy. She just couldn't.

But she knew less now than she ever had, and she could not escape that feeling.

Poor Kerrigan's revelation hadn't told them anything new about Brian and Sarah.

It had told her something new about Zach.

It had shaken everything.

She cleared her throat. "You think Brian was a sociopath?"

She nodded definitively. "If not that, a narcissist. I think that's one reason he enjoyed pursuing relationships with a young girl like Sarah, and it's one reason I believe there were more. I can't imagine that there weren't. I think it was a pattern."

"Right. That would make sense."

Gail looked at her, considering. "I'm actually more concerned about you, Margo. How are you?"

"I'm doing okay."

"I can't tell you how much I wish… I wish this could be over for you. You don't really need to concern yourself with me like you have been. Worry about yourself."

"I don't want to worry about myself. It's just driving me… insane." She laughed. "I guess that's overstating it."

She hadn't told Callie this yet, and she thought maybe it was strange to admit it with Gail there. But…the poor woman was already opening a vein talking to her about any of this. So why not?

"I thought I saw Poppy. The other day. In the woods. In her rainbow tights. And it was so real. It was so vivid. I made Dane pull over and I got out of the car and I ran after her."

Jaden came in and started to wander aimlessly in the dining area. Back and forth.

"You want some cheese?" Callie asked. That she turned her focus to Margo and frowned. "When was that?"

"A couple of days ago. We were driving back from the storage unit."

"The storage unit? I saw you right after that."

"I know. But I'm still dealing with what it means. With how I feel about it. Because it felt so real, and Dane was so convinced I was making it up."

"It's not making it up," said Callie, looking down. "I used to think that random men walking by were my dad. I think it's just hoping. Wishing."

"Yeah. Well. Like I said. It's literally making me crazy. If I can think I see her standing in the middle of the woods…"

"Poppy's in the woods," said Jaden.

Margo looked up at Jaden, who was looking just to the left of her.

"What did you say, Jaden?" Margo asked.

"Poppy's in the woods," he said.

"That's what Margo was saying she thought," said Callie. "It doesn't mean that she's there, buddy. I'm sorry."

Jaden shook his head back and forth five or six times. "No. Poppy's in the woods."

"Jaden," said Callie. "She isn't. She's missing."

"No," he said. "Poppy's in the woods."

His persistence and irritation were growing. And Margo felt an answering hysteria bubbling up inside of her.

She knew Jaden. She knew that it was easy for him to take pieces of a conversation and stitch them together, to get the wrong idea about what people were saying and latch on to something that wasn't actually true or relevant.

But there was something about the persistence. Something about his tone. It made her feel like he wasn't simply repeating information back, but that he was telling them something.

"Jaden," said Margo. "Did you see Poppy in the woods?"

"Yes," he said. "When we go on the school bus."

"Who got on the school bus?"

"We did," he said, pointing at himself.

"He means himself," said Callie. "He gets pronouns and stuff mixed up. When was that, Jaden?" Callie asked.

"Couple days ago," he said.

"Can you remember which day?"

"April 29. 7:05 a.m. When we get on the bus."

Margo knew that conversations with Jaden were often circular, and that Callie got frustrated with them. But she also knew that Callie listened to her son. His verbal expression was limited, but he was smart. He often appeared like he didn't understand or perceive what was going on around him, but they all knew that wasn't true.

"What else you remember?" Margo asked.

"Poppy's in the woods."

"What was she wearing, what does she look like? What was she doing?"

Jaden put his hands over his ears. "Why are you talking so fast?"

She took a deep breath. "I'm sorry, Jaden. But it's just important. It's important."

"Mom," said Callie, "would you be okay taking Jaden back to the house for a second?"

Gail nodded. "Of course."

Jaden was agitated now, pacing a bit more, and flicking his hand at the wrist. "Jaden," said Margo. "Did you see her?"

He nodded. "Poppy's in the woods."

"Thank you," said Margo, her heart pounding wildly. Gail put Jaden's coat back on him, and walked him out of the house.

"I just don't want you to get... He isn't meaning to make anything up. But he heard you say that, and I just think maybe that's where it's coming from. I feel like if he'd actually seen her he would've said something to me. You know he loves her. She was his little friend. And I think he misses her. And I actually feel like that was just him being excited that you thought you saw her in the woods."

"Why did he have a date and time?"

"I don't know. Something else could've happened on that day. But it's not always a straight narrative from him. He doesn't mean to make anything up, but sometimes everything just gets lost in verbal communication. He might've been thinking about her that day especially. It's really impossible to know. I'm sorry. I just... I feel like that probably got your hopes up more than it should."

"I thought I saw her too. When I say that I thought I saw her, I mean it felt real. It felt concrete. It didn't feel like something that I was making up, Callie. And I get why Dane thinks it was. I even get why you do. But I really do think that I saw her."

"I know. I feel like you probably need to feel that. I feel like you probably need to think it. I'm just really worried about you. You went from nothing, so much nothing, to Zach's body. And now Dane is in your life, and I'm so glad that he is, but it's a lot of changes, Margo. And maybe on some level you feel guilty. Maybe that's why you think you saw her. Because you're…having a life. While you don't know where your kid is. I know you. You have one of the strongest minds of anybody that I know."

"So why would you think it would betray me like that?"

"Because you're so smart. Because your mind is so strong. It's like Jaden. He has all those details because the way that he thinks is concrete and clear. But it expresses itself in different ways, and he does get twisted around himself sometimes. That doesn't make you less. It doesn't make you crazy. It just makes you a mom who really loves her kid, who is trying to wrap her head around what the hell is going on. And how you can be with Dane, and miss Poppy, and maybe even miss a piece of Zach."

"I don't miss him. If he wasn't dead I would do it myself."

That was how she felt today. It was less definitive other days.

"I know. I know. Just… I don't ever want to tell my son that I don't believe him, just like I don't want to tell you I don't believe you. It isn't that. It's as complicated as believing that whatever your brain is doing right now is to help you live. To help you function. To help you protect yourself, it gave you that moment. Maybe it's a sign. To keep hoping."

When Dane came home that night, she didn't mention what'd happened with Jaden.

She didn't want anyone else to tell her it probably didn't mean anything.

"We got called out for a job," said Dane over take-out Chinese food.

"Where?"

"We have to go to Little Rock. I'm hoping it won't be a super-long excursion, and if it goes more than a couple of days I think they're going to have to get along without me."

Of course the dive today had turned up nothing.

There were no new clues. There was nothing.

"Yeah. That's fine. Listen, don't worry about me. She was missing for six months, and we didn't get any leads, we didn't get any movement. I highly doubt that's going to change. No matter how much you dive. She isn't there. You would've found something."

And that only made the fire in her chest burn all the hotter. He didn't find Poppy because she wasn't in the river. He wasn't going to find her there. Maybe Callie was right. Maybe the sighting was a sign. A sign that she was still alive. Being kept safe by someone.

Unless he'd trafficked her.

That was a horror that wasn't fresh, unfortunately. She'd had the thought before.

It was one she didn't let herself turn over too often, or for all that long. There were certain things that were too horrible to contemplate. The idea that her husband might've sold their child was one of them.

She lay there that night and listened to Dane breathing. She was not happy at the idea that she was going to be alone in the house again.

His breathing, his presence, it kept her from hearing her daughter crying.

She didn't want him to know that. She didn't especially want to acknowledge that in her own head.

She had gotten used to him. And maybe Callie was right. Part of her felt guilty for the little bit of happiness that he brought her.

But when he was gone, she would be able to work obsessively. And she did like that.

Her feelings for him forced balance. And she didn't feel particularly balanced at the moment.

She couldn't sleep. So she went back to her computer.

She stared at the pages that she wrote earlier.

Poppy's in the woods.
Poppy's in the woods.

Those were the only words that she'd typed.

19

DANE HAD AN early flight, and he drove himself to the airport in spite of Margo's protestations.

Much of the team had started driving the day before, but a few of the team members would be joining them by air.

She had a feeling Dane had opted to go that way so that he could spend more time with her. Which was overly nice of him.

Or maybe he just cares for you.

She was about to head to bed when she heard crying. She didn't think she heard it anymore. It came from inside her. Maybe it had been her crying all along.

She spent the whole day in her office. Writing, reading files. Sitting in the implications of the night before. Until she looked up and saw that it was dark.

Restless, she decided to take herself out for a walk. Only a couple of houses still had lights on by then.

Two houses down, she saw a light flicker off.

And then her neighbor Julie's lights went off a moment later. And the whole neighborhood was dark, except for the streetlights.

Margo didn't walk toward the gate—she walked back deeper into the neighborhood.

It was so quiet. And it should feel restful, not ominous.

But she couldn't let go of the vague disquiet that settled over her shoulders like a cloak.

How could she ever really feel safe in this neighborhood again?

How could she ever feel safe anywhere?

Gail Archer's words echoed inside of her.

How could she ever trust someone again?

Well. She knew Dane. Had known him for a long time. She did trust him. Trusted him to be there for her. To look out for her.

Why do you trust that?

Maybe because she'd loved him for so much longer than any of this had been going on.

Maybe because she loved him before her illusions about humanity had been shattered with the disappearance of Brian and Sarah.

Maybe because he was part of a time when she'd been hopeful.

And maybe it was naive. To believe that in the middle of all this she could find somebody.

Maybe.

But one thing she remembered, clear and deep from her father's eulogy at her mother's funeral, was that he had wished for more time. More years.

They had married young, and had kids young. She knew that her parents had had struggles. That everything hadn't been smooth and easy. But they'd loved each other, and neither of them had been a narcissist. That was important, she was beginning to understand.

They had wanted more time.

So perhaps the best thing for her and Dane to do was to take the time presented to them.

She blew out a breath, and could see it in the cold night air.

Obsessing about Dane was maybe better than turning over endless thoughts and worries about Poppy.

The worrying didn't fix anything.

The worrying didn't bring her any closer to finding out the truth.

Looking does.

She turned and walked quickly back toward her house. She opened up the garage, and got into her car.

The electric engine whirred to life almost silently, and she backed it out of the driveway, and headed out of the gated community.

She paused and entered the code, and the gate swung open and released her into the wild.

Jaden's school bus would turn left.

It would take her along the same road that she and Dane had been on when they'd been coming back from the storage unit.

The same stretch of woods.

He wouldn't know that. He wouldn't know to say that. To make it up.

She drove along the edge of the dark woods.

There was nothing. She couldn't see a damn thing.

She parked her car on the side of the road, and reached into the glove box, taking out a flashlight.

Dane would be pissed. She pushed the button and turned her car off.

Dane wasn't here.

She respected that he had other things to take care of. But she had things to take care of too. If it was in her power to answer some of her own questions, she was going to damn well do it. She wasn't waiting for anyone or anything.

After she shut the car off, the headlights went off, and it was dark. Fully dark.

There were no streetlights out here.

There was nothing.

She heard the sound of tires on asphalt beginning to approach, and she stepped into the trees without turning on the flashlight.

She didn't want anyone to stop, didn't want anyone to think she was a distressed motorist.

Headlights became visible, drew closer, and passed by.

She let out a breath and flicked the flashlight on.

It illuminated the trees around her, catching on pine boughs that were right in front of her face that she hadn't realized were there.

It was so dark. Not even the flashlight beam made it easy to see more than a few steps in front of her.

The thick brush around her made it nearly impossible.

But she kept going.

What do you expect to find?

She had no idea what she expected. No idea in hell.

Maybe she expected nothing. But if she was hallucinating the presence of her daughter, why couldn't she do it again?

This would be the perfect time. The ideal conditions. She was desperate.

Desperate for a glimpse of her.

And it was dark. Everything was seen in flashes and snatches, so why not Poppy?

Why not?

But no matter how much she tried to will her into being, she couldn't find her. Couldn't see her.

She found that oddly comforting. Because if she couldn't simply manifest Poppy out of thin air now, why would she have been able to do it then?

She didn't believe that it was guilt over enjoying sex with Dane.

Maybe panic over the reality of Zach's death.

Of realizing fully that he *wasn't* out there taking care of Poppy.

She should be able to see Poppy whenever she felt like it if she was manifesting her. Dammit.

That was what made sense to her.

If it was a hallucination, then that hallucination should be on tap, right?

Dane would probably tell her that wasn't how this works. But she would tell him that he wasn't an expert anyway.

He was a lot of things. He was wonderful.

But he wasn't an expert on the kind of intuition that drove her now.

Or maybe even the kind of desperation. It didn't matter what it was. It only mattered that it was strong enough to have her out in the middle of the woods in the dark, desperately clutching a flashlight and hoping that all of the predators in the area were well fed.

Because God help her if not.

The only sound was her boots on the soft ground, muffled and precarious, because every so often a vine would catch her toe, or she'd slip on a slick fern leaf.

She stopped for a moment. And listened.

She could hear trees groaning, settling. The slight whisper as wind rustled the needles.

And very little else.

There was nothing out here. She wasn't out here.

Poppy's in the woods.

There was nothing out here.

She let out her breath, long and slow.

It was so quiet.

But there was no peace in it.

Everything was quiet. Everything in her life was about absence.

She would give anything for presence.

Even a bear.

Something. Something to fight at least.

It wasn't fair. She didn't even have a villain.

Her villain was dead.

And she had nothing. No insight.

She was reaching in the dark. All the time.

This was the entirety of the past six months made literal around her.

There was nothing. No matter how much she wanted there to be.

When she walked out of the woods, she was more certain than ever. She had seen her daughter that day.

There was no other explanation.

20

MARGO SPENT EACH one of the three days Dane was away in the woods. Looking. Listening. Hoping.

It was all she had. It was the only lead, the only indication that Poppy was alive and that she was in the area.

It was one thing to write herself off. But Jaden's words were an echo inside of her.

Dane was frustrated when he got home.

They had met with opposition from local law enforcement, who were confident they'd done everything they possibly could. And when his dive team had located the vehicle, they had kicked them all out of the area and cordoned it off. Done the recovery themselves.

"We don't care who recovers the body," said Dane. "But when law enforcement has been negligent in their search, it gets damned frustrating when they act like we're hurting them instead of helping them. And that's because they know they made mistakes. They didn't listen to the wife. She said her husband might've gotten confused while he was driving on his route, she said she was afraid he was in the river. Ten years. Ten years and nobody looked."

"That's terrible," she said, putting food down in front of him. Food that she had made.

Well. She had boiled the pasta water and heated up some meatballs. And heated a jar of sauce with it. That was as much cooking as she did. Dane seemed happy enough with it, though.

"Anyway, the rest of the team is driving back, and we can resume searching the last part of the river."

"You aren't going to find anything."

"I hope not."

She'd searched the woods. She'd tried to make her daughter appear. He was back. They had time. She could tell him now.

"Jaden thinks that he saw Poppy."

"Do I know Jaden?"

"Callie's son."

"How old is he?"

"He's nine. But…not fluidly verbal. He's adamant though. He gets like that. He repeats things over and over again. He repeated that he saw her."

"And does Callie think that means something?" He asked it very carefully.

"No. She thinks that he heard me, and was echoing me, because Poppy was his friend, and he misses her. And that could be, Dane. But I just don't think so. I went out in the woods last night, and I just stood there. And if I could've made her come out of the air, then I would have. If I could've manifested her right then, I would have. I wanted to see her. If that was happening, in my head, in my body, then it would've happened then."

He started to speak, but she interrupted.

"Don't tell me that's not how it works. I went through all of that in my head last night. That you would say exactly that, but you don't know how hallucinations work. Or how a mother's intuition works."

He shook his head. "Margo. I think that you are amazing.

The smartest woman I know. And a fierce fighter for your girl. There are a lot of mothers missing their kids."

And they didn't magically find them just because they wanted to. She heard that. Heard the underlying truth of it in his voice. She got it.

She had to believe she was different. She realized that right then.

She'd gone through this incredible slump, of accepting—kind of—that she was the same as everybody else. That she didn't have magic insight. That she wasn't going to solve this just because she had solved something else. But she couldn't go on that way. She had to figure out how to change. To go forward.

Until she brought Poppy back from the void.

That dark, empty space of nowhere. The place she couldn't picture her in. The place she couldn't imagine.

The not knowing. The nothing.

She had to bring her back from there.

She had to.

And maybe it would be…his way. Or the way that he believed it was likely to end. She understood that he thought that. It was what he saw every day.

But he'd told her to keep believing, so she was going to.

"I'm torn," he said. "Because what I want more than anything is to tell you that everything is going to be fine. What I want is to fix it. Dammit, I want to fix it. But I also want to spare you."

"You realize that I have been through every dark possibility. You realize that if my daughter is dead, it doesn't matter whether I thought it now, all along, or whether I *hoped*. If she's dead, everything crumbles. If she's dead, it's not going to hurt any worse if I was realistic or fantastical about it."

He nodded slowly. "That I do understand. I've watched a lot of mothers get that news. I've given it."

"It's the worst thing," she said.

She'd been there too. She'd watched other mothers be told their children were never coming home.

"Yeah."

"Thank you," she said. "For doing the horrible, practical thing of searching for something you don't want to find. Because I really need you to do that. I do. As much as I need to believe you won't find anything, I also need you to look."

"I get it."

They were silent for a moment.

"Is there going to be a funeral for Zach?"

"My mother-in-law's going to have to handle that. And I think right now... Who knows what to say about him? I think right now, while we look for Poppy, there's just no way anyone can deal with it. At least that's what I assume. I'm not really speaking to her. I assume this has been really tough. But I can't handle her sorrow... Not combined with mine."

"Closure. That's what everybody needs."

"Yes. It's tough when you're afraid of it, though. Yeah. I know it's what we need."

"One last stretch of river to cover tomorrow."

And what he didn't say was that not finding her didn't give a definitive answer. She knew that. Of course she did. Because the possibility of her simply being washed out to sea existed.

But they would know for sure she wasn't in the river. They would know that.

"Dane, I... I think we need to be focusing on the woods."

"I know what you think you saw..."

"I saw it. Jaden saw it. That's not just me."

"I hear you."

She nodded. "I've been in the woods every day. Just listening. Looking. Covering all the ground I can. I can't see anything. I can't find anything..." She stopped. "Do you know anyone with dogs? I mean, I might be able to get the police to agree to bring out a K-9 unit, but I kind of doubt it given they've already been to the woods."

"I can make a call, yeah. But they may not be able to come out today."

"That's okay. We can do it another day but...we should do it. If we're going to look, we need to look."

He nodded and looked at his phone for a second, then lifted it to his ear. "Hi, Ryan? This is Dane Hartley." He looked at her. "Yeah, been a while. Hey, I was wondering if you had a team in proximity to Portland." There was a pause. "Okay, great, I have a hunch and I can't bring police in on it yet—they won't come on what little we have." He laughed. "Just wanting to be honest with you, the hard evidence isn't there." He smiled. "Yeah, you're right, that's why we do what we do. Because we can work around all that. Great. Yeah, I'll give him a call." Another response she couldn't hear. "I will. Bye."

He hung up. "He says there's a team with three dogs in the area, and I can call and get their availability."

"Who was that?"

"A guy we've worked with before. They have a network of dogs, mainly cadaver dogs, but they can follow a specific scent, and they help out with the fresher missing persons cases and often get involved before the law will, or will follow more tenuous leads."

"Thank you," she said.

Cadaver dogs.

That chilled her.

But she had to look. She knew they had to look.

He made his call and turned to her. "They can come tomorrow. We have one last stretch of river past the car that we need to dive. Then tomorrow, we'll search the woods."

21

DANE RETURNED FROM the dive with nothing to report, and it was interesting to feel like that chapter of things was closed.

There had been nothing else. Zach's car had been there, Zach's body.

They had gone to the bridge and done some investigating. There were no tire marks but there was damage to the railing. They'd pulled info off the car's black box and they were able to determine that he was traveling on the bridge at eighty miles per hour, and that there were two points of impact. The investigators assumed it was first with the bridge as it went up and over and rail, and then the water.

It seemed like a case of reckless driving.

If he'd done it on purpose there were other, easier ways of getting a car into the river.

Daniels had told her, with care, that going into the river intentionally would make the most sense if Poppy had been present. A father might not be able to kill his daughter with his own hands, but driving a car into the river, faking an accident, that was something law enforcement had certainly seen before.

But the fact remained: it would be easier to drive off an embankment than to try to get the right angle and velocity to get over the bridge. It was an accident that would have required a specific rate of speed, specific road conditions.

Humans were never so lucky as to have something like that go their way. They were only unlucky enough to have it all come together in a perfect, disastrous storm.

But they couldn't find Poppy. The things that he had taken from the house that same night were in the car, which was evidence that she might've been there.

But not proof.

There wasn't proof.

That night she had to go into Poppy's room and find something for the dogs to scent.

She stood there in the middle of the perfectly preserved space.

Like Sarah's room for so many years. Left just as it was in case she came back.

Would she still be standing in this perfectly preserved museum of her daughter's childhood six years from now? Ten years from now? Eighteen?

The room of a five-year-old, never changing as she grew older.

The ache in her throat nearly overwhelmed her.

She walked to the bed and looked at her toys. The ones she'd slept with every night. She picked up a white horse and fought the urge to hold it close to her chest.

She needed it to smell like Poppy.

She had to hope it still did.

The idea that her daughter might have already been gone for too long made her ache down to her bones.

When she got up the next morning to get ready to go into the woods, she was resolved. There was a pit in her stomach that wouldn't go away.

And there was no insightful running monologue in her head. No way that she could figure out how to write about this.

This feeling like she was desperately searching for answers she wasn't sure she wanted. Doing something that might end in devastation, but knowing she needed to do it anyway.

It was the strangest thing.

This experience of being driven to turn over rocks knowing that there might be ugly things underneath.

Maybe it was why she resented her beautiful neighborhood so much right now.

Because it was all a lie.

They were all rocks, all those houses. With ugly things underneath.

She could remember being a child and her dad telling her that if she was going to turn rocks over she needed to do it with her foot, so that if there was a scorpion underneath her shoe would protect her. If she did it with her hands, she was going to get stung.

There was no avoiding being stung when you were turning over rocks and there was the possibility that you might find your daughter's body.

There was no protection.

She felt bare and raw as she zipped up her coat and put her boots on. She got into the car with Dane and they began to drive toward the woods, where they were meeting a man named Michael Clark, and his associates, and their dogs.

When they got there, there were already three trucks pulled up to the edge of the trees.

They got out of the car and Margo introduced herself to Michael, and to his partners, Joel and Shelby. All three of them had dogs on short leashes.

"You brought something of hers with you?"

"Yes," she said.

She took one of her daughter's precious stuffed animals out of the truck, and gave it to Michael.

The dogs were given the scent.

"I'm going to keep it with me," he said. "In case we need it again."

She watched as the white pony disappeared into his camouflage backpack, and she ridiculously wanted to snatch it back.

She didn't want her daughter's toys reduced to evidence.

She didn't want her daughter's toys reduced to memory.

Right now, that was all she had, and if they didn't find anything, it would be all she ever had.

That wasn't acceptable. So here they were.

"We don't usually have family members with us on the search," said Michael.

"Margo wants to be here," said Dane.

"You sure?" Michael asked. "Because there's no telling what we're going to find."

"I get that," she said. "I do. But I just had this feeling. I believe that she was here. I feel like I saw her. And I've been out here every day for the last four days. And I just… I feel like this matters. I feel like I need to be here. I lost faith in so much. Basically in everything. But this… This feels right."

"If you really want to, we're happy to have you. Happy to have you too, Dane. Ryan has told us a lot about you."

"Well, he found the body, I found the car. It was a good group effort."

Margo made a note to ask about that later, but she didn't care about it right now. Later, though, when she needed a distraction for her brain, she would want the story.

"We're gonna go ahead of you. We'll let the dogs go do their thing. If you want to follow behind, or you think that we missed something, feel free to contact us on the radios." He handed one to Dane. "The dogs are trained. They know what they're looking for. They're good scent hounds."

"And…cadaver dogs, right?" Margo asked.

"Tallulah is," he said, scratching his bloodhound behind the ear. "The others aren't trained for that specifically, but in a search like this it's always good to have a cadaver dog. She's highly attuned to places where remains were in the past. She knows the difference between human and animal."

She nodded. It was good to have Tallulah. It was good to be sure. Just like searching the river. But she didn't think she had seen an apparition. Didn't think she had seen her daughter's ghost.

Right then, she thought...if that was the case, if she had seen Poppy in the place where she would find her...even if it was her body, then maybe she could believe she still had a connection to her no matter what.

In her exhausted, grief-addled mind, that sounded better than this nothingness.

Maybe it was. Maybe it wasn't. She could imagine that for a moment, a strange moment, having a body would be a relief. But after that Poppy would just be gone forever. And that was the thing that she couldn't cope with.

Michael took his position across from the trucks, Joel and Shelby spread out on either side of him, and then they let the dogs off leash and followed them into the woods.

Margo stood there for a moment with Dane.

"Are you okay?" he asked.

"Just assume the answer is no. But that I'm standing here anyway."

"Yeah. I can understand that."

Margo and Dane walked into the woods behind the fast-moving dogs.

"I suppose I don't really need to be here. I'm not contributing anything. But I'm tired of waiting by the phone. It just so... It's terrible. And every time I see a text from you, every time the phone rings, I just get this vicious knot in my stomach. It's more than that. It's like the whole world stops. It's terrifying. At least I'm here. At least I'm here."

It was so dark and ominous underneath the trees. But it had become a comfort for her in the past few days, because it made her feel like maybe she was closer to Poppy. And she hadn't seen her again, which reinforced to her that she hadn't just been hallucinating.

It had to be deeper than that. More complicated.

Even perhaps that she'd actually seen her.

She hoped so.

Dammit all, she really hoped so.

They walked on. For forty-five minutes. Deep in the trees.

"The community is somewhere to the left of this," Dane commented.

"Really? I mean, I guess I know the houses back the woods, but it's just disorienting to be out here and trying to figure out which direction home is, because of the way the road moves around."

Suddenly, a barking dog split the silence.

It was incessant, coming from somewhere off to their right.

Did the dog have a scent?

She didn't even think, she just started running toward the sound.

And Dane didn't try to stop her.

She heard the radio go off behind her, which meant that Dane was following along.

She heard the radio, but she still didn't stop.

She kept going. She kept running.

And then, Michael and Tallulah came into view. Tallulah was standing still, pawing at the ground, barking.

"Oh God," said Margo.

"Margo," said Dane, wrapping his hand around her, holding her chest, pressing her against him, her back to his body. "I think it might be best if you go."

"No," she said. "I can't. I can't leave. I can't leave. What if it's her? I can't leave her."

"Tallulah thinks there's human remains there."

"She thinks it," Margo said, laughing, because…because everything hurt. Because it was absurd. "She ever wrong?"

He shook his head. "No. She's not. That's what she smells. So that's what they are."

"God in heaven," she said again. And other words tumbled out of her mouth, but she wasn't quite sure what they were. If they were curses or prayers or just incoherent groans from her soul. She would never know. Because it was just…unthinkable. To be standing here at this moment.

The dog had found a body.

"We're going to go ahead and call local law enforcement," said Michael. "Because we tend to want to get their forensics unit out here before we touch anything. This is a crime scene. If a body is buried, it's not ambiguous."

"Yeah," she said. "Of course."

She wanted to get down on her knees and start digging with her fingers.

In fact, it was easy to imagine herself doing that. Pulling out of Dane's grip and digging through the soft earth on her own.

Just like she'd wanted to jump out of the boat. Because if her daughter was there, even if it was just her body, she needed to be near her. She needed to know.

And right then, it was like a string was cut, between herself and her feelings. Right then, it was like she was released from the resounding pain inside of her.

It was shock, maybe. Or her brain and body protecting her. Because what she had felt a moment before wasn't something you could endure for an extended period of time. That was for certain.

"The department's on their way," said Michael.

"And they know… They know they need to start digging, right?"

"I told them. That I've got a cadaver dog with the scent, so yes, they know."

Waiting was torture. Absolute torture. And she knew it would take time, she knew how far they had walked into the woods, and still she felt…like she was losing her grip on everything.

Eventually she ended up sitting against Dane, who was against the tree. He was warm, she was cold. She was grateful that he was there holding her, or she would've fallen right apart. Finally, after what could've been minutes or days, the police came.

With equipment. Bags.

Body bags.

Officer Daniels looked at her. "I don't think you should stay," he said.

"I'm not leaving. I can't leave."

"I would advise you at least to sit with your back to the proceedings. And then Dane can let you know…"

She shook her head. "I get it. I turned away when the car came out of the water. I turned away and I didn't look at Zach. I'm not turning away now. And maybe I'll be haunted by it the rest of my life. But if my daughter is there, I will never be okay again."

"But what do you want your last memory of her to be?"

She thought of Poppy. Spinning and twirling and happy.

Poppy, the only child other than Callie's that she had ever thought was remotely interesting.

She had never liked kids as a general rule. Had never been one to babysit. And then she'd had her own, and she'd been shocked by how instantly she'd felt a fierce and glorious connection.

She didn't want to lose that. That life-altering, soul-shifting love. She didn't want it shattered. She didn't want to know if her child was gone from this earth. If only her body—that tiny body she'd grown in her womb—was all that remained.

God.

It would kill her.

But she also knew one thing for certain. If she didn't see her, she wouldn't believe it. Because it had been more than six months of not knowing. And if this was the answer, she needed to see the answer herself. She couldn't take someone else's word for it.

"I have to see," she said. "Because I didn't know where my daughter was all this time. If she's here, then I need to see her. I haven't seen her. I miss her. I just miss her and if she's here and this is my last chance I need to see her."

Maybe it was unhinged. She was unhinged.

Dane, for his part, never argued. Not like he did at the water. He simply stood by silently, the support that she needed to keep from going to the ground.

And then the team started. Cautiously digging into the soft earth. Tallulah barked. And barked and barked. Like the scent was getting stronger for her. And undoubtedly it was.

It did hit Margo that maybe there should be a scent to them as well. But maybe it was too late for that.

She was grateful that she was numb.

She needed to be numb.

It was what was going to get her through this. It was what was going to get her through the next part of her life. Maybe even the rest of it. Numbness.

She'd had wild, glorious love before.

Maybe now this was all she had.

"I've got something," said one of the officers. He knelt down, with gloved hands, and began to clear away some of the debris.

Margo's heart froze.

"This is skeletal," the officer said. "Completely. This isn't six months old."

She let out a sound that had no name. Relief, anguish.

It wasn't over.

She hadn't wanted it to be over like this. But she'd been standing on the edge of over. Nothing had changed.

It was all just unknown.

But in the unknown was *hope*.

It was a story she could tell herself.

She'd been so angry at herself, for her stories about Zach.

She needed a story now.

"This is years old," he said, continuing to push back the debris. "Not a child."

The team of officers continued to dig around the remains.

One of the shovels hit something that made an off sound. Another officer bent down and uncovered it. "We've got a bag."

He held up a purse. Leather.

And she felt Dane go still beside her. "Open it," Dane said.

"Okay," said the cop, like he wouldn't have thought of it anyway.

He opened the flap, and pulled a wallet out of it. And then opened it up.

"Well, holy shit," he said.

She looked at Dane, at the grim set of his jaw.

And that was when she knew.

"That's Sarah Hartley's ID, isn't it?" Dane asked. "He found my sister."

The silence was clear. More like a gunshot than real quiet. It tore through them all.

The officer nodded slowly. "Yes, sir. I'm sorry."

And then it was his turn to lean against Margo.

She wished to hell that this wasn't how she had found a functional relationship. He had let her take all of his strength, he had been prepared to stand by and watch her endure this. And instead, it was him. He was the one going through all this grief.

"I'm sorry," she whispered, turning to him and putting her hand on his face. "I am so sorry. I brought us out here. I didn't know, I did…"

"I know you didn't. Why would... Why would you ever believe this is what we would find?"

"We'll have to do an autopsy to be sure," said Officer Daniels. "But the ID..."

"That bastard," said Dane. "That bastard killed her. And skipped town. Instead of bringing her with him. Why the hell... Why the hell would you do that?"

She could tell that this was one of the few scenarios he hadn't been prepared for.

Or maybe the idea that you could be prepared, after eighteen years or six months, was a fiction.

But he was right, it didn't make sense. None of this did. "That letter was on Sarah's computer, it doesn't make any sense."

"Unless she thought they were leaving together, and he was just getting out of Dodge," Dane said. "He didn't actually want to bring a sixteen-year-old liability with him. He might've had someone else. He might've been done with her. Who knows how a bastard like him thinks."

"I don't know. I wish I had answers."

"You gave me an answer. You found her."

It didn't feel good. There was no triumph in this. Because a moment ago she'd thought it was maybe her daughter's body, and now she felt the full complexity of what this kind of closure meant.

Eighteen years of wondering where she was, and she'd been right here the whole time. It was just... It was awful.

They stood there, while they excavated the remains. That Margo found she couldn't watch. She held on to Dane, who watched everything. And she understood why he needed to do that.

She was put in a bag, and then on a stretcher. To be carried easily out of the woods.

She and Dane followed behind, along with the dogs and their handlers.

A funeral procession with the stately pines on either side of them.

"I'm going to need to go speak to my mother."

"Do you want to wait for an autopsy?"

"No. Since they were able to visually identify the bones are female, I don't think there's any reason to suspect it would be anyone else. No one else was missing from here. And my sister's purse was there. I just think...we know. I think we need to go to my dad as well. In person."

"I understand that."

"I'll just fly up and back in the same day. Just to Seattle."

"You don't have to do that."

"I saw how close we were..."

"That Sarah was here doesn't mean we were close to Poppy. I don't know why this was the place I was obsessed with searching. I don't know why I saw Poppy here."

She didn't believe in ghosts. But it was hard not to feel like maybe Poppy's had led her to Sarah.

Then lead me to you. Please.

Her prayer went unanswered.

There was no voice in response.

No visions.

No crying.

Just a grim walk through the woods. Through the dark.

With grief an ever-present cloud.

And an ominous feeling encircling her.

They had gone to look for Brian Archer's car in the water, they had found Zach's. They had gone to look for Poppy, they had found Sarah.

She couldn't find the link. And yet she felt like it was there. Circling.

But it didn't make sense. It just didn't make sense.

She couldn't make it connect. And that was maybe the grimmest thing of all.

That all the sadness just felt random.

She drove Dane back to the house, and he went to his truck. "I've got to go see Mom."

She nodded. Then she took a step toward him and kissed him. "Drive safe, okay?"

"I will."

"I'm sorry I…"

Then he looked at her, his eyes shining bright. "Thank you," he said, holding her hands tight. "Thank you. Because we know now. She didn't leave us. She didn't stay gone for eighteen years. She didn't forget about her family." His voice broke. "She was taken from us. She didn't want to go. I really believed she didn't. I would've loved if she was alive, but you know that meant… she didn't want us. That was okay. It was nice sometimes to imagine she was out there living her life. But now we know. She never left. She was always right there."

She nodded. And took a step back from him. "You don't need to thank me. I was trying to figure my own self out."

"But you've been doing all of this. Trying to find answers. Trying to fill in Sarah's story."

"I promise you this," she said. "If Brian Archer is still out there, I'm going to move heaven and earth to find him. He'll pay."

"And I really do believe that if anyone can find him, you can. All this time. All this time, and she was right there."

He shook his head, and went to his truck.

"If I'm back it will be late. Otherwise, I'm staying with Mom. But I'll text you."

"Okay."

She went straight upstairs to her computer. She opened up the desk drawer, and touched the lid on her Adderall, staring at it for a second.

No. The adrenaline of the day was enough to keep her going. That was for sure.

I used to think that answers were the most important thing. But I'm not sure about that now. I found answers today in the woods. Had a sense that something was there, but it wasn't what I thought.

Today, we found Sarah Hartley.

She wasn't a runaway. Not a Lolita. She was a girl who was the tragic victim of what was most likely violence at the hands of a man who was already sexually abusing her. It is such a common story.

When you work on true crime blogs, when you do investigations, you see it so often it becomes a cliché.

The mystery is the part that gets your brain going. That fires you up. The answers are often just sad. In the motive is often worse.

It's entitlement. It's anger. It is a fundamental disregard for the victim's personhood.

And so many men are quick to visit those things upon the ones around them they see as less.

The ones they don't see as people in the way that they're people.

I wanted this answer.

But the truth is sad.

But with this revelation comes more determination. I won't let Sarah's killer get away with this. If he's out there, I will find him. And if he's gone, I will find him anyway. I'll drag his name through the mud.

He will never be able to be remembered as anything other than Sarah Hartley's killer. He will no longer be a loving father, a loving husband. A middle manager. A quiet neighbor.

That's my vow.

When I get my hands on the person responsible for this, all of his pride will mean nothing. All of those petty, angry reasons he felt entitled to take her life I will take from him. Even if he's dead. I will harm his legacy even if he's in the grave.

Right now, for me, answers aren't enough.

I need revenge.

22

DANE DIDN'T COME home that night. He texted her to let her know that he was staying at his mother's house, and the next morning, Margo went straight to Callie's.

"This is going to be in the news," she said. "But I wanted you to hear it directly."

"What?"

"Yesterday we went out with dogs." She stood up from where she'd been sitting at Callie's kitchen table and started to pace. "I wanted to see if…if there was any truth to Poppy being in the woods. We gave some dogs her scent. But those dogs were cadaver dogs as well, and they are trained to respond to human remains. A dog scented some remains. And for a while, I was afraid that it was Poppy, but it wasn't. Yesterday they found Sarah Hartley."

Callie covered her mouth. "Oh fuck."

"She's been there the whole time. There's… That's what the age of the body suggests."

"He killed her," she said. "Margo, he had to have killed her."

"That would definitely be the leading theory," she said.

"I'm going to be sick," she said. Then she sat there for a second. "No, I'm serious." She ran out of the room, and Margo heard retching coming from the bathroom.

"I'm sorry," said Margo, looking straight ahead. She said it more to herself than to Callie even.

This was like ripping open a badly healed wound.

It hadn't been fully healed, no. It hadn't been resolved. But it had settled. It had been in one state for a long time. And this had just made it new. Bloody and fresh.

Callie came back in, her eyes watering. "Not Sarah," she said, sitting back down at the table. Tears slid down her cheeks. "I just really liked Sarah. Always. I've always felt so bad that my dad was the one who…took her away. I didn't think he killed her. I never thought that. I never thought that… I never thought that he would do that. It that not ridiculous? Somebody is a sexual predator, why wouldn't they do that? Why wouldn't they?"

"You aren't stupid," said Margo. "For not thinking that. Nobody thought that. I had entertained the idea that maybe he'd done something to her after. But I never thought she was dead before she left."

Dane's words echoed again.

They're usually dead before you know they're missing.

"My mother is going to be devastated," Callie said.

"Maybe let's hold off until the body is formally identified. Her ID was with her. It was enough for Dane. He's in the process of telling his family. Maybe we don't need to tell anyone else right now."

"I'll have to tell DeVonte."

"Of course. Tell your husband. You're my best friend, and I couldn't keep that from you. I couldn't let you find out another way."

She nodded. "Thank you. I appreciate it." It was so weird. How polite Callie was being. But there was no…handbook for this. It was all weird.

"This is just… It's not how I thought it would end. I think I maybe thought it might never end. But this isn't how I thought it would."

"It's still not over. We still have to find your dad."

"Yeah," said Callie. "Please find him. He needs to pay for what he did." Her chest hitched. "I am really tired of not having answers." She paused for a while. "You know, in a way I'm glad that I never knew this until now. I was…deeply distrustful of men. There's a reason I didn't date all that seriously, you know, not with the intention of getting married."

"I recall you being pretty hung up on different boyfriends."

"Sure. But I always told myself I wasn't going to get emotionally involved, and I did. But I really didn't mean to get married. DeVonte changed that. He made me feel like I could trust someone. It was bad enough knowing that my dad was a sexual predator. Knowing that he was a murderer I think might've broken me completely. It would've kept me from this. From this life. And I love it. I'm glad I made this choice. I'm glad I married that man. Because he's a good man. I know there are so many shady ones out there, but my husband is a really good man. He is a good father. He would never leave the kids. He would never take the kids. Jaden had his problems, and it took us a while to figure out what they were. DeVonte is always so patient. He gets him. I am so glad my dad didn't keep me from having my life."

"I'm glad you have your life."

And she didn't say that she'd been pretty damned confident in Zach too. But then, she hadn't quite looked at Zach the same way that Callie had looked at DeVonte.

Margo had been so sure she knew Zach.

"I thought it mattered, finding the truth. But before when I did this I got to walk away. The story was the way I unraveled it all. The way I got to the answers. But I don't think I've ever fully grappled with what the answers mean to the people left behind. And now… I'm here. This is my community. It was your dad. It was my… Dane's sister."

Callie's face crumpled. "Is he okay?"

Margo looked down at her hands. "He was stoic. It's been eighteen years and he recovers the bodies of missing people for a living. He's not an optimist. But it was his sister."

Callie nodded. "I know. I'm so sorry."

"We'll keep going. Because… I have to believe there's something better on the other side of this. And I don't know if answers heal anything, but maybe they can build bridges to something new. We can't be stuck forever. Look at you, Callie. You have this life. You have this life because you decided that you wouldn't let the dark things hold you back, and I respect you so much for that. I'm going to need to figure out where you get that strength from." She took a ragged breath. "I wanted better answers from today. It's just more pain."

Callie nodded slowly. "Yes, it was. But you're here, and we're friends. DeVonte will be home tonight after work, and he loves me. My kids will come home from school and have a fight. The good and the bad are just there together all the time. Dane has you, even though he lost the hope of something today."

Margo had such a hard time seeing good right now, but Callie was right. She'd experienced it. Her friendships sustained her. Her remaining family supported her. Dane brought her companionship and pleasure she hadn't expected. In the middle of the darkest nights.

She stayed with Callie until she convinced her to call DeVonte and have him come home from work. Once she was sure her friend was taken care of she texted Dane to find out where he was.

He got back to her house in the late afternoon.

"How did your mom take it?" she asked.

"Not great. It was rough. I'm going to need to go talk to

my dad tomorrow. I need to do it before anything ends up in the press."

She looked around the house. She hadn't stayed one night away from the house since Poppy had disappeared. Just in case. Like leaving the porch light on. Letting her know she was home.

But Poppy could be anywhere.

"Do you want me to go with you?"

He looked surprised. "Sure. If you want."

"I can let you speak to your dad alone, but you shouldn't have to make a trip that far alone right now."

"No. Can you come with me to speak to him?"

She felt like it was a big deep ask and it made her feel good. In the way complicated things did. When the good mixed with the bad.

They all go together.

"Of course."

23

THEY TOOK THE 5:00 a.m. to Seattle out of Portland the next morning and arrived blearily early. They went to a coffee shop in a neighborhood near Joe Hartley's place and sat together until eight, and then Dane texted his dad.

I need to come by for a visit. I have some news.

"You know, it's really impossible to figure out how to do this without creating extra tension when you just really think you need to tell someone something in person." He scowled at his phone.

Margo put her hand over his wrist. "I know."

You're in town?

Dane sighed. Yes. I can head over now if you're ready.

Come on by.

It was quicker to walk than try to get a car, so they headed out the coffee shop door and down the blustery street.

The house was up a street that was on a steep incline and Margo was breathing hard when they reached the top. Apparently wandering around her comparatively flat neighborhood hadn't given her the quad strength for this.

She tried to catch her breath as they walked up to a white house with a red door, and Dane knocked. This neighborhood was older than hers, a little shoddy, but in a charming way. Mid-century homes with paint that had seen better days, cheerfully shining the colors of their original era.

She wondered if he'd chosen something this different on purpose, or if it was incidental. If this was the first new house he'd lived in since leaving Conifer or if he'd lived in many places since.

Joe was a more theoretical figure to her than everyone else in the family. He'd usually been at work or out fishing when she'd come over to visit.

The door opened, and a man answered that Margo would never have recognized as Dane's father. He had once looked like a businessman, except on the weekends when he'd looked like a polished outdoorsman.

His hair went down to his shoulders now. Not unkempt, just sort of bohemian. Or maybe an early-day hipster, or a Silicon Valley tech executive determined to look down-to-earth. He was wearing a sweater and jeans. His feet were bare. He had round black glasses on.

"It's good to see you." He pulled Dane in for a hug. But there was concern vibrating off him. He stopped and looked at Margo for a long moment. "You were one of Sarah's friends."

It jarred her that he knew that. That he recognized her, even if not by name. She had no concept of him really, but maybe that had been her teen hyperfocus and not him at all.

"Yes," she said. "Margo."

Dane cleared his throat and took her hand. "Can we come in?"

His dad looked at their hands. Margo was grateful she'd taken her rings off months ago, otherwise the poor guy was going to think this was about an engagement announcement and not the real reason they were here.

Not that anything would soften it or make it worse.

"Yes. Please."

The house was clean, but not in a strict minimalist way. There were throw pillows and blankets. A basket of reeds. A lot of extraneous decor.

He led them through to the kitchen table, which had candles at the center. Margo looked around the kitchen.

He had a calendar on his fridge.

It was marked up in blue with all kinds of engagements.

"Dad, I wanted to come up here to tell you in person. Yesterday we found Sarah's body."

His dad's amiable face went completely flat. "You did?"

"Yes."

"Where?"

"The woods off of Highway 66."

"How…long was she there?" he asked, his voice breaking as he looked at his hands.

"Eighteen years, most likely. They're still getting confirmation but it would seem that…she was there the whole time."

"Eighteen years," he repeated. "She was…gone. She was gone the whole time."

That truth was so heavy. It took the past eighteen years and changed every thought. Every theory. At least for her.

But she could see something else on Joe's face.

He nodded slowly. "I knew. I always did." He nodded faster. "I did know. I… It's just very final."

Margo's stomach was so tight she could barely breathe. Watching a parent process the loss of their child, even eighteen years after they'd last seen them, was too close to home.

But he didn't rage or scream or cry.

He'd known.

Debbie Hartley hadn't. She'd kept the room for Sarah. She'd hoped. She'd been angry at her being out there and never coming home, but she'd tried to believe she was alive even though it broke her heart.

"If I could have done something..." He closed his eyes. "I would give anything to trade places with her. To give the last eighteen years of my life so she could grow up."

She heard the honesty in that. The gut-wrenching desire to turn back the clock.

"I'd give anything to keep her safe."

Keep her safe...

She thought of Zach and Poppy. He'd do anything to keep Poppy safe. He'd shown that. He'd demonstrated it. For the five years of his life he'd been a father he'd been caring, he'd been careful.

He'd been invested, interested.

He would have done anything to keep her safe.

I kept them safe.

Her stomach twisted.

The idea of safe could get skewed.

Someone could convince themselves that death was safety. But...

She didn't think so.

She didn't think Zach had done that. She didn't think Zach could have made that leap. Not the man she'd known who was a hypochondriac-by-proxy. Who was worried about every cough, bump and scrape. Death and the fragility of life terrified Zach.

It made her almost feel bad about his death.

About what had surely been a terrifying way to go.

But one thing she knew for certain, he would have never had Poppy unbuckled in that car. Because Zach would have given his life for Poppy.

She didn't know why she still felt so confident in that.

It wasn't out of loyalty to him.

Fathers did kill their children.

It happened.

I knew.

He'd known. And on some level Margo believed she would know. Maybe that wasn't fair, because Debbie had clearly believed something different. Her need to hope had blotted out intuition. Maybe the same was true for Margo.

No. She knew. She *knew.*

Poppy was alive.

She'd seen her that day in the woods.

All of the death, all of the tragedy had taken her to a dark place, and for a while she'd been unable to see any hope.

But she knew Poppy was still out there.

They stayed with Joe the whole day, and for a while Margo sat in the living room on her laptop while they talked privately.

Then when the sun was setting, they walked in and she stood.

"I'm glad he has you," Joe said.

"I'm glad I have him."

They got a Lyft to a hotel and decided to get room service. It was a nice hotel near the airport, and they were on an upper floor that gave them a view of city lights.

She ordered steak and a chocolate torte, because she was trying to weave more good things into the bad.

They ate, they showered, they lounged around in robes not speaking. They made love in the hotel bed and it was electric and intense, and just what she needed to make her mind blank.

Of everything but his mouth, his hands, his sculpted body.

"I suppose we have to have a funeral," he said, his lips pressed against her hair as he spoke.

"Yeah. Will your mom and dad... Can they be in the same place together?"

He nodded. "Yeah. Their split wasn't acrimonious. I think

they couldn't care enough to hate each other. But he couldn't live with the hope that she was still alive, and my mom couldn't stand him thinking she was dead."

"Neither of them were wrong."

"No," he said. "They weren't. They both believed what they needed to. If my mom had thought she was dead all this time she'd have grief all the same and worry right along with it. My dad…he became a different person. I think he needed to. In a lot of ways he's a better person now. And I've always enjoyed visiting with him. Well, since I got my life together. I was angry at him for a long time because, you know, I couldn't believe she was dead either."

"Did you…did you think she was out there?"

He sighed heavily. "You know, I don't believe in most cases a person is still out there if they've vanished without a trace. It's so rare for that to happen. And especially as technology improves…to never get identified anywhere, it's unlikely." He stroked her hair and she felt herself relaxing against him. "But I hoped. In a corner of my heart. Because it's like you said, you feel like you have to. There was that note. I hoped that they'd run away together. I hated him, and I hoped that she was out there with him happy somehow. I hoped she was living her life and she'd had three of his babies and they were some star-crossed lover shit." He laughed, but it was broken. She felt something wet land in her hair. It was a tear, she knew. But she didn't look at him because she knew he wouldn't want her to see. "Wanting her to be alive made me wish all that even though I hated him with everything I am. I hate that she's gone. I'm…glad in some ways to know she didn't choose to leave us. And that's selfish."

"It's human. If there's one thing I'm learning from all this, from this tangled, horrible web, it's that we're all messy enough that we're allowed to feel complicated feelings. Sometimes I think it's this dedication to fake narratives, to the idea that people's thoughts and feelings and nuances can be distilled into a short text or internet post or a one-minute video is part of what makes these breaks. People have to hide who they are. Because they have to be acceptable and not real. And one day they break."

"Maybe. Brian Archer is a disgusting sexual predator though, and a murderer. He should have suppressed that."

She huffed a laugh. "Yeah, no argument."

"I feel both things," he said. "And part of me finds it so easy to keep pretending she's out there. She was gone for eighteen years and we had no idea. I can just pretend yesterday didn't happen."

"It's why you had to see," she said.

"Yes," he answered, his voice rough.

"That's why I kept watching at first. If it was Poppy, I knew I'd need to see her. Or I'd keep pretending."

"Do you have any pet theories on where she could be?"

"I don't know," she said, her voice choked. "I really don't. I just don't think he'd have put her in the car without buckling her up."

"We finished with the river anyway."

I knew.

She didn't *know*. But she wanted to push, just a little more, at that theory.

"Maybe you should look above where you found the car."

"That wouldn't make a lot of sense."

"If she wasn't buckled she could have been thrown from the car." The words were so awful and vile spoken against that white hotel linen, in a different environment than she'd been in all this time.

Because she couldn't leave this behind.

It was too much a part of who she was.

"Yes, that's possible."

"And she could be hung up somewhere. Stuck in the roots upstream. You looked downriver because she might have floated down and got stuck there but what if…" The words caught in her throat.

"Yeah, that could be."

"Just do one more dive," she said.

She wanted to prove she was rational as well as hopeful.

Or maybe she wanted to validate her hope.

That was enough.

It was enough for her.

24

WHEN THEY GOT back the next day they'd talked about her coming to the dive, but she'd decided she didn't need to stand on the shore for hours unable to see anything.

I'd come get you if there was anything. If we found anything.

She'd felt compelled to be in the woods because she was certain Poppy was there. This drive...was more about being certain of where she wasn't. It was something she couldn't easily explain.

She decided to work on her book. She was trying to get the pieces she'd written stitched together.

She pulled up her email and decided it was time to contact her editor.

Re: The Next Book
Hi Kate,
Sorry that it's been so long since I was in touch. As you know, things in my personal life have been challenging. But I have been trying to work on the next book. I decided it wasn't working and switched focus, but I didn't want to come to you about it until I

was certain there was something there. It's another cold case, but this one is from my hometown. And just three days ago we found the body of a girl who's been missing for eighteen years. I feel like this will be another book that centers on solving a cold case, and it will be worth the switch.

Let me know what you think.

Margo

Her email dinged five minutes later.

Re Re: The Next Book

Margo, Jesus Christ you just found your husband's body and your kid is missing no one is worrying about the book.

But this sounds great. Do you have a time frame?

Best,

Kate

Re Re Re: The Next Book

Hard to say. I want to keep pushing. We have some unanswered questions to get through. I'm exploring some links with

She sat there staring at her cursor.

What was there to say? *This feels like it has to be connected to what happened to me because I saw a vision of my daughter in the woods and it led us to Sarah's body?*

Likely not.

She hit the backspace key.

I want to keep pushing. There's more here. I'll keep you posted, but just wanted you to know I'd changed focus, and that I didn't forget about the book.

She went back to the manuscript, which was so far disparate observations she'd been writing down after new things had appeared. She wanted to keep what she'd written about Brian and Sarah before she knew Sarah was dead. She thought it made the whole thing read better. She could never recreate the work she'd written when she hadn't known Sarah was dead. All of her questions, when she really didn't know, needed to be left as it was.

She was good, but nothing would ever be as good as the truth.

What she did was try to add in her personal details.

I couldn't sleep. That was normal. When it gets too quiet I think I hear my daughter crying. But I can't find her. I can't hold her. I can't stay still either. That night I decided I needed to get answers—from anywhere, about anything. I just needed some mysteries solved so I could sleep, so my brain would stop moving in vicious loops all night—I went for a walk out of my neighborhood.

She heard a sound, and she jumped. It was her phone vibrating on the desk.

It was Dane.

Her stomach crashed, her hands shaking instantly. She thought she was going to be violently ill.

He could be calling for any reason. But it wasn't time for them to be finished.

He wouldn't call you. He would come to you.

That made her relax. Because it was true. As much as he would want to let her know right away if they'd found something, he would be at her side when they did. He wouldn't let her know over the phone.

She picked up the phone and held it to her ear. "What?"

"Not her," he said.

"Thank God," she said, the blood rushing back into her face suddenly, making her dizzy. "But you did find something?"

Her mind was moving quickly. There were a lot of possibilities for what it could be. Even...whoever Zach's other woman was.

"We found another car," he said. "Thirty feet upstream from the bridge."

"What?"

"We found Brian Archer's car."

"Holy shit," she said.

"He's in the front seat. Brian Archer is in the...front seat."

Brian was dead. Brian's body was in the car.

Her thoughts were a tangle and she knew there was something there that wasn't fully clicking.

"I'm coming down there."

"You can, but don't tell anybody else yet. We need... We need a little bit of time. I am contacting the police department to find out for sure if the plate matches. But based on a search that I did of the vehicle description, and the plate they gave on that, I believe it does. Making allowances for very strange discrepancies, you know... You don't want to accidentally tell someone you think you've found their father's body if you haven't."

"Yes. Definitely."

"I'm about to go back down and go through the whole vehicle. Just to see what else we can find. It's incredibly silted in. I have to verify that it's him somehow, not easy to do. We're talking bones."

"But you think it's him?"

"Yeah. We need to call law enforcement down, but yeah, I do."

"I'll be there in a minute."

She ran out of the house, typing up a new email to Kate, not even realizing she wasn't wearing shoes. And she had to run back in and put them on.

Kate,
Big news. I have another body for the book.
Margo

I assume this was a body you wanted to find?

She got into her car and turned the engine on, holding her phone with shaking hands. A body she wanted to find? That was hard to say.

It's one we needed to find.

She hit Send, and then it was like adrenaline caught up with her. Hard. She was shaking uncontrollably and had to take several breaths to keep from passing out.

What would you have done if it was her?

It wasn't her.

They'd found the car. They had found Brian Archer.

Sarah…

They would never be able to get answers about Sarah. They'd be able to put scenarios together but unless there was a waterproof written confession in the car, their prime suspect was dead.

Without really wanting to, she began to build a picture in her head. She knew what it looked like when cars had been underwater for that long. The older car from the Incline Valley Killer case had looked rusted. It'd been covered in silt. The inside had been packed full of it, and they'd had to take the body inside out through the window and put it in a bag. From the elements. They'd looked more like sticks than like a human being. If Brian's car was moved, she knew that the bones would be sucked out the window. The skeleton would wash away. And that they would be left without crucial evidence.

When she got down to the shore twenty-five minutes later, Dane and one other diver were about to go in.

They had equipment. Body bags. And the police were there.

"Officer Daniels," she said, moving to stand beside him.

He looked grim.

"Well, it's possible he drove the car into the river out of guilt after he killed her," Daniels said.

"He didn't deserve that. He deserved to live, and to have to answer for this," she said.

"It looks to me like it's been down there for eighteen years," Dane said, his voice rough. He was angry, she realized. Almost shaking with it. "So that's a definite possibility. Whatever happened between them, he didn't want it to go down that way and felt so guilty he took the easy way out."

She hoped then that it wasn't the easy way. That there was some justice whatever was after this.

If hell was hot, she hoped he'd found out.

But for her part, she'd mete out justice in this life. Sarah's story would be in her book, and he would be the villain. The least interesting part. Reduced to *rapist. Murderer.*

She would erase any last hint that he'd been a well loved teacher. A prominent member in the community. A husband. A father.

Those things wouldn't define him.

His sins would be all he was.

She would make sure.

She stood on the shore as Dane went back into the water and disappeared beneath the surface.

This didn't feel like when she pulled Zach from the water.

But it didn't feel like it had when they found the girls in Lake Tahoe either.

It didn't feel like they were on the verge of something exciting. It was far too close to home. The reality was, this would hurt her best friend.

And when she thought of taking away Brian's identity beyond what he'd done to Sarah, she knew that wouldn't take what he'd been to Callie away.

For Callie, for Gail, this would be devastating.

It would also be closure. The end of something.

It would be a lot of feelings.

And Margo felt nothing but grief over the fact that Callie would have to cope with it.

It was also a different story.

It would be an answer to a question. One that had haunted Conifer for so many years.

One that had shaped Callie. What would it be like to have an answer at last?

Dane was underwater for an hour.

His partner emerged with a closed black body bag, which he dragged to shore.

"This is all that we could get easily of the skeleton."

"Anything else?" Daniels asked.

"There will be, for sure. Hartley's diving through the back of the car, and he's going to open up the trunk. Try to see what's going on in there. It is packed full of silt. It's difficult to get down to the bottom of everything. Two windows are down."

"How is the car?"

"Upright," the guy said.

He gestured out straight in front of him. "The nose is facing the opposite shore, the back is facing us. It's almost like it drove straight into the river. Right into the middle. And just rested there. A good fifty feet under. All that suction is keeping it from moving. Keeping it locked in place."

"Like he just drove in?"

That seemed to support the suicide theory.

Zach's car had gone over a bridge. It was on its top.

Everything pointed to it being an accident. This was the kind of thing they'd have expected if it had been deliberate.

"Yep."

"Was the seat belt fastened?"

"No."

"That's strange."

"Yeah. The body was in the passenger seat."

Margo frowned. "What?"

"Not buckled in, in the passenger seat. It is possible that when the car went into the water he panicked, and because he wasn't belted in he moved for some reason to try to get out the other door. Hard to say."

In the passenger seat.

The scenario was possible.

But it was just so… It was so weird.

As if all of this wasn't weird.

But if he'd committed suicide by driving his car into the water, why would he switch seats? That seemed to undermine the possibility. It could have been an accident. If he was distraught after killing Sarah, maybe he hadn't been paying attention and had driven in because he was distracted.

Dane surfaced, and came out of the water holding a bag in his hand.

He took the respirator out of his mouth. "Just to be certain, I made sure to look in the whole vehicle for another body, as this body was in the passenger seat," he said. "Absolutely no confirmation of any other remains. I've got a pair of men's sneakers, from the front seat. Passenger side. Foot bones in it."

After everything they'd seen and been through in the past few weeks that didn't even faze her.

"Feel like that's pretty decent confirmation that the remains are that of a man, though the height appearance made it seem to me like it was. Same with other clothing fragments."

"Why wasn't he in the driver's seat?"

"We're going to have to turn the bones over to forensics to find that out."

"What do you mean?"

"Two likely scenarios. He panicked, and that's where he ended up when he realized he couldn't get out. He passed out, whatever. The other option is that he was in the passenger seat when the car went into the water. Or there was another driver, who somehow got out of the car and was maybe swept down-river. And never told what happened. Or the car was pushed and he was already dead."

But who would have done that?

There would have certainly been people who would've wanted him dead if they'd known about what had happened with Sarah, but if someone had known, why hadn't they reported it?

Daniels looked grim. "We were having the coroner in to do an autopsy on the remains we found in the woods tonight. We'll have this done tonight too."

The remains we found in the woods.

Sarah.

She squeezed Dane's forearm, just subtly, so no one else would notice.

"Thanks," said Dane.

To Daniels or her, she wasn't sure.

She wanted to smooth the brackets by his mouth. To offer him comfort she knew wouldn't mean much right now.

"The human remains are in the bag?" Daniels asked, gesturing to what Dane was holding.

"Oh yeah. Here you go," he said, handing it to Daniels.

"We'll get a crane down here," he said.

"I'll call Callie…"

"Wait. I'm going back to see if I can find a wallet. Once I do, and we can get ID, I'll have you call her. I just don't want to give her any unnecessary trauma."

"Yes, fair."

She waited. And this time Dane was back fairly quickly. He had a wallet in his hand.

He opened it. It was an old-style driver's license. State of Oregon. Brian Archer.

"Well," she said. "That's a lot."

She blinked hard, staring at the water. It'd kept its secrets. But for some reason, they'd all come up now.

Because of Dane. Because of her.

Because they were looking.

Hope. Hope had driven all of this.

The ending was so grisly, and it made her feel like her hope was the thing that would get answers, but that the answers might just be decay.

Hope was the thing with feathers. And death was the thing with creeping icy fingers insistently wrapping its fist around her throat.

That was all that had been uncovered because of this pursuit. *Death.*

Before Poppy, she had believed that the answers were comfort. And maybe after twenty years they were. But she had less and less belief in the comfort of all of this as she looked at Dane's grim face.

She decided that calling Callie wasn't the right way to go.

She drove toward Callie's house. Trying to rehearse what she was going to say. She'd had to go over there two days ago and tell her friend that her dad was probably a murderer. That their high school friend was dead.

Now she had to tell her this. She entered the code and drove back into the gated community, her chest tight.

All the flowers were still perfect. Every lawn manicured.

No garbage cans left out when it wasn't trash day.

It was early evening and the lights were all on, except one house at the end of the street that stood dark. Most everyone was home with their families having a perfect dinner in this perfect life.

She hoped, for all their sakes, their lives stayed perfect.

The poison of all of this was spreading down their street. It'd touched Gail Archer, and Callie Smith. It'd touched her, and it had touched the Hartleys' home just six houses down. It'd touched her brother's house at the very end of the street.

You couldn't keep poison like this contained.

She pulled up to Callie's house, as well lit and lovely as the rest of them. Giving no hint as to what was happening in their lives.

To what she was about to tell her.

She got out, and she walked through Jaden's flower path on her way to the door. She rang the doorbell and waited.

DeVonte answered the door.

"Margo. Is everything okay?" he asked.

Fair question since everything had been terrible recently. She decided not to answer.

"I need to speak to Callie. Dane found something."

"Not Poppy," he said, taking a step toward her.

"No. Not Poppy."

"Come in."

She walked into the house, and Callie was standing there. When she saw Margo, she grabbed hold of the back of one of the kitchen chairs. Like she *did* have some idea of what Margo was there to tell her.

"Margo… What is it?"

It felt both wrong and right to be the one to tell her. Callie had stood by her through all of this, with strength and with humor. Warmth and caring. She knew Callie felt like it was a gift that Margo had stood by her all those years ago, but it had never felt like a trial, not in the least.

Callie was her best friend. They'd been through so much together. More than any two people should have to go through together, really.

She had to be the one to tell her because Callie had stood there when Dane was working on recovering her husband's body. Margo had to be there because it was what Callie would do for her.

"Dane went back to the Columbia today with the team. They didn't find Poppy. Callie, they found your dad."

"What?"

"They found his car. Underwater. It's been there for eighteen years."

"No," said Callie. "That's impossible. They've been out there somewhere. Even if they… Even if he's dead now, he ran away after he killed her. That's what had to have happened."

"No, Dane is reasonably certain the car has been down there for eighteen years."

Callie was speechless for a moment, and then she shattered. "What was the point of all this? Of all this pain? We didn't know where they were all this time. We thought maybe they were out there, we thought… But no. No. She's dead. He's just dead. Eighteen years. Eighteen years wondering, and he has been just a few miles down the road. Underwater."

"I'm sorry. I'm so sorry. It's horrible, I know. It's not fair, I know."

"I…"

DeVonte went to his wife and wrapped his arms around her. And she turned her head into him.

"I don't understand how this is the way it ends." Callie's face crumpled. "He should have to answer for it. He should have to explain it to me."

She felt that. Like a dagger cutting her own soul.

"It's not over," Margo said. "Not an ending. It's an answer. You spent all this time without answers."

"Now I can never ask him. Now I can never ask him what the hell he was doing. I can never ask him why he thought it was…okay to take us for ice cream and then just disappear. How could he have sex with a girl my age? How could he kill a girl my age? How could he do all those things and still… Why did he seem like such a good father? I will never have the answers that I need."

Then she laughed. Sounding borderline hysterical. "And I really don't have to tell you that, do I? Because you just pulled your husband's body out of the water, and you still don't know where your child is. And what the hell is wrong with me?"

"You are allowed to be upset," said Margo. "What I'm going through does not take away from how horrible this is."

For the life of her she didn't understand why they had to go through this at the same time. Maybe this was what happened when you started pulling at a thread. Unraveling one story. It started to pull at all the threads around it, undoing the whole tapestry.

"I just… I never imagined that. Of all the things. I never imagined it. My poor mom. I just think this is going to… My poor mom. She doesn't even know about Sarah yet, this is… This is awful." She looked bleak then. "And poor Dane. Kerrigan and Debbie. It's just…" She looked up at Margo. "It's such a mess."

"I'm sorry. When I started this, I really believed that answers were important."

Callie was silent for a moment. "I still think that. Answers are important. It matters. The truth matters."

"Because it's the absence of truth that creates these situations. Secrets. You have to bring them to the light."

"Yeah," she said. "I know. There was never going to be a good answer to this. This just isn't at all what I thought we'd find."

"I'm here for you. Whatever you need."

"You always have been. Always."

Margo knew the next part would be hard. She also knew her friend. Who was strong, a warrior. She'd go to bat for anyone. And she didn't back down from hard truths. That meant she had to make sure she knew. "You don't have to come to the river. But they're pulling out his car. You won't see anything. They have…him…out of sight."

DeVonte was immediately protective. "Hey. Wait a minute, I don't know that that's a good idea."

"No," said Callie. "I need to do this. I need to see it. Our family car. I need to see it come up out of the water, because if I don't, I don't think this is going to feel real. I need to know. I need to really know."

She could see that Callie's husband didn't agree. But Margo got it. There were some things you needed far more than protection. Closure, however grim, was one of them.

"I'll drive you."

It was such an eerie echo. Of the way Callie had taken care of her before.

She drove Callie down to the river, and they got out.

It was different than when they had found Zach.

She stood with grim acceptance, knowing that this was the end of her search for her father.

A man she would never be able to have simple feelings about.

Margo held on to her, but Callie didn't need it. She was strong.

Watching the car come up out of the water, a black SUV, was somber.

It hung suspended by a crane as they brought it down onto the back of a flatbed.

Officer Daniels came over to talk to Callie.

"We're going to take the vehicle back to the station. It will be entered into evidence."

"Thank you," she said.

"I can drive over to speak to your mother, if you want."

"I would appreciate that," said Callie. "Thank you. I'll go with you. But it would be better if… It would be better if you were there."

"Do you want me to go?" Margo asked.

Callie shook her head. "No. You don't need to have a front-row seat to everybody's trauma. You have your own."

"I'm not afraid of it."

"I know you aren't. But that doesn't mean that you should

have to put up with it. It doesn't mean that you should have to go through all this."

Margo was already thinking about how to write this. She might have felt guilty about the compulsion. But something had been shifting over the course of these past few weeks. It was her need to write toward understanding that had brought them here.

Her need to write truth, the best she could.

They had found Sarah Hartley. And now they'd found Brian Archer. She had set out to do that, and her own loss had fueled the discovery. It was almost unfathomable. And yet, it was the truth of it. It was the reason that they'd found them. Because she had sent herself down this road out of obsession. Out of a desire to run away from her own problems. From her own pain.

It was her job now to try to figure out how to make this into something that would…

Make sense.

Maybe that was a fantasy, but Callie wanted answers and dammit, she was going to do whatever she could to give them to her.

She went back to the car at the same time Callie did.

"I'll drop you off at your mom's."

"Thank you."

She knew she would see Dane at the house later, but he was busy wrapping things up, processing the scene.

She trusted that he would be there.

In the middle of all of this, that was a miracle.

And she would take whatever small miracles were available. Because everything else felt like it was falling apart. And falling into place.

She had miscalculated. How it would be to try to solve something that was this personal. She had miscalculated how personal it was.

Because she had bought into the idea that there was something deficient inside of her.

This sense of dissatisfaction that Zach had instilled in her. Had made her take on board.

She had blamed her herself.

Not anymore.

She would not let the villain write the story.

And when she got inside her house, she let herself weep.

25

SHE COULDN'T SLEEP. Even with Dane beside her. The whole day had been so horrendous it was difficult to know what to do. It was difficult to find any peace.

They had found Brian Archer's body.

He had been here the whole time.

Brian and Sarah had both been here the whole time.

Separate. Not together.

She was turning over that implication when she decided to go downstairs. Down to the box of items that they had from the storage garage.

She opened up the computer again and sat there, until her eyes were strained. Until she felt like the reflection of the brilliantly bright rectangle was burned into her retinas. She opened up some of the other autosaved files. There was nothing especially compelling there.

Half-finished school projects. No hearts and flowers about Brian Archer. No plans for their escape.

There were photos of them. The friend group. Put into her

photo-editing software and given the best version of a filter that they had access to back then.

There was one where they all looked watercolored.

Four exuberant girls in prom dresses, standing in a store in the mall. Dresses they hadn't bought. Dresses they had just tried on for fun.

She went back to one of the boxes, the one that contained the photo albums.

There was one from a summer trip. Many that were just from everyday life. Trips to the mall. Trips to get ice cream. Playing around on the beach. They'd been so carefree. And all of that had been stolen.

Half of it had been a lie.

Zach had known that Sarah was being hurt.

Sarah hadn't been living the life of a young, carefree teenager. She had been navigating the abuse of a teacher.

She stared at a picture that she knew was from around that time. Right before Sarah had gone missing. And Zach must've known everything by then. They were looking at the camera, open-mouthed glee on every face.

She could almost hear it.

Why wasn't it obvious? Why couldn't she look and see signs? Why had they hidden it so well?

She started to dig down deeper, found another photo album.

This one was mostly filled with notes. Pictures that they had drawn for each other. Carefully cataloged and dated, as everything Sarah had done was.

She had been a record keeper of their friendship. Of the good times.

Everything was dated, organized and saved.

Maybe that was on purpose.

Maybe it was because of how difficult things were.

Maybe that was why she kept track of every single beautiful thing.

She would never have left.

That whispered itself through her.

Sarah had loved her friends.

She would never run. Not willingly.

Brian must've been threatening her. And maybe it had gone wrong. Maybe she'd agreed to go because she'd been afraid and had written the note under duress. Or he'd used her computer in the classroom to type it out and had printed it at the school.

She looked at the picture that she had drawn for Sarah of a dragon.

And behind the dragon was a whole short story about a lonely treasure-hoarding dragon who found himself in the mall, and was enamored of different retail outlets. Just one of the ridiculous things that she'd once scribbled down to entertain everybody. They'd all been a little bit weirded out when she got into true crime writing. Because back then, everything she'd done had been humorous.

But then, back then, she'd had a lot more faith in humanity.

It had been a different time.

A lot different than it was now.

The notes asking for the meetups at the mall dwindled as she went further into the book. It did, in a small way, show the way that Sarah had pulled back.

She had.

That wasn't a hallucination on Margo's part.

Sarah had definitely withdrawn herself.

They'd still done things, but it hadn't been every day.

The notes became less effusive, less silly, and she didn't tend to be the instigator.

She looked down into the box and saw a little cluster of notes that were folded up tight still, sunk down to the bottom.

She pulled one out and unfolded it.

Are you okay?
Zach

you have to let me handle it.
Sarah

That was dated three weeks before she disappeared.

Zach had reached out to her.

She sat there, completely uncertain of what to make of that. It challenged the way she had begun thinking about Zach.

He had reached out.

She wondered if something about this had broken him.

Had cracked something inside of him.

Because he had known. And he hadn't been able to do anything to help.

He'd asked.

She picked up another note, and unfolded it.

This one was between Sarah and Callie.

My house after school?
Callie

I have homework. Sorry.
Sarah

That told a different story. One that made her feel vaguely nauseous. Sick to her stomach.

She unfolded the last note, and stared at it.

It was dated the day before Sarah disappeared.

Will you help me?
Sarah

yes.
Zach

She stared at it. What had Zach known? What had he helped her do?

"Dane?" She shouted his name as she ran up the stairs.

She started heading up the stairs, taking them two at a time.

He opened up the bedroom door, his hair messed up, and he was completely naked. She knew a moment of total, out-of-body surreality. He was just here. In her bed. They'd found Zach. Sarah. Brian. She'd found this note.

All of these things that had been unchanged for so long were now utterly, irrevocably different.

She felt dizzy. She pushed the notes toward him.

"Sarah asked Zach to help her. Before she disappeared. Right before she disappeared."

"What?"

He skimmed the papers. "She could be talking about anything."

"Sure. It could be math homework. It could be that she was terrified of Brian and needed Zach's help. Brian Archer was in the *passenger* seat. I can't get over that. We need the coroner's report."

"There won't be a report yet."

"Do you think they'll be doing an autopsy now?"

"It's the middle of the night."

"I know. But Officer Daniels said he was calling the coroner so that suggests they're doing it tonight. We should go."

"You don't want to see that," he said.

Maybe it didn't say anything good about her that at this point, with everything that had been broken, she did.

She picked up her phone and dialed Officer Daniels. "Is the morgue open?"

"Dammit, Margo, it's one in the morning."

"And you're not down at the station?"

"I am," said Daniels, sighing. "We have two autopsies happening."

"Can we come down?"

"You are a civilian," he said, but without any real weight.

"I have been the whole time. But you know I've helped. That we've helped."

"I know."

"What's happening right now?"

"X-rays, cataloging, we've got a team in from the county. It's not often we have this much to do, and because the team had to travel we just committed to it being an all-nighter."

"Great. Dane and I are coming."

Daniels's breath was heavy. "One of the autopsies is being done on his sister."

She closed her eyes. "I'll talk to him."

She already knew what the answer would be. Dane had been there when her body was discovered. There was no protection left for him.

She hung up the phone. "Do you want to be there?" she asked.

"Yeah," he said.

They took the drive down to town, and pulled in to the morgue.

They were under strict instructions to put on protective gear, and did so when they went into the room where Brian's autopsy was being conducted.

"We just got everything arranged," said the coroner.

Sarah's remains were in another room, and Margo was grateful for that. She shouldn't be in the same room as Brian. Even now. And she and Dane didn't need to see her again. Once had been enough.

Daniels came into the room behind them and the coroner looked up at him. "They're working with us," he said. "You can disclose information to them."

"Have you completed the autopsy on Sarah Hartley?" she asked.

"We have," said the coroner.

"What were your findings?"

She checked with Daniels before turning back to Margo. "Homicide, by strangulation."

Dane nodded. Once. Hard.

It was one of the worst things, Margo thought. Just an awful way to die. Slow and deliberate. Up close with the person who did it.

She hated Brian then. More than she ever had before.

She hated men and all the shit they did to the women around them.

"And Brian Archer?" Dane asked.

"You've completed X-rays?" Margo asked.

"Yes," the coroner said. "The body is in pretty rough shape. But what I'm seeing on the skull is pretty unambiguous."

"What is that?"

"Brian Archer was shot in the head. At point-blank range. He's missing a substantial amount of bone here." The coroner gestured to the side of the skull. "And there are bullet fragments."

"He was *shot*?"

"Yes. There's no doubt about that, he was dead when he went into the water."

Margo closed her eyes, trying to wrap her head around the new information. "He was shot, put into the passenger seat and then someone pushed the car into the water."

"That's what seems most likely. I'm comfortable ruling that the cause of death is a homicide. Suicide would've been possible, but the positioning of the shot makes it unlikely. The car being in the water also makes it unlikely."

She was still having trouble wrapping her head around the implications of it.

"Do you think this is the kind of help that Zach gave?" Dane asked.

"I don't understand how... I don't get it. The note, Sarah, none of it adds up to anything. At least not the way we've been looking at it for eighteen years. It just... It doesn't make sense."

They left the autopsy room and went back outside. She was relieved to be away from the chemical smell. She felt like throwing up.

"We need to see Gail and Callie. First thing in the morning. I want to make sure that they find out before it ends up in the media," Dane said.

"That's a good idea." She hesitated. "Officer Daniels, tonight we found some things that were in Sarah's possession. Notes. I recently found out that my husband, Zach, knew that Brian was abusing Sarah when we were in high school. Now I have a note from Sarah asking him for help."

Officer Daniels stared at her for a long moment. "Goddamn. After all these years. And our only lead is a dead man and a dead girl."

"But it's a lead," she said. "More than we've had all this time."

And it was a connection. More one that she had thought she might find at this point.

They were connected.

They were connected.

It wasn't a coincidence that pulling at the thread was unraveling all of it.

She stood there, beneath the fluorescent lighting in the police department, and let that thought roll over her.

Connection.

She kept trying to find the connection.

"When you go over to Gail Archer's house...can I accompany you?" She let out a slow breath. "It's just that I've been in contact with her recently. I feel like... I feel like she might need someone with her, and Callie has been through so fucking much. I just want to be there."

"Sure," he said. "I'll give you a call."

They went back home, and she sat in front of her computer. She wasn't sure if she'd stopped shaking since Dane had called her this morning.

They say there are no coincidences in law enforcement. But sometimes things do seem haphazard. Life does. The world does. I had convinced myself that there was no way I had special insight. There was no way what I knew was special. I had convinced myself that I was wrong about the pattern. But you see, sometimes intuition is right.

Sometimes there really are signs from the universe. Or books and Little Free Libraries, delivering letters that finally found where they needed to be.

Jacob Spinner might never have gotten that letter, but I did.

And even though it was eighteen years later, I answered it. I am answering it. It's a key to figuring out what happened in my own life, I know it is.

I have to believe that it is.

Everything is pointing to a connection.

I'm back to believing that maybe the universe does speak to us. If we can only stop and listen.

She was meant to find the book.

She stopped typing.

She was meant to find the book. The book that had brought the past back into the present. Sarah's book.

She went and grabbed *Devil in the Dark* and brought it back to her desk and stared at the cover.

Cody did it. It had hit her that her husband sympathized with him because Zach had also found a way to justify his own actions. To cast himself as the hero so he could have Poppy. Cody had justified his actions because he'd made himself the hero. But he'd gotten away with it because…

Because of who else had known.

My husband was a sociopath.

She suddenly thought of Gail, sitting on the couch that day at Callie's.

My husband was a sociopath.

It had been easy to assume Gail had discovered that after she'd learned about his abuse of Sarah.

Margo's arms tingled, the hair standing on end.

What did Gail know?

26

CALLIE, MARGO AND Officer Daniels met in front of Gail's house the next morning at 7:00 a.m.

Margo had slept for two hours, and she had left Dane asleep in bed.

"What is this about?" Callie asked.

"Information about your father's death," said the sheriff.

She nodded, somewhat grimly.

They walked into the house, and Gail was sitting there, waiting.

"Have you done an autopsy?" Gail asked.

"Yes," said Officer Daniels. "Gail, it seems that Brian's death was a homicide."

There was a long pause as Gail sat there, staring at her hands.

Margo looked at the older woman, the suspicions of the night before buzzing inside her.

"What did you know?" Margo asked.

Gail looked up, her pallor gray. "Margo..."

"What did you know? Were you covering for Brian?"

"No," she said, shaking her head. "I wasn't. I just didn't know what to do."

"But you did do something," she said, her conviction only growing.

"I... I did. I had to."

It was like everything broke open.

"Mom?" Callie asked.

Gail looked at Callie, her blue eyes so similar to her daughter's. The spark there so similar to Callie's. Margo could see it all. Her rage at the injustice. A need to make something right. "He was hurting that girl. I couldn't stand it. I started to have suspicions but I was afraid to say anything. How do you ask your husband if he's having an affair with a student? I couldn't. Because I didn't want to disrupt my life. It was selfish. I spent too much time at the school. He spent too much time with her. I saw them together."

And that was when Margo saw herself. The woman who saw something was wrong, and was afraid to ask what. The woman who was scared of breaking everything apart.

"Zach came to me."

Margo's head got light, a wave of shock washing over her.

"I was his favorite teacher back in the fourth grade, and he trusted me. He told me about Brian and Sarah. He said Sarah wanted help, but that she didn't know how to get it. I felt... immense guilt. She was just a girl. Sarah Hartley was just a girl. And my husband was...doing those things to her. I know he wanted her to run away with him. He was trying to blackmail her into it. That was what Zach told me."

"That bastard," said Callie. "That fucking bastard."

"We knew that they were together, and that they were coming back to the house on a night when I was supposed to be out for a parent-teacher meeting. We waited there in the garage. Sarah was in the passenger's seat, Brian was in the driver's seat. When he saw us..."

Her expression shifted then, not the resigned woman telling a detached story. She was pleading.

"My husband had many secrets and his temper was one of them. I knew... I knew he was going to get violent. I was prepared for that. I had brought a gun just in case. I didn't plan to kill him. But I guess... I knew the moment I put the gun in my bag that night that I would."

There wasn't a sound in the room. Everyone was held captive by Gail Archer.

There was always someone who knew something.

Always.

"I pulled out the gun, and I shot him. We never exchanged words. I killed him. My husband of twenty years. It was like... the biggest problem I had was suddenly gone. Sarah was screaming. Zach was...upset. I know how to calm children. They were no different. It was...it was like getting a class through a crisis." She let out a shaking breath.

"Sarah wrote a letter saying she and Brian were running away together. We moved his body from the driver's seat and I drove the car down to the river.

"We found a place where we wouldn't disrupt anything, and we pushed it. We knew that we were all involved. They were accessories. And I had killed him. We also knew that the only way to make it clean was to have Sarah run."

She'd thought that in this instance, Gail was the one keeping a secret for the murdered. But no. Gail had committed the murder.

Zach had witnessed a murder. He'd helped cover it up.

And Sarah...

"Sarah was there when Brian was killed," Margo said.

"I don't know what happened to Sarah after. The plan was for her to run. To start over. She was... She didn't want to stay and face the fallout, but she knew there was no way for her to be disconnected from Brian or his disappearance. She knew that Kerrigan had seen them. She said she would rather go away than see her parents' reactions and I... I let her. I shouldn't have. But I was afraid. I had my own daughter to look after and..." She shook her head. "I would tell you. If I knew I would tell you. I have nothing left to lose. I bought her a plane ticket to Seattle. She had a fake ID. Brian was pressuring her to run... It was why she asked Zach for help. She was afraid." The anguish on Gail's face was real. "I wanted Sarah to live."

"My husband saw you kill your husband. You just...saw him in the grocery store, on the street and then...and then when we moved here you brought us a casserole and welcomed us back to the neighborhood like nothing happened? You just waved at each other from across the street, every day for the last seven years?"

Gail's eyes went glassy.

"You forget," she said. "When you write a good enough story, you forget. It was easy for me to believe that Brian and Sarah had run off together. It was the story I told everyone, over and over, and somehow it became true to me too. The truth didn't feel real. Then you found him, and I knew that there was only a limited time before that came back to me. I had decided last night that I was going to confess. I lived all this time without consequences for my actions. I was afraid then. I'm not afraid now." She smiled softly. "I decided a few years ago that if this ever came to light I wouldn't deny it. I'm not a criminal. I married the wrong man. What he did... I felt like I had to stop it. Like it was up to me. So I ended it. But I understand that comes with consequences."

Callie was sitting, frozen. She had said nothing. Her face was drained of blood.

"You looked at me every day," said Callie slowly. "And you lied. You said that Dad left me."

Gail closed her eyes. "He was *going* to."

"But you knew where he was."

"And what good would telling you have done? You would've just lost both of your parents. I had to wait. At least until you were grown. I knew that. And then you married DeVonte, and you had your kids. They are the lights of my life. I never wanted to give this up. I still don't. But nothing stays hidden forever."

"Gail Archer, you're under arrest for the murder of Brian Archer. Anything you say can and will be used against you in a court of law…"

Officer Daniels, who had known kindly fourth grade teacher Gail as long as any of them, proceeded to read her her rights, and put her in handcuffs.

She had killed Brian.

She had killed him.

But who had killed Sarah Hartley?

27

THEY DECIDED THEY needed to be together, and for once, Margo didn't bury herself in writing to try to avoid the situation.

It made her feel like she was sitting in her mom's hospice room and she hated it.

Maybe that was why she avoided these feelings. Distanced herself from them.

She'd had to be there. Glaringly present while her mom had slipped away, and she really had no desire to ever do that again.

But she had to be here. For Callie, and Dane and DeVonte and the kids.

Callie had lost her mom now, after she'd already lost her dad, and her whole vision of everything was shattered. The past eighteen years of her life had been a complete lie.

And Sarah had been alive when Brian had been killed.

Brian hadn't killed Sarah.

But Gail was a murderer, so she supposed none of these truths were very helpful to Callie at the moment.

Though Gail's description of the moment made it seem like it had almost been self-defense.

But she wondered...

Was it possible she'd killed Sarah too? If Sarah had threatened to tell? All these years, Gail had kept that secret, so clearly it was something she hadn't wanted revealed.

It all felt tangled up. It all felt like a mess.

Maybe Zach had been right. Sometimes answers just dredged up more pain.

Callie sat at Margo's kitchen table holding a mug of tea until it went cold. It felt far too much like when Sarah had gone in the first place.

Except they were the only two left who weren't dead or just not speaking to each other.

Dane, who had always been there, but not with them, was sitting at the table, his hand resting on her knee beneath it.

"I'm sorry," Callie said.

"It isn't any more your fault now than it was then," Margo said.

"But I feel like every disgusting part of this is...in me."

"Your mom tried to help Sarah get away," Dane said, his voice rough. "She stopped your dad from hurting her or anyone else. I don't think she's the major villain here."

"What if she is?" Callie flexed her fingers on the table, then curled them in. "I mean... Sarah witnessed that murder. Sarah was sleeping with her husband."

"What do you think, Margo?" asked Dane.

"I don't know what I believe. What Gail said about believing the story, that's powerful. I can believe that. That eventually you start to buy into the story that you told everyone else. Because it's what they see, it's what they believe. I understand that. We all do it. We fill in gaps and we...we miss things."

She frowned. She had been very focused on that for a long time. Missing things.

What had she missed?

What had she missed?

That was the problem, there were gaps. Gaps that had to be filled in by people who were there. That could no longer fill the gaps in.

Gail could fill them in, but would she?

"There is of course the very good question of why she would admit to killing Brian, but not admit to killing Sarah," she pointed out.

"Well," said Dane. "It's excusable to shoot your statutory rapist husband in the head. Damned near sympathetic." He looked apologetically at Callie. "Sorry."

"Don't be sorry. I… It's true, it is what she did. And you're right." She laughed. "It's almost sympathetic. In fact, given a few days I might think it is."

"Sarah was strangled," Margo said. "It takes a lot of strength to strangle someone, and I'm not saying it wouldn't have been possible for Gail to do it, but I think unlikely. Why not shoot her? She'd already done that."

"Strangulation is personal," Dane pointed out.

"Feels male," Callie said.

They were quiet for a moment.

"Well, that is true," said Dane.

"I need to go home," Callie said. "I just…need to be with my kids. And sleep for a year."

"I'll see you tomorrow," Margo said. "Should I walk you?"

"I'm three doors down."

"I trust nothing."

"Who's going to walk you?" Callie asked.

"Me," said Dane, standing up. "Come on, let's all go."

They walked Callie back to her house, then took a slow walk around the neighborhood together.

"I want answers," she whispered. "We're so close now. That's the thing. You made me believe that we can get some answers, and now I want them. We know Sarah is gone. We know Brian's gone. And we know none of it went the way that we thought. We need to finish the story. The true story. Not the one that's been out there. Not the one that we believed. The real one."

The truth.

"I don't think Gail did it," Margo said. "I don't. I think…"

She felt like there were things eluding her.

What had she missed?

She quickened her pace, releasing her hold of his hand. "Maybe I've been looking at this the wrong way. I've been asking myself ever since Zach left what I missed. We all asked ourselves ever since Sarah left what we missed. But everything we've found so far…it's not about that." She put her hands on her temples. "Zach and Kerrigan saw Sarah and Brian together. Gail saw Sarah and Brian together. A lot of people did. It was what they hid, not what they didn't see. It was…" She shook her head. "I don't know."

He sped up to keep pace with her, and reached out and took her hand. "Well, if you were conducting an investigation as a police officer, what would you think?"

"Honestly? We would have to look at Zach. Because he was one of the last people to see Sarah alive. He was there when Brian was killed. He helped her dispose of the body."

"But why?" he asked.

Why was all she had when it came to Zach. *Why.*

Why any of it?

There was nothing but vagueness. Emptiness where a person that she could no longer ask used to be.

"I don't know. But how can I say for certain he wouldn't?"

"You think you can be certain he didn't hurt Poppy."

"That's different," she said. "Because I know what kind of father he was. I know how he was with her. It's different, because… Zach wasn't a manipulator. Not a good one, anyway."

"He managed to hide what he was planning to do."

"Yes, but not by convincing me I was crazy or anything. It wasn't gaslighting, he was actually so clumsy. He was cheating on me, he accused me of cheating."

"You could call that gaslighting."

"Not the way he did it. It was just like a kid telling a story. A kid trying to convince himself he was right. Or what he was doing was okay. I helped with that. Because I wrote half the story for him. I saw what I wanted to see in him."

"You knew him in high school."

"I know…" She put her hand over her mouth, pressed it there for a moment before lowering her hand. "He really…he really identified with the killer."

"What?" Dane asked.

"When we read *Devil in the Dark*. Callie thought it was a stranger, she was afraid of it being someone close. Sarah thought it was the man in power. He thought the boy was innocent."

"Well, he might have been when the book was written."

"I know," she said. "I know. But it… I keep seeing him talking about that. Making his case. The way he justified all those actions the kid did that really were red flags. He saw it as someone else's fault. I think that's him. I thought all this time that added up with him taking Poppy. But now I'm wondering if it was more than that."

"But if he killed Sarah, he'd be…a sociopath."

"He wasn't, though. But people don't have to be sociopaths to kill other people, that's the scary part. If there's one thing that all the true crime has taught me it's that ordinary people sometimes become killers. Like Gail."

"She had a reason."

"But people always think they have a reason. That's what I'm saying. He was so good at coming up with reasons."

They walked on in silence, beneath the soft glow of the street lamps, the air damp and cold.

They sat on the couch and watched TV for a while, and Dane fell asleep, the strain of the past few days taking a toll.

He'd had to be part of the recovery of his sister's body.

He'd had to go tell his parents that their daughter was gone.

He was being an older brother. Even in the end. Fighting for her. Fighting for Sarah as best he could.

She wanted to find that closure for him.

But she couldn't sleep.

She went upstairs and sat down in front of her computer, and pulled up her document. It was all still patchwork. Like everything. There was no through line.

There was no connective tissue.

She felt like it was there. The truth. The single golden thread that could be drawn from the beginning to the end. The thread to replace the lies they'd picked out, used to unravel everything. It was there.

She just didn't know what it was.

She started typing.

I know my husband was having an affair. I know that because I counted the condoms in our nightstand. I know there were condoms missing that he didn't use with me. I saw his mood change. I saw his support get thinner the more successful I became. I watched him become more paranoid that something might happen to our daughter.

I watched him begin to show doubt about my parenting skills. I started believing him.

I also saw him with our daughter. I saw how much he loved her. I watched him dote on her, care for her.

Those elements were enough for me to begin to write a new story for myself. One where his failures were actually mine.

The trouble is, when you get so deep into a narrative, you honestly don't know the truth anymore. And I can't ask him.

Why did you take her?

What changed?

Who were you, really?

I'm so aware of the great, blank voids where information should be. I am so aware of the void that exists where my daughter should be.

I rewrote so much history to make the present bearable, and now I can't find the truth.

I even doubt the things I know I've seen.

What did I see?

She paused and thought back to the notes.

Will you help me?
Sarah

yes.
Zach

Back then, Zach had offered help. Sarah had wanted it.

And six months ago, maybe for the past few years, Zach hadn't trusted Margo.

She hadn't quite thought of it that way before, but it was true. Zach hadn't trusted her.

He hadn't trusted the way that she parented Poppy, he hadn't trusted her enough to talk to her about his issues. He'd accused her. He'd demonstrated his lack of trust that way, but none of it was ever about solving it. Because he had made up his mind already.

Of course he had.

He had decided that he wanted to leave and he'd been building himself a case for that. These were reasonable things she could fill in based on what she'd seen.

He hadn't wanted to leave Poppy with her. He had found a way to decide that she wasn't a fit parent. That was his story.

These were the words that he'd use to write it.

I would do anything to keep her safe.

Safe. Zach would've done something to keep her safe. He would've sent her somewhere.

She was back to the other woman. There had been another woman.

He'd been smart enough to not leave a trail. There'd been no contact between himself and the other woman via a phone.

She frowned.

There'd been no contact between them via a phone.

He must've had a burner, but they hadn't unearthed one in the car that night. There was only the phone he'd thrown into the trash in front of the house.

Poppy is in the woods.

She stood up from her computer, and she went downstairs. And she stood by the front door for a moment. But she already knew where she was going.

Poppy is in the woods.

She knew what she'd seen.

She knew what she had seen.

She didn't know the story yet. But the story didn't matter. Because it wasn't true.

She knew what she'd seen.

Zach had been paranoid. Why had Zach been paranoid? His paranoia had grown along with her career.

She'd thought that it'd had to do with insecurity about her making more money than him. About her being with Dane.

No. Because he'd been cheating, so that hadn't actually mattered. Except as an excuse. He'd been paranoid about the digging she was doing.

It was about the digging.

He'd said. He had said that he didn't think these kinds of answers helped anybody. Because there was no fixing something like that. She had found it undermining. What if it wasn't meant to be?

What if it was desperate?

She couldn't know what she didn't know.

But she knew Zach had never shown strong emotion about Sarah. It had all seemed like support for Callie. Male stoicism. But he hadn't liked to talk about it.

And he'd definitely never indicated that he'd had a friendship with her that was deeper than the group. The kind that passed private notes and shared a secret.

He'd never told her he'd known Brian was abusing Sarah.

It could have all been because of his involvement in hiding Brian's body.

She knew that he'd been involved in that. It was a crime, and he'd known she was relentless. He had in fact often found her too relentless.

Was that, on its own, enough to have made him want to take Poppy away?

A fear that she might have discovered that he'd been an accessory to the murder of Brian Archer?

And what would you have done?

You would have made him turn himself in.

She would have.

Taking only what she knew and laying it out on a virtual evidence table in front of her, she could see why Zach would have been worried. She'd circled Sarah's case so many times over the years and none of it would have seemed worrying.

Until she'd solved that case.

Zach had never wanted to hurt Poppy.

She knew that.

She also knew she'd seen Poppy in the woods. They hadn't been back since they found Sarah. Because she had been distracted. Partly convinced that perhaps that's why she had been led there, but that wasn't it. It was never it.

Poppy was what had driven this entire thing. Poppy had driven her out of the house that night and down to the Little Free Library.

The letter that she had found in the book to Jacob Spinner didn't mean anything. It only connected because she wanted it to connect.

And it turned out that it had connected, but looking back she didn't think she could have reasonably known that.

It'd just been drive. Drive to find her daughter. That relentlessness that Zach had hated.

Zach had feared.

It was like she was seeing everything through new eyes now. She looked over at the couch. Dane was sleeping, and she wasn't going to wake him up. But she wasn't going to stay home either.

She put on her jacket and slipped out the door, into the garage. And gave thanks for the fact that her car started up silently.

It eased out of the garage, and onto the street.

It was still early enough that many of the houses were lit up.

She drove out toward the gate.

She needed to go back to the woods.

It was what drove her. It was the one concrete thing she could hold on to. She'd seen her there, she knew she had. If she couldn't trust herself, then there was nothing left. She was relentless.

It was what he feared.

She repeated that mantra as she drove.

She was relentless.

And she would be relentless for Poppy.

Forever.

It didn't matter if she was holding out hope like Sarah's mother or grimly realistic like Sarah's father. She didn't care if she was wrong. She believed she could find her. She believed it.

She believed that the signs mattered, because she had to.

Maybe she was crazy.

Maybe she was a fool.

Maybe she was seeing things.

If she put any of this on a true crime board she'd get called a nutjob.

Any true crime aficionado knew the parents were often to blame, and even when they weren't their instincts were colored by grief and desperation.

But she didn't care.

Something had been pulling at her, relentlessly, since Poppy had disappeared.

Maybe it was grief.

Sorrow.

Insanity.

She'd follow it. To the end.

She'd unravel it for her daughter.

All that had relentlessly led her to Zach's body.

To Sarah's.

To Brian's.

It had led to death.

It wouldn't lead to Poppy's, because she knew.

She knew.

She got there, to the edge of the forest. And she took her flashlight out of the glove box. She shoved her phone into her pocket.

And she got out, heading into the trees. She stood there for a moment.

She looked to her left, and headed that direction toward the back of the neighborhood, rather than heading in a straight line for the deepest part of the woods.

The flashlight provided poor illumination, but it was something.

She held it tightly and pressed into the trees.

She wasn't going to question herself. And she wasn't going to fall back on hopelessness because of what she couldn't know.

She knew what she'd seen.

And she'd seen plenty.

She believed in herself.

She kept moving until she saw breaks of light shining through the trees.

And then one went out. Then another. And another.

That was it. It was the gated community. That safest of safe havens in Conifer, Oregon.

The backside of the houses.

She moved closer, her heart thundering hard.

And then her flashlight went out.

She stood there for a long moment, quietly.

Just quietly.

She could hear her own breathing, and it made her feel nervous. Edgy.

Then she took a step forward, and another.

Until she could see three houses, unobscured by the trees.

She saw movement inside one.

Dane, she realized, moving around in her bedroom.

Probably getting dressed. Probably pissed at her for not telling him where she was going or what she was doing.

She reached into her pocket to look at her phone, because he'd probably texted her in irritation to ask where the hell she was.

The screen lit up, and then she heard a child crying.

It's not real.

It's not real.

She heard another sound. Another voice.

The hair on the back of her neck stood up, and she jerked her head back up quickly, this time looking directly into her neighbor's second-floor window.

And saw her.

28

SHE HAD BEEN there the whole time.

There she was.

A child. With her hands pressed against the glass. Her blond hair illuminated by the light behind her.

"Poppy," she whispered.

What had driven her nearly off the boat and into the river, what had driven her to her knees, drove her forward now.

She ran forward. As fast as she could. Launching herself at the wall, pressing her palms against the top, her feet scrambling up the side.

She cut her forearm, her knee, as she managed to pull herself up to the top.

And launched herself over into Julie's yard.

Her heart was hammering. She felt like she was going to throw up. She straightened and felt blood tricking down her forearm to her wrist.

She went straight to the glass door at the back and tugged on the handle. It was locked. Panic rose inside of her. She was right there. Poppy was right there.

Nothing would keep her from her.

And then she looked around for something. Anything. She saw a bistro table on the patio. And she picked that up by the legs and slammed the tabletop through the glass door.

Glass cascaded around her, some of it fell on her arms. But if it'd cut her, she didn't notice.

She walked over the broken glass, through the kitchen, to the stairs.

She tried to figure out which room it was based on what she'd just seen.

And ran.

She went to the door, and tried the doorknob. But it was locked.

She started banging on it. "Poppy!"

She heard a muffled sound behind the door, and she hit at it with her shoulder. She started looking for something to break the door down.

"What are you doing in my house, Margo?"

She turned and saw Julie standing there. In her pink scrubs. Holding a gun.

She should be afraid. That would be the normal response to that, she knew.

She couldn't find fear. Only rage.

"Are you going to shoot me, Julie?" she asked, rage making it impossible for her to be as afraid as she should. Her daughter was on the other side of that door. "You took my child from me. You psychotic bitch. Did you kill Zach too?"

She shook her head, moving her hands along with it, the barrel no longer pointing directly at Margo. "No. No. I don't want to… I didn't want it to come down to this. I didn't want…"

"What are you going to do? Kill me? Disappear with my child?"

"I didn't… I was supposed to just hang on to her until he got back. He didn't come back. And I didn't know what to do. I didn't *know what to do.*"

"Open the door. Put down the fucking gun and open the door."

She trained the gun back on Margo. "I can't go to jail."

And Margo needed her daughter back.

"Then go to hell," said Margo, closing the space between them. Julie flinched. The gun didn't fire. And Margo hit her with the full weight of her shoulder, taking her down to the ground. The gun flew out of her grip and against the back wall, and Margo called upon every skill she'd learned in her women's self-defense classes and punched Julie in the face.

She'd never hit anyone before. She'd never had to. She was surprised how much it hurt her fist.

And even more satisfied by just how much it seemed to daze Julie.

She got off her, ran across to the gun, and picked it up. "Open the fucking door," she said.

"Please don't kill me," said Julie.

"The only reason you're not dead right now is that my kid doesn't need to see it."

Julie was shaking and crying. Fetal. She wasn't helping with anything. She stood there and looked at that useless, limp woman. This woman had her child? *This* woman?

"Get me a key."

"There's a pin," she said. "It just opens with a straight pin. It's on top of the door frame."

Margo went over, keeping an eye, and the gun, trained on Julie. Then she reached up and grabbed the straight pin, jamming it into the lock and undoing it.

Then she stood in front of the door, her heart hammering.

She heard glass crunching downstairs.

"Margo?"

Dane.

"Upstairs," she shouted.

"I called 911 already," he said as he made his way up the stairs. "I was outside looking for you when I heard the glass shatter." Then he looked down at Julie, and at the gun in Margo's hand.

"Poppy is in here," said Margo. "Take the gun. Please."

He stepped toward her and she found it hard to let go of the gun. Her fingers were so tight around it that when she released it to him, she realized she had impressions from the stock on her hand.

That she opened the door slowly.

Poppy was huddled in a corner, her knees drawn up to her chest, her blond head tucked down. "Poppy?"

She lifted her head, her eyes bright.

"Mom," she said, the word half a whisper.

Margo dropped to her knees, all the air sucked out of her lungs.

"I found you," she said. "I finally found you."

Poppy still didn't move. She looked afraid. Like she couldn't trust what she was seeing.

And why would she?

What would make her think that she could trust any of this? "I'm really here," said Margo.

She sat down, and held her arms out.

"I'm here."

And then slowly, very slowly, Poppy crawled to where she was, and got into her lap.

Margo held on to her daughter tight. Memorizing the feel of her body against hers.

It wasn't long before sirens split the night air, disrupting the silence of the gated community.

She was there the whole time.

The whole time.

The crying. It had come from inside her...

But it might have come from here too.

She had been here the whole time.

Paramedics came, and evaluated Poppy physically.

And Margo was told she would have to undergo a psych eval

without Margo, which made her want to kill somebody, because she couldn't see how it was rational to expect her to let go of her child after six months.

She wasn't permitted to attend the psychological evaluation Poppy had to undergo, but she had been able to find a way to get them to schedule it during Julie's interrogation.

She sat there on the other side of the one-way glass, listening in as Officer Daniels question Julie.

"Were you and Zach having an affair?"

She nodded slowly. "Yes."

"How long had the affair been going on?"

"Margo was never home. And when she was she was spending all of her time working on her book. He felt like she wasn't paying attention to him anymore. And there was… There was more. He was… Zach was a really good man. You have to understand that. He was so good. Such a great father. And so good to me. He wanted to start over. He said Margo ignored Poppy. That she didn't care about her. He told me that she left Poppy in the playground. That she lost her. He wanted to protect her. Because he said… Zach told me everything. He made a mistake when he was really young. But he wanted to take that back. He thought that Margo and Poppy were his chance at having a life."

"What mistake did Zach make?"

"You'll think he was a monster. He didn't want to tell me, because he thought I would judge him. I know… I know what it's like to love somebody so much that things just can get out of hand. I know what it's like. I didn't judge him for it."

"What did Zach do?" Daniels asked again.

She put her head in her hands. "It's going to make you hate him. He isn't here to defend himself. And you don't understand. And when you say it, it sounds so crazy. But when he said it, it didn't."

"No one is going to judge you," said Daniels, his tone light and conversational. "It's okay. You're okay. You're just talking to me."

That right there was a reminder of how disingenuous Daniels was being. Because she wasn't just talking to him. She was talking to Margo and Dane.

"He was in love with her. This girl. Sarah. He found out that she was sleeping with a teacher. And it devastated him. Then she said she wanted his help. He wanted to give it to her. They killed the guy. The one that was hurting her. He risked everything for her. And then he was trying to help her run away, and he wanted to go with her. He wanted to go away with her. But she just wanted to go by herself. She wanted to start over. He said that he loved her and she rejected him. She said it wasn't like that. Not for her. He helped hide a body for her. That's how good of a man he is. He was helping her start over, and that was how she thanked him. She rejected him. He got emotional. He didn't mean to. He kind of blacked out, he told me. And when he... He was too rough with her. When he realized what he was doing, she was already gone. He blacked out, and when he could see again, his hands were around her neck. They'd already made it look like she was running away. With the guy that they killed. So he buried her in the woods. Because he didn't know what else to do. She was already... They'd already made her vanish."

Dane made an inhuman sound and sat abruptly in the chair in front of the glass. He put his head in his hands.

Margo took a step toward him and put her hand on his back.

It fit. With what she knew.

"He felt guilty about it. But he tried to forget. He tried to pretend that she was off somewhere. But he was always afraid that God or whatever was going to take his daughter from him. Because he took somebody else's daughter. He tried to forget. He told me he did a good job of it. Until Margo started digging around in stuff. And he knew she was going to be the one who ended up destroying his perfect life. And if he went to prison he was going to lose Poppy. So we started planning. To get away. To make a new life. New identities and all of that. He said we were going to be a family. But he had some things to get in order. He had some paperwork to pick up. Fake passports and stuff. I had to go up to Seattle to do it, but he couldn't fly. Because he didn't want his movements tracked. So we had to drive. He told Margo that he was taking Poppy to dinner. She never left the community. He just walked her over to my house. He dumped his phone in the garbage can.

"And then he just never came back. And he didn't have a phone. Not even a burner. He didn't have anything on him. And I had no idea what happened to him. I didn't know if the people he'd gone to get the documentation from had done something to him. I didn't know. All that time, I was worried sick. I had Poppy. And I knew that I couldn't... I just decided to wait. I decided to wait for him to come back. But he didn't. He just never came back."

"And what did you do with Poppy all that time? Did you keep her up in that room?"

"Mostly. But I took her to play in the woods a couple of times. Because I couldn't have her play out in the yard. So I had to hide her in the car and drive her out of the community, and I took her in there to play because I knew that no one would see us."

"Except I did," said Margo. "I did."

Julie put her face in her hands. "And after you found Zach's body I knew that it couldn't go on, but I just didn't know what to do. I was devastated... I knew that if I said that I had her the whole time I was going to go to jail. I took her to the woods because I thought about just leaving her there. And scaring her. Telling her not to tell anybody, but I got afraid. I thought about killing her. But I couldn't. I'm not a monster. Not a monster. That's the thing. I didn't kill her because I'm not a monster."

But there were different kinds of monsters. And monsters seemed to find a way to believe they were heroes. Margo was the monster to Zach. The person that could take away the life he tried to build. The person that could shine the light on his story and tell the truth.

Margo was so relentless, and he'd known it. It was why he hadn't liked it.

It was why he had gotten more paranoid when she'd solved the Incline Valley case. It had never been about her success.

It had been about what he'd been afraid she might discover next.

It would be easy for her to decide that the thread was Zach. The golden thread that ran through all of it. The connection to both things.

To both tragedies.

But she was going to take that away from him.

The golden thread was the way that people who loved those they were missing never gave up.

She was meant to find the book. *Devil in the Dark*. It had brought her here. It had. It had shown her who Zach had been. Gail's part. The book had spoken to her, beyond the actual words in it.

And it was worth celebrating.

The evaluation went better than could be expected. Poppy hadn't really known where she was. She hadn't realized she was in a house next door because Zach had gone out of his way to confuse her before he dropped her off. It had been dark.

And Julie always made her hide in the car when they drove to the woods, so she never saw them driving past her house.

Dane went home for the first week after Poppy was back.

Margo grappled with a lot of paranoia that she tried not to pass on to Poppy.

But thankfully, she had Callie.

And Dane.

Callie brought the kids over to see Poppy after it had been a few days.

Poppy looked up at Jaden shyly.

Jaden lifted his hand and waved. "You came back from the woods."

Poppy wrinkled her nose. "Yeah," she said.

"Good," said Jaden.

Margo lifted her hand, and offered Jaden a high five. "Thank you," she said to him. "For telling me that you saw Poppy. It really helped me."

Jaden nodded, and then looked down at his phone.

"I think the kids are going to be all right," said Callie, looking at Jaden, and then at Poppy.

"I think so."

There would be a lot of things to untangle for Poppy. It was going to be hard for her to understand why it was wrong what Julie had told her about Margo. But her dad really was gone. He wasn't going to appear.

"Did Daddy tell you what was happening?"

She shook her head. "He just said that I had to stay at the house for a while."

And then she decided she didn't need any more answers. She had Poppy. And that was what mattered.

Margo's book ended up taking shape again. It wasn't until six months later that she was able to write the last part of the story, and get a very important opening. *Close to Home* was rushed into production and released six months later.

Gail Hartley was sentenced to less than six months. She was found to have acted in imperfect self-defense. That felt like justice to me. Especially as I sat there holding my friend while she cried. Because her children would be able to have their grandmother back.

Because she didn't have to lose both of her parents.

Because there was no reason to compound tragedy like that, and it was just a good thing that the judge and jury had agreed.

Zach Corbin would have gone to trial for the murder of Sarah Hartley, but he died before he was able to be brought to justice. However he spent the last several years of his life in the hell that he'd crafted for himself. Afraid of the people around him. Afraid that he would lose a life that he knew he hadn't deserved.

In the end, he sabotaged himself.

In the end, he couldn't tell a story good enough to convince himself that what he'd done was justified.

It would be easy to think that the sinister truth of the story is that you can't trust your neighbors. That danger is hiding closer to home than you might think.

That can be true.

I've seen it. The danger was inside my own house, next door. Right there all along. But that's not the story I choose to tell myself. Because it isn't only murderous husbands and adulterous neighbors who tell themselves stories. We all do.

I could tell myself danger is around every corner. As I go on to raise my daughter, to tuck her in at night, I could tell myself that I might lose it all again.

When I wake up and look at Dane's face, I can tell myself I don't know him, and never can, that he could trick me too.

But I won't do that.

In literature, happy endings are often treated as the lesser choice. As safe, or far too neat, or delusional.

As someone who loves to interrogate the messiness of humans and the darkness of true crime, I might have once agreed. But as I sit here in the happiness I chose, in spite of it all. As I watch my daughter go outside and play, and laugh. And as I let her even though sometimes terror over losing her again grips me. As I tell this man I love him, and believe him when he says he loves me. As I watch my best friend carve out a happy life with her husband and children, in spite of it all, I realize that happiness is not the easy way out.

It is a choice we make. A story we tell, not because we don't know that there's darkness out there, and inside as well, but because we know. And we choose to find joy anyway. We choose to love. We choose to live.

Hope is the thing with feathers that perches on the soul.

If we can find the strength to choose it. And I do.

If I give my daughter one gift, it would be the understanding that she can choose her story. And that she can make it as bright and happy as she wants it to be.

One Year Later...

Foreword

Dear Ms. Box,

I first became aware of your work when I Kept Them Safe released. Your dedication and honesty, your dogged pursuit of truth, humbled me.

Now to read this book, which is such a heartfelt and personal account of your own experience going through hell and back to find your own child, I find myself wishing I could embody even half of your bravery.

It surprised me to learn I played a part in this story. That a letter I never got, tucked into the pages of a book I wrote twenty years ago, became the catalyst for finding the truth.

You told me when we met you were relentless. I think you are nothing less than relentless in your hope. It was hope that made you see that letter as something more than ink printed on paper. It was hope that drove you when others would have sat down and accepted all was lost.

Of all your triumphs, it is your hope that shines brightest.

I read all your books.

I thought I would tell you.

Sincerely,

Your Biggest Fan

Jacob Spinner

* * * * *